THE VAMPIRE HUNTER'S DIARIES

Blood Moon

David Clark

"Blood Moon"

- An optical illusion created by the scattering of light through the Earth's atmosphere.
- A sign of the start of the end of days.
- A sign portending death.
- The opening of a path to explore the darker side of yourself...

1

September 30th

Dear Diary,

Okay, so this whole diary thing is kinda weird, but like, whatever, right? People in movies always start with "Dear Diary," so I guess that's what I'm supposed to do. I honestly don't know. This is my first-ever diary entry, and it's not even really a diary. Thanks, Grandfather. I turned sixteen today, and he handed me this old-school, leather-bound journal thing. Brown and boring. Super sweet of him, right? Not. It's my official journal to record my encounter and kills now that I have "arrived." Like, what even is that? He's been training me forever, but I've never seen an actual vampire. Not that I'm complaining, but I mean, do I really want to be a vampire hunter? No one bothered to ask me. My grandfather and his "associates" just decided it for me. Apparently, it's in my blood or whatever.

So, I'm supposed to hunt vampires, but I've never even met one or seen one up close. Makes total sense, right? So, no kills to brag about in the journal, and zero encounters. He's trained me like some kind of ninja, but he keeps me away from the real action. Fine by me, honestly. I'm not dying to meet vampires. I'm not even sure how I feel about this whole vampire hunter gig. It's just what I am, apparently. Predestined. Birthright and all that jazz.

I asked Grandfather why he's kept me away from vampires and not taken me on his hunts, and he just said I wasn't ready. No explanation. It used to bug me, feeling like an insult. Now? Don't care. I just wanna be me, survive high school, and hang out with my friends. Speaking of which, birthday wish? A car or my driving permit, instead of this journal. That was a big no and no. Most of my friends get theirs on their birthdays, but not me. Why? Grandfather's rule number one, no attachments, no real names, no records. We're ghosts, blending in and disappearing. I'm Maria Foster, but here I'm Elizabeth Winters. Not the coolest alias, but whatever. Lana Perez was the coolest. I wish I could be her again.

That rule makes school trying. I'm to just do the work, learn, and don't get attached. No activities, no real connections. Easier said than done. Blending in means not being a total loner, but not too social either. Perfect balance. I've got it down, mostly. Sometimes I slip up and let someone get too close. I can't help it. I'm human. Sometimes hearts speak louder than brains. I'm worried tonight's one of those times. My brain was screaming no, but something else, I'm not so sure it is my heart, was screaming yes. It has screamed yes before, but not as loudly as tonight. My grandfather will kill me if he catches me sneaking out, but that wasn't my biggest concern. That was the concern that I had slipped up again, and Lucas, the nerdy gamer I met at school and spent hours at his house playing video games with, had become an attachment.

"Want these?" Lucas sat up in his bed, dangling my panties on the end of his finger.
"Keep them," I said with a quirky smile.
"A souvenir?"
"A reason to come back."
I checked the clock on his nightstand. It read 2:12 A.M. I didn't plan on staying this late. I didn't plan on a lot of what had happened this evening, but it did. Just like I didn't plan on stumbling over his shoes on the floor as I searched his room for the rest of my clothes. My hand located what felt like my shirt and I pulled it on. My skirt was right next to it on the floor, and so were my flats, which I slipped on.
"Maria, you could stay the rest of the night and leave before my parents wake up." Lucas suggested, sitting up in his bed and sporting a smile so white it practically glowed in the pitch-black room. His hand reached out for mine. I didn't yank mine away, but I didn't grab his either. I just let the distance between mine and his remain. It was a familiar distance. One that defined what Lucas and I were. One that defined most all my relationships, if you could call what Lucas and I had one of those.

"My grandfather would kill me." He probably will anyway. I knew what Lucas was going to suggest next, that my grandfather was fast asleep, and I would be home before he knew it, but that was a lie. He was still up in the living room waiting for me, just like he did every night. Part parental, part other.

"He wouldn't know. He Is probably asleep."

An easy prediction to make from an outsider's view of my life. Perception is often not even close to reality. "Trust me. He already knows." A check of my cell phone confirmed that. Several texts asking if I was okay. Then about a half dozen ones just with '911' in it. That is our code for an emergency. An absolute overreaction to a missed curfew. Especially when I did it as often as I did.

I held up my phone and shook it for Lucas to see while giving him that awkward and quirky smile that said he had already caught me.

He mirrored my smile and got out of bed naked. I diverted my eyes. Why the sudden shyness, I didn't know. It's not like I hadn't seen him like that for the last few hours. When he attempted to hug me, I hurried to his bedroom window, putting that distance between us. With both hands on the window, I quietly slid it open.

"Maria, you can use the front door."

I ignored Lucas and stepped out onto the slanted roof just below his window. "See you at school tomorrow."

He leaned out the window, and I quickly kissed him. Why? My brain didn't give me a response when I asked, and I rolled my eyes at myself while walking to the trellis. The climb down from the second floor was easy. Well, easy for me, and not because I had done it a few times. It was child's play. I only looked back once up at the window I came from. Lucas was there watching me, so I gave him a quick wave. *Distance girl. Distance.*

Halfway down the block, I felt an urge to look back again, but I resisted. I cringed when it returned. I knew my own rules, and any such feelings completely broke them. Lucas wasn't someone I would consider a boyfriend. He was just someone I considered. Someone I consider when I want to hang out. Someone to consider when I want to go out. Someone to consider when I want to do what we did tonight. Someone just to consider when I want anything. He was not alone. There are others. I only considered some for certain things, like Rob Carter, despite being the quarterback of the football team and the desire of every girl in school. I only considered him a few things, and not the one he wanted. I don't fall for that whole more muscles than brains jock type. They have their purpose. Their uses, but that was it. I wanted depth, and he is anything but deep.

Most, including me, considered Lucas a little nerdy. He reads a lot, and not just what they assign in school, but I liked that. There were never any awkward silences between us. There was depth there, and I like depth, which was hard to find in this shallow, superficial world.

What was I doing? It's like I was making an argument about why Lucas could be that one. That one I dropped my shields for. I can't, can I?

Absolutely not. I shook my head to clear the thoughts from my head. Blaming the afterglow of what had just happened for it. But then again, thoughts crept in and not about the sex. That little smile I see when he looks at me across our chemistry class. The way he waited for me at my locker every morning. The way...

A cool breeze chases me around the corner and to my home. Feeling it against my stomach shocks me out of my internal discussion and forces me to check the buttons on my shirt. Thankfully that happened, or I would have walked in at home with my shirt only half buttoned. I probably forgot to do it in my rush to leave. Walking in like that would have been a disaster and given my grandfather even more to lecture me on. I was already in for one about being late, or was I?

I expected to see a light glow in the front windows from the lamps on the other side, but they were all dark. In fact, all the windows on this side of the house were dark. That wasn't a good sign. It's an ambush. He was probably sitting there in the dark, just waiting for me to open the door. Probably with his cane in hand, waiting to slam it down on the floor to scare the crap out of me. To be sure, I walked by and checked the other side for any signs of life. I found nothing. Every window down that side was dark. Even the little half bathroom window, which should have a little glow to it from the nightlight he kept plugged in. I've told him several times I didn't need that anymore. It's more of a thing you would have for a child, which I was not anymore. That was a bigger sign than anything. He never turns it off. I was being set up. That was for sure. Well, two can play that game.

Instead of going in through the front, I walked down the driveway and headed for the backdoor. I reached for it carefully, not wanting to make any noise, but almost gasped when I found it unlocked. That was practically blasphemous against his principles and the training he instilled in me. Doors were always to be locked.

Everything was dark inside, just like I expected. It was dark and quiet. The television wasn't on. No radio. Not even a fan, which my grandfather always slept with. I crept down the hall while I debated going to the living room, where I knew he would be waiting, or heading straight to my room. There were both good and bad to each decision. There was no way I was going to avoid the lecture, but I could delay it. That might raise the intensity, though. Might as well just take my medicine and get it over with.

I put my purse down on the counter in the kitchen and headed down the hall to the living room. Out of nowhere, a hand wrapped around my face, clamping over my mouth, and then yanking me backward into my room. I tried to turn around to see who or what, but I felt a long wooden rod press across my back and pin me against the wall face first.

"Don't scream," whispers my grandfather. "Understand?"

I nodded, and he removed his hand. The pressure across my back let up enough that I could turn. I found myself looking right into the whites of my grandfather's eyes. "I'm sorry I am late." I expected a lecture, not the accosting I just suffered. This was extreme, even for him.

"Not that. Grab your bag and follow me. Now." The cane dropped to his side, freeing me from the wall.

"Bag?" I asked, as I started for the kitchen where I left my purse.

"Bag," he whispered. "They found us." Then he pointed at my closet. When I saw my grandfather holding his bag, *the bag*, in his left hand, panic piled on top of my confusion. If he had that bag in his hand, it meant one and only one thing. I grabbed mine from the closet, being careful not to jostle any hangers or the door. With it in hand, the panic ratcheted up about the looming threat that must be there; I realized this was the end of who I was.

"Let's go," he whispered and then hurried down the hall for the backdoor. Now I knew why the backdoor was unlocked. He prepared a quick egress path. When my own footsteps joined his, I heard something fall to the floor in the living room. My pace quickened, but my grandfather continued to move slowly until we reached the backdoor, then we ran for the car. I slammed the door shut as the first dark creature emerged from the house and gave chase.

    The car cranked without issue, which was not the norm, and my grandfather put it in reverse, backing out just as the pale face of our pursuer came into view. He leaped on the hood, landing with a thunderous bang. That was going to leave a dent. I broke the promise I made to my grandfather earlier and screamed. I screamed my lungs out, and when I thought I couldn't scream anymore, I found more air just as another pale figure exploded out the front door, hitting the car with his shoulder, sending it skidding across the road.

    When it stopped against the curb, my grandfather slammed it into drive, and sped off with a chirp of the tires. I turned to watch; they gave chase for a bit and then stopped. That didn't mean I turned back around and stopped watching for them. I watched as they stood there. It was only after we made several turns and I didn't see them following that I turned back around, but that didn't stop me from looking in the rear-view mirror, watching that life disappear behind us from time to time. Once it disappeared into just the darkness of night, I settled in for the ride.

    We drove long into the night. My grandfather constantly fiddled with the radio, trying to tune in the weak signals of the stations as we passed between towns. He wasn't after anything particular, setting on everything from talk radio, sports, country music, and about a half an hour of some evangelistic church preacher reminding us we were all sinners every minute or two. Praise the Lord! According to what he said, he was the one that could save our wretched souls. Too bad we drove beyond the range of his station before he brought us to salvation. Eventually we reached the official middle of nowhere, which was too far for any signal to reach, so he turned off the radio, leaving us with the rumble of the engine and the sound of the tires on the road.

    "How the hell did that happen?" I yelled, finally breaking the silence of the last few hours. I wasn't asking anyone in particular. My focus was out on the moon, which was illuminating the flat featureless landscape that lined the freeway we were traveling.

"I don't know. I took precautions, just like I always do, but somehow, they found us."

"I know." I reached over and patted him on the shoulder. My frustration wasn't aimed at him. It was just the situation we found ourselves in. My grandfather took precautions to keep this from happening. He always did, and so far, this had only happened once before. Not to say we hadn't left our home in a rush under the cover of darkness before. I had lost count of how many times we had so far. All but once before was because he finished his job. This was only the second time like this. The twitching in my grandfather's jaw meant the machine inside him was running at full power. Details were being reviewed for anything he missed, and revisions were being made to my training to adapt, one of his favorite words.

"Why were you out walking in the open so late?" The question was calm leaving his lips, but the expression was stern, and intense. The next statement echoed how he looks. "You darn well know the night is when they are active. How stupid…" My grandfather bit off that last comment, and even took a glance out of his own window, away from me, instead of focusing on the road ahead.

I didn't know how to answer. He was one hundred percent right, and even worse, I didn't even consider that fact. At that moment, I was being a teenager. Of course, I am anything but. My childhood was anything but normal. A parade of schools, homes, and friends. I think we only lived in one town longer than a year. Even then, it wasn't much more than a year. I spent days listening to my grandfather tell me the history of our family and undergoing physical drills to improve my reflexes and coordination instead of playing with dolls or learning to ride a bike. I could do a backflip when I was six. I didn't have much of a choice. If I didn't, the rope my grandfather swung would smack me in the head.

Life as a teenager wasn't much different. The training now included offensive moves. It was something my grandfather added after he felt I could defend myself and survive. A status he forced me to prove against what he called one of his brothers of the order. The man was someone I had never seen before, and such visitors were rare. Just one or two passing through from time to time. He never introduced them to me and kept them hidden in a backroom.

Ironically, their comings and goings were always at night, like ours were.

"Are you listening to me?" He sounded agitated as I came back to the present, accepting this was just another move, like so many times before.

"Yes. Sorry, Grandfather. I don't know what I was thinking. It was just my birthday, and I..." I stopped myself. Something about admitting the truth to him of what I was thinking about and what I was doing seemed worse.

"That rule is for your own protection, and one you must follow." He let out a sigh and then brushed a hand across his brow. He was tired. I could tell. My hand reached for my phone to check the time, but my empty pocket reminded me I left it on the counter. But, then again, he would have had me throw it out the window shortly after we left town, anyway. No attachments. Nothing that could be traced. Thems the rules, as he always said.

"Why don't you pull over and let me drive? You must be tired."

"I'm fine," he said, but his eyes were barely open. "Where were you tonight? I tried calling you as soon as they showed up. I really should have left."

"At a friend's."

"That late?"

"Yes, we were watching a movie." It was just a little lie to save me a larger lecture. "I'm sorry. It won't happen again."

He sighed again, rubbing his eyes, and then let that hand crash down on the armrest next to him. There was something about his demeanor. Something I hadn't seen before as he sat there shaking his head a little from side to side. "Look," he started. The sting was gone from his voice, and it wasn't from exhaustion. "I know it's hard. You want the life you see others having. We just can't. Remember, we don't choose our life. Life chooses us. Our only choice left is if we will live it..."

"And we can't say no," I said, completing his speech for him. It was a mantra I have heard him say for as long as I could remember. I even pointed out once that there was no choice at all. He didn't disagree with my point. "I know. It won't happen again. Now, why don't you pull over and let me drive?"

"Okay," he agreed.

At the next offramp, he turned on the blinker and pulled off and into the closest gas station he could find. I offered to gas us up while he grabbed some snacks and drinks. He didn't answer verbally, just walked toward the store. He returned with a grocery bag of sodas and sandwiches and put them in the back seat next to the two bags we grabbed on our way out. I saw the same scene that he did. He stood there and took it in for a few seconds. Everything we own, the totality of our lives, there in two bags in the backseat. But it's like he said. We don't choose our life. Life chooses us. He didn't want to be a vampire hunter, and neither did I, but that is who we are.

"I keep going over it. It was just a recon, but somehow, they followed me. I didn't know until they came in through the door."

He appeared shaken. My grandfather was not a young man, but he had nerves of steel and reflexes like a ninja.

"They just followed you. That's all. Nothing you did wrong."

"Not possible." He shook it off.

"Just stop thinking about it and try to get some rest."

He didn't fight my suggestion, opening the passenger side and collapsing down into the seat. He leaned back in the seat and slammed the door shut. I filled the car with as much gas as I could get in it, then took my spot in the driver's seat of his blue and rust colored 1970 Impala. The shocks squeaked as I shifted around and adjusted the wheel. I leaned over and hugged him. His arms attempted to hug me back, but the exhaustion I knew he felt had set in.

"Where to?"

"Get back on the interstate and keep driving west until you find some place to stop for the night." He settled back in the passenger seat and leaned against the door.

"And then what?" I asked, but I had a feeling I already knew. This wasn't my first rodeo with this. It didn't matter if my grandfather had completed his assignment or not. Our departures were always in the middle of the night. No goodbyes or anything. We just disappeared from where we were, hoping anyone we had crossed paths with would forget who we were quickly.

"You know the protocol. We go somewhere safe...," he replied, already half asleep.

"Yep, and we wait," I whispered under my breath, turning the key, and pulling the shifter on the column to "D". The car lurched forward under my less than graceful touch. Maybe if he had gotten me my learner's permit and given me a few lessons, I would be smoother. At least I didn't have to shift. I pulled out and worked my way back on to the interstate and did as he said, drove west, watching the signs for a hotel of some type — well, not any type. If my grandfather were awake, he would pick some off the wall, hope you aren't killed by the caretaker, rat infested location to pull into and rent a room for the night, or a couple of days. How long we would need to stay there we never knew. I was looking for a brand name. Something that will have clean sheets and towels, and maybe a working television.

I passed a few exits that had signs for the brand name chains. Something inside wanted to put more distance between us and what we had just left. Not that I felt there was a chance they would find us. It had never happened before, and I wasn't sure if that was even the reason for feeling that way at all. The further away we were, the easier I found it to put that life behind me. To consider it as a distant memory. Why this time felt harder? I wasn't sure.

After another hour, I pulled in, and following my grandfather's training and example, I pulled the car around the back, and walked around the entire hotel looking for… to be honest, I don't know what I was looking for. We haven't gotten that far into my training yet. I mean, I had seen vampires before, kind of. Just flashes here and there when they chased us. After a second lap around the two-story square structure with a pool in the center, I found myself standing at the office door and so far, no creatures lurking in the shadows had attacked me. It must be safe, so I went in and reserved us a room for the night. Our standard room. Nothing in the interior. It had to be exterior facing, with the car parked right outside the door. What I wouldn't give for pool side? Not that I would go for a swim. Well then again, maybe I would just to relax. Just watching the water and the reflected ripples it created would be a relaxing view. Instead, we had that luxurious view of the rear of a green 1970 Impala, which I was now backing into the parking space in front of our room.

A little nudging was all it took to move my grandfather from the passenger seat to the bed in the room. He sat down on the edge of the bed and dropped his bag on the floor, still half asleep, and attempted to stand.

"I need to clear the room," he mumbled.

"You need rest," I said, while doing my best to help my grandfather slide up further on the bed to the pillow. "I can take care of the room."

There was no protest at my suggestion, just a point at his bag on the floor. I knew the objects I needed were in there. I had watched him do this more times than I could count since the death of my parents when I was six. The first time I thought he was nuts, but now I understand both the symbolism and importance of every step. Some of which I thought were overkill. I could only imagine what the housekeepers thought about us once they saw a room we had cleared.

I opened his bag and dug through it past the few changes of clothes he had packed in his emergency bag. At the bottom was the simple wooden box I needed. I pulled it out and placed it on the floor, carefully opening the top and laying out the contents in the order in which I would need them.

First were the cloves of garlic dangling on the end of ropes and a handful of old rusty iron nails. Every door and window leading to the outside needed a clove dangling over it. He didn't pack a hammer. He never had. I watched many times as he stood on a chair holding a clove on a rope in one hand and a nail in the other hand. With a single violent stab, he affixed it to the frame, every time. It took me a few times to make it stick in the frame, but I finally got it. The windows took less of an effort. Then it was time for the vial of holy water he kept packed. There wasn't much left, so I needed to use it sparingly. I dabbed a bit on my finger and ran it along the edge of the windows. I was afraid there wasn't enough to surround the door, so I just ran a little on the door handle. The cloves should cover it. My next-to-last task, placing crucifixes on the floor in front of the door, and on each window ledge. He had six packed for that purpose, but I only needed three. That left me with the last task, which I felt was the one that made us the scourge for hotel housekeepers across the country. What I needed was not in my grandfather's little wooden box. The box wasn't big enough to hold it. It was the bag that was under the clothes in my grandfather's emergency bag. A simple bag of salt. With it, I drew a line in front of the door, and a circle around the bed. With that done, I repacked the box and the bag of salt.

"The call," my grandfather moaned.

Oh, yes. The call. I reached back into the bag and pulled out a simple white card with a phone number printed on it. I stood up and walked over to the other bed in the room, and sat, studying the simple card the entire time. This was another step I had never performed before, but I had seen him do it many times and knew what to do. My hand picked up the receiver of the room phone, and then I dialed the number. It rang twice before the other end picked up the call. I counted to three, slowly, and then hung up and leaned back against the pillow. Sleep was something I probably needed, but it probably would be nothing more than a distant desire. My mind was racing faster than the cars on the interstate outside.

2

October 1st

Dear Diary,

Feels pretty silly doing this, but here I am, scribbling away. What else do I have to do? My phone is back on the kitchen table. Even if I had it, my grandfather would've smashed it. No traceable stuff allowed. Time for an upgrade anyway. So now, all I've got is this diary and the TV, which I can't even turn on 'cause he's a light sleeper. Seriously, he'd wake up if a fly snored.

I should be catching some Z's, but my brain's doing the Indy 500. Here I am, peeking through a crack in the curtain, watching cars zoom past on the interstate. My thoughts are going warp speed. Maybe this diary thing ain't so bad after all. It might not be the kill log he wants, but maybe writing about how I feel will help.

So how do I feel? Tell me Miss Foster, how does this move make you feel? I needed to lie down on a couch for this therapy session. Well, doctor diary, this move hit differently than the others. This time, I felt like I left something behind. Weird, 'cause I always felt that tug a little. This time it is stronger. Much, much stronger. Maybe it's just fresher. In a few days, once I settle into whatever life's got for me there, I'll forget all about this one. Just another chapter in my many lives. That's not right. Maybe I made a mistake in this one. I let more of me be the real me than before. People liked that <u>me</u>. Lucas liked that <u>me</u>. Oh Lucas... I can't get out of my head that I will never see or talk to him again. Why him? Why not anyone else? Maybe in ten years I'll circle back and pay him a visit. What harm could *that do? Maybe he'll still be single. Not likely. He was too good of a guy. Someone else will realize it one day.*

STOP IT! No attachments, remember!

On to the next. Supposed to be all hopeful for the next one, but there's this looming dread. The restart. The whole "starting a new" routine. Been there, done that, lost its shine ages ago. Just hoping for a better name this time. Knowing my luck, I'll probably end up a Wilhelmina or something just as dorky.

Laters

When I closed my diary, I held it in my hands and allowed my fingers to explore the worn leather cover. It had character, more character than this cliché of a room. What did I expect? I picked a brand name. There were two beds, with simple white sheets and pillows, and a dark navy comforter. Colors that wouldn't offend anyone. Neither too bold nor too bland. As was much of the furniture. It was all plain and unadorned dark wood. Every room in this place was no doubt the same. Just like the headlights of the cars passing on the interstate. Each set appeared the same as the one before it and the one behind it. My life, or make that lives, felt the same. I sat here at the window looking out at the night, the traffic flashing by on the interstate in the distance and thought about all my past personas I had to create, and the more I had created, the more they all seemed to be the same with varying bits of the real me poking through, if that was even possible. Part of this moment of retrospective was an effort to catalog who I had been, so I could construct who I needed to become. As I considered what parts of me to allow to show through, my snarky side, my sensitive yet not vulnerable side, I started wondering if those were really me, or just a me I had created to fit one of my new lives.

It was a good thing I still remembered my real name. Maria Foster. Not that many even called me by that name anymore. To be honest, I couldn't remember the last time I had heard it out loud. My grandfather made sure to call me by whatever name I was supposed to be. He was always fully committed to the illusion. The last time I had heard my name might have been when he showed up at the hospital when I was six to claim me, after the death of my parents. From then on, it's been the longest game of make believe in the world.

Don't get me wrong, there were benefits to this. You could be whoever you wanted to be. At times, I would add in a little of the personality of a friend I met in a past life. Mostly out of admiration of that trait, or my running out of ideas. And there is the fresh start. Now it was just nerve-racking dread. Who would I be? Could I be believable? I was sure this time would be the same as all the others. They would give us the basics, our names and backstory, and my grandfather and I had to fill in the rest. I probably needed to wait to at least have the basics before I decided which of my past lives to carry forward into this one, even how much of the real me I would include. I often wondered how much of the real me remained.

I would have to ponder that further later. Sleep beckoned at my eyes, and their lids were hearing the call. Maybe it was the rhythmic passing of the cars in the distance, and the drone of the air conditioner that almost put me out, but there was no fighting it. I was going down for the count, so I slid down in the chair right where I was and closed my eyes.

My eyes sprang open to the sound of three thunderous bangs. I jumped up from the chair. The blanket someone had draped over me after I fell asleep fell to the floor. Sun formed blazing bright lines along the edge of the curtain. I looked around the room, which was no longer dark. Besides the knife edges of sunlight coming in around the windows, the flicker of the television, a 24-hour news show, illuminated the room. Two white takeout containers were on the table. I heard the banging on the door again and jumped.

"I'll get it," my grandfather announced as he walked out of the bathroom, rubbing a towel across his wet hair. He never looked at me on the way as I stood there, surprised and shaken. With a quick check of the peephole, he opened the door. The light of what had to be almost a midday sun exploded in. A large dark figure stepped in, blocking it, before my grandfather closed the door behind him. The dim light of the room was enough for me to recognize the features of the man, and I felt my shaking subside until a click behind me startled me, but that was just my grandfather turning on the bedside lamp.

"Maria. Jonas." He greeted each of us as if he would an old friend. And why wouldn't he? Micheal Langston had been a figure in my life for as long as I could remember. Almost like a guardian angel swooping in to rescue us anytime we got into trouble, like we had now. He was also the one who handed out the assignments for what I had only heard referred to as brotherhood.

"Morning, Mike," my grandfather said, still drying his hair with the towel.

"So, it's time for a move?" Mike reached out and pulled the other chair out away from the single round table that was positioned in front of the window. He first took off his trench coat, which he wore no matter that time of the year, and folded it over the back of the chair, and then sat on it.

"I'm afraid so. They found us. I was really careful…" my grandfather rushed to explained.

"Oh, I know you were. Jonas, you are one of our best. It just happens sometimes. And it has happened so seldom with you, it's not a worry."

"I still feel horrible though."

Mike raised a hand to wave off any lingering concern my grandfather may have felt. I know that wouldn't really take care of it. He would obsess about it over the next few weeks to adjust his routine to avoid a repeat in our next location, but he would drop it now.

"So where are we going now?" I asked, wanting to cut right to the chase.

"Well, hello to you too," Mike replied, slowly turning his head to look at me. "You okay? You look like you've seen a ghost, or something else." He raised an eyebrow.

"She wasn't there when they arrived, but she saw them coming after the car when we left."

Mike turned back to my grandfather and leaned forward. "They followed you out?"

"It was night, and they attempted to attack the car. There is probably a good dent in the passenger side now from them," my grandfather explained.

Mike leaned back in the chair, balancing it on its back legs while pulling the curtain free from the window. The blast of light brought his weathered but friendly facial features under a mop of salt and pepper hair, clearly into view. That was the face I had grown up calling Uncle Mike. "I see. I know a few that can help pull that out, or you could finally upgrade. It's a few decades out of warranty."

"There's nothing wrong with it that a good dent pulling won't fix," my grandfather said. Always the protective one about that car any time someone suggested that he trade it in.

"Nothing wrong with old things, but there are times for new things." Mike let go of the curtain, returning the room back to its dim, single lamp setting. He allowed the chair to settle back on all four legs and then leaned against the table with one arm. "Speaking of, how is your training going, young one?"

"It's going…" my grandfather started to answer.

"Nope, I'm asking her," Mike said, interrupted my grandfather. The arm leaning on the table slowly rotated, and he pointed right at me. "How is it going?"

"I think it's good," I said, looking to my grandfather for confirmation. I really didn't know. He never graded me or gave me any kind of status report of where I was in his plan, if there was a plan. My only source of feedback was when I did something wrong or took a risk outside of my training that I shouldn't have, like sneaking out.

"Keeping up with the physical training?"

I nodded. It was a daily activity for me down in his basement, or on rare occasions outside in some field, well away from anyone. It was a mix of gymnastics and mixed martial arts. I could spring out of the way of anything in a flash, while delivering a blow right to a target at chin height, thrusting one of many types of blades into a chest, or slashing across a throat before my target knew what happened. Some days, it was fun, like I was some kind of badass superhero, and other days I had to force it. Either way, we did it every day.

"That's good. What about the tracking side?" he asked, looking toward my grandfather through the side of his eyes.

I struggled to understand what he meant.

"We haven't started that yet," my grandfather said, bailing me out. I had no clue what Mike was referring to.

"Why not?" Mike asked pointedly. "Most start that around age fourteen or fifteen." The hand that was pointed at me slapped down on the table under its own weight. "She's late."

"By who's clock?" my grandfather asked scoldingly. "Really? By whose clock? I am training her. I will decide when she is ready. Not some schedule put down on paper." He balled up his towel and slammed it on his bed.

"Now Jonas, no one is questioning your methods. I was just asking, as a friend," Mike responded defensively.

My grandfather sniped back, "I bet." Then proceeded to his bag to pull out a fresh shirt.

Mike turned and looked right at me before making his next point. The tension in the conversation was not evident in his expression. Who I saw looking at me resembled someone I may consider, and have considered, an uncle that was concerned about his niece. We weren't true family, but outside my grandfather, he was the closest thing I had to an extended family. "Jonas, just remember, you aren't doing her any favors. She needs to know how to protect herself, and I know she is more than ready."

My grandfather let out a huff as he slipped into his clean white shirt. Mike mouthed in my direction, "you are more than ready."

I replied with a silent, "Thank you."

"So, how do you two feel like visiting the south?" Mike leaned forward and reached back, pulling his coat off the back of the chair. Then he unfolded it as his hands searched through one of its pockets. His left hand pulled out two white envelopes. After a quick glance at each, he slid one across the table to me, and then tossed the other one on the bed in front of my grandfather. "Savannah, Georgia, to be specific. It's on the coast."

I didn't hear the description of where we were going, or any of the business side of things he started told my grandfather. That wasn't much of my concern or interest. I rummaged through the various papers in the envelope for what I was most curious about. It would be a smaller, aged-looking piece of paper, and it was always in the envelope. It was a necessary piece of information to establish my new life. I found it in there, folded up, and pulled it out and laid it on the table. With one deep breath, I opened it and read the name off of my new birth certificate.

"What the..." I screamed and then stopped myself before I let out a line of profanity that would make a sailor blush. I slung the paper and the envelope back on the table.

"You don't like your new name?" Mike asked, reaching over to gather the envelope. His hand searched through the envelope for something. I slid the birth certificate back in his direction before falling back in my chair. Did I like the new name? No, I hated it. We were supposed to blend in. Be both noticeable and forgettable. This would not be the latter. No way. No how.

"Raven Cross? Really?" I complained and leaned my head back against the chair and stared up at the ceiling.

"I thought it was a cool name. Very mysterious."

I held my hands up and shook them as I let out a creepy sounding, "Wooo."

"That is what we need for your cover story. Maria, your style won't exactly fit in here. Hoodies and black eyeshadow aren't exactly the common fashion where you're going. I thought, instead of asking you to change who you are, this time we adjust the persona we give you to match the real you, except your hair color. You're supposed to be a blonde. I have some bleach out in the car."

I almost spat back, asked if he knew who the real me was. I wasn't completely sure I did anymore. How could anyone else? The change of hair color was the least of my concerns. So far, I've had every color known to man, and one I created in the bathroom of a hotel just like this one.

"Let you be you for a change, and here," Mike tossed a small piece of plastic across the table. It was maybe four inches by six inches and had a picture of me on it. "This might make it better."

I reached for it, almost not believing what it was. It couldn't be, could it? My eyes confirmed it once I picked it up and looked it over. Okay, maybe this would ease a little of the frustration over that choice of name. I felt things flutter inside as I looked at the picture of me, ignoring the blonde hair and the name next to it. With a huge grin on my face, I held it out toward my grandfather for him to see.

"She hasn't taken the test yet," was his response.

"Oh, come on Jonas. She has been driving you around from time to time since she was thirteen. She knows how to drive, and if she doesn't, you need to teach her. She has a car waiting for her."

That word caused me to spring out of my chair and around the table with a squeal, giving Mike a hug around the neck. He didn't resist it, and accepted it, but added a caution to temper my excitement. "Now, don't get too excited. It's an old beater. An original beetle, with some dings, but it runs."

Nothing he said mattered to me. I heard the word car, and that was all I heard. The grin it produced felt like a permanent fixture on my face. Nothing could remove it. Not even the look my grandfather gave us both as I turned toward him holding the license.

3

October 2nd

Dear Diary,

     Ugh, I don't even know why I'm bothering to write in you right now. It feels weird pouring out all this stuff onto these pages, like I'm spilling secrets I keep locked up tight. I mean, hello? I'm supposed to be this tough vampire hunter, not someone who spills her guts to a book.

     Today kicked off yet another round of "new school, new me." Raven Cross. Seriously? I was half-worried they'd give me some dorky name, but this might be worse. It's so unforgettable, and I bet everyone else will think the same, which is a major headache. I've lost track of how many times I've been the newbie. It's always the same drill—faces I don't know, awkward intros, and that constant feeling of being an outsider. Sad part? It's starting to feel like the norm. I've never stuck around anywhere long enough to get comfy. Not that I never had friends. I did, in a few places. Some were even super close, but in my world, nothing lasts.

     Good news though: I've got wheels now, and it's not half bad. Checked out the car last night when we rolled in. Got a couple of dings, but nothing tragic. So, I'm driving that baby tomorrow. Sayonara, bus rides or my grandfather dropping me off.

     But then there's the downside: my room is a disaster. Who thought a canopy bed was a cool idea? Am I 10 years old or what? I wanted to tear that thing off last night, but grandfather insisted I wait till today. Something about noise and his beauty sleep. Pliers are ready on my nightstand for the minute I'm back this afternoon.

'Til next time, which I guess is tomorrow. Later, diary.

Mike said the car was an old beater of a Beetle. The outside didn't look too bad in the dark last night when we arrived, but I got my first good look at it when I came out to drive it to school this morning. There were a few scratches in the spots of light blue paint that remained, a rust spot or two by the gasket around the back window, and one dent that looked like a shopping cart hit the driver's side front fender, but all-in-all not bad for a free fifty something year old car. The inside was relatively spotless, with a little fraying around the edge of the seat, which still had enough padding to use the word comfortable in the description. That was where it ended. Once I turned the key, I knew the meaning of the word beater. It was going to beat the hell out of me on the drive to school. It spit and sputtered to life, and when I backed out, the lack of any type of shocks or springs in the car announced the transition from driveway to street with a bone-jarring slam. The same bone-jarring slam greeted every bump and paint stripe all the way to school. A chiropractic appointment might be in order after this drive. Of course, that was my thought before I hit one of the cobblestone roads in downtown Savannah. Comfortable was no longer a word I would use to describe the seat. With each stone, I felt the metal frame of the seat rearranging my spine.

I survived one last painful bump, a speed bump in the school parking lot placed just inside the fence to deter any burnouts or other reckless displays of power on exit. Bump or no bump, I wouldn't be able to take part in those. It took a quick pump of the gas pedal just to make it to the top of the bump. My front wheels rolled down the back side of it. One more pump helped my rear tires clear it. I coasted the rest of the way into the spot I found I could safely and discreetly park in. It was just inside the gate, but far away from any of the groups of students mulling around their cars before class started. I had seen this scene before. It was pretty standard. No one wanted to go inside until the first bell rang. Usually, my grandfather dropped me off at the front. I would then pull my hood close around my face and make the trek straight inside to the office, avoiding anything beyond a few odd stares the new student always received upon arrival. That was just fine with me. Now I needed to perform the same trick. This time, it was a tougher task.

Where the main office was, or so the sign said, required me to walk through the crowds. Not just a few crowds either, mind you. All the crowds. The thought of looking for a spot closer was tempting, but that wouldn't qualify as discreet. From my front seat, I eyed the situation and noticed the walkway along the side of the gym. It wasn't more than a few feet away and led straight to the sign denoting the location of the office, but most importantly, there were only a few groups camped there. My other option was sitting here until the bell rang and just be late, but that option was worst of all. That had happened a few times. None of them were on purpose, and each time they were complete groaners. Coming in late to a class as the new girl, where the teacher could have you stand in front of the class for several moments while you hope she didn't ask you to introduce yourself, which most never missed the opportunity, was sheer torture. My plan was to complete my paperwork and get my schedule early enough to race to my first class and have that awkward introduction moment with my teacher before anyone else had arrived. With over half an hour before the first bell, I had a chance, but every moment I sat here brought me closer to what I wanted to avoid.

The driver's side door creaked open, and my body cringed. I looked around to see if anyone had noticed. It appeared no one had, but just to be sure, I pulled my hood up over my head, cradling my notebook with a pencil stuck in the spiral tight against my chest, and all but ran for the walkway. I didn't look up as my feet reached the sidewalk, and I turned toward the sign. There was no need to look for friendly faces yet. Maybe by the end of the week things will change, but not yet. I moved quickly, feeling beads of sweat forming on my forehead and body. The heat and humidity this morning were stifling. I could swear my hoodie felt moist. *Great*, I thought, *I was going to be the new smelly student.* Talk about making a first impression.

I reached for the door handle, wanting to feel the welcoming blast of air conditioning as I stepped in. Instead, I caught the door right on my cheek, sending me spilling to the ground. I did so rather quietly, but the cause was anything but.

"Oh my god, are you okay?" the attacker with the door screamed. He didn't even offer me a hand to help me up. This jeans and white button-up shirt wearing goof, he had to be a goof, just stood over me looking down at me with his brown eyes under a mop of freshly dyed blonde hair like I was some kind of animal in the zoo.

I pushed myself up with my elbow, ignoring the throb in my cheek, and rolled to my left, looking for my notebook that became dislodged from my grasp by the impact of the door. That was when the horror of all horrors became clear. At no fault of my own, I was now the center of everyone's attention.

At least they weren't laughing. That was one silver lining. The other was how close I was to the door. I rolled over to my knees and gathered my notebook, pulling it tightly against my chest again as I stood up. Without looking, I knew everyone was still watching, which fueled my next move to the door, ducking under the hand that now reached down to help me up. The door was closing, and I hurried and twisted my body to slide in before it closed. I should have let it close, and then pulled it open. I would have saved myself the further embarrassment of colliding with the door again and sending me sprawling on the ground. My notebook again flew from my gasp as my hands attempted to catch my fall I missed, only cushioning my landing, avoiding slamming my face into the dirt that was beside the path.

"Oh, crap!" A female's voice said behind me. "Let me help you up."

I felt her leaning over me. Then she kneeled down next to me, grabbed me by the shoulders, and tried to help me up, but I didn't notice her. It was everyone else who had my attention. I was sure they were all looking at me and laughing. Hell, I probably would have if I had just watched someone run into the same door twice. But no one was. Not a soul. Some looked at me, concerned, and others appeared perturbed by my interruption. Maybe I should apologize. Not! Before pushing up, I made another scan around. It would appear I was no longer entertaining, and everyone had returned to regularly scheduled whatever they were doing. That was all except two. They stood there, leaning up against a sleek silver European sedan. Both peered at me from under their own hoodies with two sets of mesmerizing blue eyes set inside faces chiseled from marble. They watched, but I didn't mind. Why? I couldn't explain. Then they walked in my direction.

In a panicked movie, I readily grasped the hand of my latest assailant, but I couldn't take my eyes off of them as she helped me to my knees. The world around them was just a blur. I didn't even notice as she whisked the dirt from my clothes. When she brushed my cheek, now that was a different story. A shot of pain made me wince, and I averted my attention to my attacker. "Crap! That hurts!"

"Oh dear. We need to get that looked at," the girl said. I looked in her direction and saw a pleasant-faced girl. Not beautiful, slightly plain, and thin, wearing just a t-shirt and shorts. Her hands rummaged through her purse for a moment before they produced a tissue that she used to dab at my cheek. Each dab caused me to jerk uncontrollably. "Here. Let me get you to the office. The nurse needs to look at that." She reached down and grabbed my forearm, helping me to my feet. I looked around for my notebook, and when I found it just to my side, I leaned down to pick it up, but she beat me to it. With a hand on my back, she led me through the very dangerous door and into the office that was the first door to the left.

"Mrs. Marshall," the girl yelled.

A reply emerged from inside an office. "Yes, Jamie. What is it?" The source, a woman in a navy-blue dress, walked out of the office. At the sight of me, her hand cupped over her mouth. I must look like something out of a horror film. "Oh dear. What happened to you?" she asked, walking through the pass-through door next to the large counter that separated the front area from the offices.

"The door hit her," Jamie reported.

I held up two fingers, and added, "Twice."

"Oh dear," Mrs. Marshall exclaimed, again. She joined us up front and had taken the tissue from Jamie.

"Come with me. Sit down." She guided me over to a chair. "Julia, the school nurse, isn't here yet, but I think I can handle this." She stood up, studying my face. "I'll be right back," she said with a raised finger, and then sped back through the pass-through.

Jamie sat down next to me and brushed a little dirt off my other cheek. It didn't hurt, so I had only destroyed one side of my face. "I'm afraid that is probably going to bruise."

"Great," I sighed.

"First day?"

I nodded.

"I'm Jamie Langston," she held out a hand.

I reached over and shook it, pausing for just the briefest of moments while I remembered my new name. "Raven Cross."

"Oh my god," she responded, surprised. "That name is so beautiful."

"Thanks," I replied, looking straight ahead. My cheek throbbing.

Mrs. Marshall appeared again, carrying a grocery bag. She kneeled next to me and emptied the contents of their makeshift first aid kit along the floor. "This is going to sting a bit," she said, tearing open an alcohol wipe. She was right. It burned like hell as she dabbed my cheek. When she was done, she blew on it, as if that would make it go away. She handed me a cold compress and said, "Hold this against your cheek."

I took the ice pack from her hand and pressed it against my cheek, feeling the unmistakable soreness of a new bruise developing. Talking about making a first impression. This, without a doubt, was the most eventful first day of school I had ever had.

"So, you're my new student, Raven Cross, I presume."

I looked over and nodded. "Yep. Some way to make an entrance, huh?"

"Psh," Jamie spewed. "You aren't the first, and you won't be the last one to be hit by that door. It's almost got me a few times."

Mrs. Marshall stood up and walked away. It couldn't have been for more medical supplies. She had half the supplies from a trauma unit spread out on the floor beside me. All that was missing was something to shock me back to life, and that wasn't something I needed yet.

"It could be worse."

I pulled the ice pack away from my cheek, turned, and smiled at Jamie. She returned a grin. It could be, but not much.

"I think I have some cover-up in my locker. I can help you with that."

"Thanks," I said reluctantly. It was a kind offer, but not one I was considering. With how badly this was hurting, I didn't want anyone touching it. Plus, I knew how to cover bruises up all by myself. A practice of my trade. My training, at times, took on a rather physical nature, and accidents happened. Accidents had a habit of happening a lot. "It will be fine," in a few days.

"Here it is." Mrs. Marshall walked through the pass-through door holding a small piece of yellow paper. She held it out in front of me, displaying it for me to see. I reached out and retrieved it. I knew what it was, but that didn't stop her from telling me. "That's your schedule." She stepped back, crossing one arm in front of her while propping her chin on the other. "I think we can hold a few days to do a student ID."

That sounded like a great idea to me. There was no need to immortalize this moment in plastic. I didn't know how swollen my cheek was, but the pain made it feel like it was at least twice its normal size. It wasn't that bad yet, but it wouldn't be long. "Thanks."

I looked my schedule over, mostly studying the room numbers, not that I knew where they were in this school. The classes didn't matter. They were probably the same classes I had just left, and at first glance, I saw they were. Right down to my elective, drama. That was where Lucas and I met. I would have to thank Uncle Mike for that later. He, or someone in the brotherhood, always called ahead and delivered the transcript from whatever my last school was. Which kept the school from reaching out themselves, and finding out that Lynbrook High School in San Jose, California, had no record of a girl named Raven Cross having ever attended there. Uncle Mike could only do so much.

"Let me see that." Jamie ripped my schedule from my grasp. She studied it with several grunts and groans. "Not the worst schedule I have seen. You and I have drama together for fifth period, and we have the same lunch."

"I'm glad you approve," I replied, reaching over and taking it back with a swipe.

"Pretty good teachers. You avoided Mrs. Beltrand, good god she is boring."

"Be nice," Mrs. Marshall warned Jamie, giving her that universal look.

Jamie replied with the universal teenage pout which started with dropping her shoulders. I had tried that once with my grandfather, and he found it humorous. "I'm sorry, but she is boring. If you have her after lunch, it's a snooze fest."

Mrs. Marshall shook her head and reached up and pulled the ice pack from my cheek. "Tsk. There is no avoiding it. That is going to bruise." She looked up at the clock on the wall above my head as she lightly pressed the ice pack back into place. "Why don't you take that and hurry on to your first class. That will let you avoid the rush."

"That might be safer," I remarked.

"Come on." Jamie stood up. "Let me walk with you and protect you from doors." She looked down at me, and I waited to see a smirk following her commented. Every second that passed without one made me squirm. She wasn't joking. What a first impression I made. Then there it was, and relief ran over my body, and I allowed myself to stand up and join her.

We walked through the empty halls. Jamie acted as my tour guide, telling me what classes were down each hall. She didn't waste an opportunity to point out all the doors, and I did my best to hold the cold ice pack against my now throbbing cheek. This was going to more than bruise. It was going to bruise and swell. It already felt bigger than my damn head.

"Here you are. Room 137. Mr. Fletcher. English," Jamie announced, standing at the door. I half expected her to open it for me to make sure I didn't hurt myself, but she let me do that all on my own.

I was almost inside, using one hand the best I could while clamping my notebook against my side with my elbow, my other hand still holding the ice pack to my cheek, before she called back to me. "Raven, if you aren't doing anything for lunch, you are welcome to eat with me. I am next door to your class, and I can wait for you."

Well, this would be a record for me. I had my first friend within the first few minutes. Normally, it took me weeks before I let anyone in. It's not like I had much of a choice. "That sounds great."

"Perfect. I'll see you after fourth period." Jamie all but skipped away from the door, waving her fingers bye, leaving me there standing with my back to an open classroom door with a teacher behind me. I felt his gaze on my back. I turned, hoping he wouldn't have questions about my present condition.

"Hi, I'm Raven Cross."

I approached Mr. Fletcher, offering my schedule with my free hand. Mr. Fletcher sat at his desk. A jacket hung over the back of his chair. Stacks of papers littered the top of his desk. He was a pleasant, but tired looking man. A hand reached up and ran through his thinning salt and pepper hair before reaching out to take the schedule. He didn't even look at it before dropping it down on top of his desk and spinning around in his chair to the half bookcase behind him, returning quickly with a textbook in hand. He dropped it on the desk and then picked my schedule up and put it on top of it before grabbing a pen and scribbling something next to his name. Then he picked them both up and handed them back to me as his head returned to the paper he was reading when I walked in. "Take a seat anywhere. They're not assigned."

"Okay. Thanks," I said, unsure what to make of that less than personal greeting. It should be something I looked at as a blessing, but it was off-putting, to say the least.

With a whole classroom of desks to choose from, I took the easy way out and headed to the back row, hoping to just blend into the back corner. My experience of dozens of first days should have snuffed out that hope long ago. If it hadn't, seeing every set of eyes turn in my direction as students started piling into the class did. I was on a pedestal that was easy for everyone to find. A few even turned and looked back in my direction as they took their seats. My appearance, being the new girl, sitting there holding an ice pack against my cheek dressed like something out of a grunge music video, didn't help me blend in, so I removed the ice pack, hoping the bruising hadn't started yet.

"Oh, look. It's the door girl," a feminine voice with a deep southern drawl called out from the front of the class. I looked up into the southern belle's face. She was even pointing back in my direction as she stood there, her books clasped tightly to her chest by her other arm. A snicker emerging from her bright red lips, below her startling blue eyes and a mass of curly blonde hair. Stuck on her hip was a mass of masculinity, wearing a letter jacket in the school's colors, which I guess were green and yellow. From the look on his face, it appeared the elevator didn't go all the way to the top. Typical jock. I've seen hundreds of them in every school I have ever attended.

I waved a single hand in response. Why? Who knew? Some stupid automatic response in my brain to do exactly what I didn't want to do, attract more attention my way. It wasn't my best move of the day. It ranked right behind running into the door twice. I sank and affixed my eyes straight ahead.

"That's enough. Take a seat, Gracie," Mr. Fletcher warned. "You too Todd. And two different seats. You can't share one."

"Sure thing, Mr. F," the lug-head replied. How he sounded confirmed my suspicion.

The final bell rang, and a few straggling students came in, filling the seats in the rows in front of me. There were only two empty seats left, and they were both back here in the last row with me. Mr. Fletcher stood up from his desk and walked across the room, holding the stack of papers he was reading when I walked in. With a quick look down the hall, he closed the door, and then started passing out the papers. His presence at the front hadn't drawn the attention of most of the students. They still turned around in their desks, looking back at me. My hand reached and lightly wiped my cheek. It came away clean. With how everyone stared at me, I expected to find a little blood or a smear of mud.

The door opened, and every head spun around, even Mr. Fletcher's, and in they walked. The two mysterious guys from the parking lot. Their icy-blue eyes, set in their ashen complexion faces with chiseled features, cut through me, and I found myself in the same trance everyone else was, watching their every movement. Neither held a textbook as they walked in. Both looked like they had just stepped out of an Abercrombie and Fitch catalog, wearing jeans, buttoned up dress shirts with the sleeves rolled up to a simple cuff, and dark hair that looked salon fresh. The hoodies I saw them wearing earlier were probably in their lockers. As hot as it was today, only a fool would wear something like that all day long. Of course, I still had mine on, and I was sweltering inside. Both seemed as cool as an ice cube as they split the center aisle of desks, walking on either side of it back to the last row. One of them was walking directly towards me.

He stopped right at my desk. His eyes drilled a hole through me, but he had a hint of a smirk on his lips, almost as if amused by something. I guessed my little show outside had entertained him and knowing that made me squirm a bit. That amused him more. "

"Okay," he said, before spinning around to the seat next to me, where the other one sat, and finally taking the seat next to him, still looking at me and nodding. I felt the desire to shrink out of existence and pulled my hoodie up over my head.

"Adrian. Elijah. Nice of you to join us today. Can we start?" The question appeared to be rhetorical as Mr. Fletcher continued handing out the papers and began what sounded like a group critique of the quality of those assignments.

I wasn't as lucky in my next two classes as I was in Mr. Fletcher's class. Each had me stand up and give an introduction about who I was, where I had moved from, and something fascinating about me. Each was part of the backstory Uncle Mike, or someone, had written for me on a folded piece of paper in the envelope. The handwriting was rather feminine for it to be his, but I was told a long time ago not to ask questions about how any of this works. Just accept it and do as I was told. That was what a man claiming to be my grandfather, who I had never met before, told me, a six-year-old who had just lost her parents when he picked her up at the hospital. I didn't even question that. But that was then, and now I had questions.

"I'm Raven Cross. I moved here from San Jose, California—I have never been there. Something interesting about me. Well, I am being raised to hunt vampires." Well, that wasn't exactly the introduction I gave in each of the classes. It was something less dramatic. "I'm Raven Cross. I moved here from San Jose, California. I like to read and surf." That is what someone wrote for me. To add some authenticity to it, I held up my hand and extended my pinky and thumb out while I shook it slightly. It was something I had seen surfers do in movies.

Miss Gracie Jones was also in my third period class, and while I did my introduction, I braced myself for her to add in my new moniker of "Door Girl." To my relief, she didn't. At least not out loud. She sat in the back of the classroom, whispering back and forth with her court.

In fourth period, I believe I found out why I had such an odd encounter back in Mr. Fletcher's class with, who I have now learned to be, Adrian. I didn't ask anyone his name directly. I didn't have to. All I needed to do was wait and watch them walk out ahead of everyone else and watch all the other girls swoon over him and his brother, and how all the guys leered at him. Then the girls started like a gaggle of hens. Adrian this, Elijah that. One thing I have learned about being the new kid in a school, you can learn more by listening than asking, and I had so much practice at this I could teach a masterclass. As it would appear, I was in his seat. A detail I discovered on my own when I… I guess… I did it again. He gave me a quirky smile and commented, "All right." Then he resigned himself to his fate and sat in the seat in front of me. He turned a few times to talk to his brother, sitting next to me, and I had to divert my eyes to keep from swooning myself. Even then, I found myself becoming mesmerized by the perfection that was his features, having to force myself to look away to avoid being caught.

Jamie was right where she said she would be after fourth period. Plastered against the wall outside the door of my class. Our first stop was my locker, which I didn't know I had. My schedule had the number written on it. I guess it was a little detail Mrs. Marshall had forgotten to tell me. My arms were killing me, holding now four textbooks and my notebook. It's not that it was all that heavy. They were awkward, and no matter how I tried to hold them, the edges of a book or two cut into either my ribs or my arm. Jamie helped me with the combination after my first attempt failed. She got it on the first try. The door popped open with a metallic rattle, and then I saw it. A reflection of my face in the mirror glued on the inside of the door. I had done a number on my cheek. Green was an excellent color on me, but not on my cheek. There were several bruises forming. I only remember the door hitting me twice.

After I deposited the books, Jamie whipped out her coverup and did her best to repair me while not killing me. Things were touchy, and I jumped the first few times she touched it. She did the best she could. Our skin tones weren't a match, so it looked like I had a light spot on my cheek when she was done, but it was better than the bruising.

The trip to the cafeteria was uneventful. I even passed through several doors without incident. It was a typical scene: long lines, crowded tables, and teachers roaming around to keep order. In most ways, it resembled what you see in prison movies, except we weren't wearing orange jumpsuits. We got our food and settled down at a table. We both opted for chicken sandwiches and fries, the more fast-food variety of offerings compared to the casserole in the hot food line. Throughout lunch, Jamie waved person after person over to introduce me to them. I guess she felt I was her new responsibility. Most of them I met with a mouth full of chicken, bun, or both. A couple sat down at the table with us. Stephen Moore was the first. Caroline Webb was next. Both were drama students and in the class with Jamie and me after lunch. The level of gossiping that happened at the table, which Jamie disguised as helping me become familiar with everyone in the school, reminded me of why I usually took my lunch somewhere else and ate by myself. It was too late to escape now.

Over Stephen's shoulder, and across the chaos, there they were again. Sitting at a table in the back of the cafeteria, with no food, and only one other person, a female, that, like them, seemed more in place on the cover of a fashion magazine than in a public high school cafeteria. I couldn't stop myself from looking, except when Elijah caught me, and I looked away and back down at my sandwich.

I must have jerked or something. Stephen noticed and asked, "What's wrong?" Then he turned around and looked back. "Oh," he said, turning back around. "She has only been here for four periods, and she's already caught in their spell."

Caroline cast a look back in their direction and sighed, "It's not hard."

"I hear that's what their girlfriends say," Stephen remarked, and then caught an elbow from Caroline.

"Who are they?" I finally asked, while casting another look over Stephen's shoulder. They were gone. My eyes darted around, looking for them, but all I caught was a door closing.

"They are the royal pains," Stephen started, but another hard elbow from Caroline cut him off.

"The homeschoolers," Jamie said, but that answer didn't appear to satisfy Caroline. She leaned across the table, practically climbing up on it.

"That's the Starlings. Adrian, Elijah, and their sister Miranda. No one knows much about them, but their family is huge in this town. Their name is everywhere. I even think they named the hospital after them. Their father is some major international business tycoon or something. They live in an older house that is a palace over on Drayton, in the Forsyth Park area, so they have a lot of money. Those three showed up here last year out of nowhere. Rumor has it they have been kicked out of all the top private schools, so they are now homeschooled, and they only come in to take tests. Today is a history test. They are in my class for that."

"You picked a good day to start," Jamie added, "but I would just keep them as a picture in your mind. They rarely speak to anyone, and from what I've heard, one of them is an ass, but that isn't the biggest problem. If you try to speak to either of the brothers, you will face the wrath of Miranda. I wish she was more like her brothers and never talk to anyone." Jamie groaned and leaned back. "Eat up, we need to get to drama. You can take a few more mental pictures of them there."

4

October 3rd

Dear Diary,

The plan was to do this once a day, but... it was the first day in a new school and I need to vent, ABOUT ME. I am a total klutz. 100% klutz. It's who I am. I can't hide it when I try. When I try, like today, I am a bigger klutz. While ATTEMPTING to sneak into school unseen today, I ran into a door, twice! Yes, that is correct. Not once. Twice! Chalk that as a big fail!

Well, I can't call today a complete failure. I got my schedule. I don't really hate any of my classes yet. I think I have a friend. But, then again, it could be some kind of Florence Nightingale situation. She did come to my aid and help me to the office after my face crashed into the door for the second time. That is one door I will avoid for as long as we are here.

Schools are schools. This one's nothing special, but Grandfather will want the usual rundown. High schools are like clones of each other, same drama, different day. Cliques are everywhere, and even the anti-clique crew doesn't get they're a clique too. It's like a soap opera, seriously. Who's dating who is like a big deal, just the usual teenage craziness. Not like anyone bothered filling me in on the deets, though. I'm just chilling, overhearing stuff while pretending to be deep in thought. It's my thing, okay?

But hold up, there's this weird thing. Two siblings in school that seem low-key royal or something. I've seen the whole clique hierarchy thing, but this is next level. Intriguing, right?

Oh great, Grandfather is calling me to come take a ride with him. I sure hope he hasn't already been discovered. Later.

"It wasn't that bad." I said, answering my grandfather's question about my first day of school.

"What happened to your face?" my grandfather asked, glancing in my direction from the driver's seat of his car.

"I hit a door," I explained briefly, leaving out the bit about me hitting it twice. It was one of the only details that I had left out as I began my usual first day task, the debrief.

It usually occurred while sitting across from my grandfather at a table, probably in a kitchen. Like some kind of criminal interrogation, I had to recount every detail of my day, with some cross examination coming from my grandfather if he felt I glossed over something. Now, he wasn't interested in any of the fluffy stuff, such as who was nice to me or not, or what my classes were like. To be honest, I wasn't sure he was interested in any of it. I felt this was more about the art of the report, and how perceptive I was to the world around me. I mean, why the hell would he be that interested in which girl was the most popular, and who was dating who in high school land? I could barely stomach it myself. This was all about the art of recon. That was skill number one. Not to be confused, the list of the rules he had was a list of skills he said I needed to be a master of, and knowing the world around me was at the top of it. Even if I never took over the reins from him, I needed to master this to stay safe. So, the afternoon after every first day of school since I came to live with him was the same. My telling him who I met, how I met them, what I knew about them, what I perceived from their personality, and that was just about the people. To give him the physical recon on the school at the detail he wanted, I practically had to draw him a map of the school. Come to think about it, the first time I did have to draw a map of the school. Now it was something I could do on autopilot. He cared little about the details I reported, just how I reported it and the level of details. Doing it in a moving car was different.

"Recon?" I asked, thinking he was finally taking me with him to check out a target.

My grandfather looked straight ahead, and without even a flinch, he said, "Training."

I let out a loud sigh and slumped down in the seat.

"It's been a while, and you need all the work you can get."

The validity of his point didn't stop another loud sigh from escaping past my lips. This was the last thing I was in the mood for.

"Keep the report going," he urged.

I picked up right where I left off; a variation of the skill I had learned over time. He often would throw a distraction in to see if he could get me to lose track of my thoughts. So far, he was a big 0-for there. It never worked, which brought a curl to the corners of his mouth. Come to think of it, that was as close to a smile that I ever saw from him. He wasn't a gruff person, but he also never let his guard down around me. That's not to say he was cold to me. He just wasn't warm. Much like I might imagine a grandfather who had lived alone for a while and out-of-no-where had a kid to take care of. How long he had lived alone before I arrived? I wasn't sure. I didn't know when my grandmother died. He never talked of her. I hadn't even seen a picture of her sitting around the house. Of course, with how much we moved, such things were a novelty we didn't have space for in our escape bags. The only picture I had of my parents was the one I saw when I closed my eyes.

I was finishing up my report about where my locker was physically located in relation to the doors when I threw a distraction his way. "Why aren't we training in the basement? This house has one. I checked it out last night." It did, and it was cleaner than any of the others I remembered. It was partially finished with dark hardwood floors. Probably something the original owners had planned to make into a family room, or even a man cave, to watch sports in. It was a ton better than the house before the last one we left. The floor was dirt, and from the stench, I was pretty sure the sewer system was leaking.

"It's not set up for such activities yet, and we need more room. Continue."

As requested, I continued with the report, giving him the lay of the cafeteria and the offerings, never expecting him to admonish me for my choice. That was not something he ever did. I gave him the run-down of the people I met, with as much detail as I knew. It wasn't like I had them each fill out a bio, but I knew the drill so well now he didn't even feel the need to ask me anymore. Over time, I would find out everything I could about them. Again, none of them were his target. This was about learning skill number one. I even went over the scene I saw regarding Adrian, Elijah, and their sister, Miranda. That gave me an opportunity to ask him something I had thought about most of the afternoon.

"Grandfather, why can't I be homeschooled? Would it be easier? No connections. No hassles or worries of being discovered. It seems cleaner…"

"You already answered your question," he said, interrupting what I felt were two more dynamite points in my argument.

"How so?" I asked, knowing a lecture was probably coming to teach me a lesson.

"No connections," he said simply.

"But–" I started, but he interrupted me again.

"No attachments. That's the rule. Attachments and connections are not the same thing. Remember, you must be both memorable and fit in, while also being forgettable after you leave. And you must live in the world to learn how to observe and read it," he explained, never once taking his eyes off the road ahead of us.

Which was hard for me to look at. We were driving straight into the setting sun, which was blinding. "Now, continue."

I almost said yes, sir, but I knew he was right, and his response didn't deserve any sarcasm. So, I picked up where I left off again, this time going right into drama class, which was the only other time I mentioned Elijah and Adrian for the rest of my report. I didn't mention anyone else either, but their presence was worthy of a mention, especially with my grandfather being such a fan of Shakespeare, something he quoted often. The class was working on a presentation of *Othello*. Come to think of it, I never saw them, or their sister, the rest of the day after drama. Since I was a late addition to the class, they assigned me the understudy for the part of Emilia. The maid. I was still learning names of my classmates, but Chad Burks, a stately and athletic looking guy with blonde hair that I was sure some girls swooned over somewhere, was our tragic hero, Othello. He wasn't exactly my cup of tea, and based on the chemistry, or lack thereof, that I saw with our Desdemona, one Gracie Jones, told me he wasn't her cup of tea either. Chad stumbled over lines right and left, triggering a few tantrums by Gracie. They were full on talent fits. Which was odd, since I had observed no talent in her either. She was over-acting every word and every reaction. Each line from here was being read, flat, with no emotion. If you closed your eyes, her performance would take you absolutely nowhere. Not that I was any award-winning actress, but Drama class had been the one constant throughout all my travels. I even went as far as studying it outside of school in books and online videos. Why wouldn't I? Every day I was playing a part, and my very life depended on delivering a believable performance.

When Othello took a swat against the head from Desdemona's script, the class erupted in laughter. Mrs. Prentice took her place between the two feuding cast members and attempted to regain control of the class as Adrian took center stage, unprompted. He was in full Shakespeare in the Park mode, reciting Othello's lines word for word with a legitimate passion that I wasn't sure even the work's master could have summoned. The classroom went silent, and jaws dropped for a brief second, until Elijah threw himself at his brother's feet and started belting out Desdemona's lines, mockingly. After a few moments, Chad stepped in between them, and attempted to take back the stage, earning him an odd leer from Adrian as he relinquished his spot, and returned to his seat, but not without looking back at me as he sat down, "This is my seat."

I felt a rush of heat and turned away, while Mrs. Prentice applauded the brother's performance.

Grandfather pulled into a parking lot of shells and rocks that hid under the shadows of a canopy of moss-covered trees. If you were looking for some place to take someone to kill them, this would be the place. There wasn't a house in sight. Just trees and a bog full of cattails to our right. He stopped the car and exited without explaining what we were here for. Of course, he already had, just not with a lot of detail. I followed him, with no other choice, but out of habit, I walked to the trunk. This wasn't the first time we had taken a "field trip" to train, and our training tools were always in the trunk, but not this time. He waited for me up at the front of the car with a curious look. I joined him and we took a few steps out into the trees. I, looking into his face the whole time, tried to figure out what was going on.

"Watch your step!"

Right then, my right foot kicked something hard, and I stumbled forward, catching my balance before I tumbled to the ground. I looked down at what had just attacked me and stepped back. It was a headstone. An old limestone headstone, stained with mildew and who knew what else. The elements had long eroded away the writing on it, and the name of the person who lay underneath was just a depression in the stone. This headstone wasn't alone. There were dozens of them on the ground among the trees. Some headstones were barely buried in the ground. Others were nothing more than cracked pieces of marble. Okay, so maybe he came here to kill and bury me.

My grandfather reached into his pocket and pulled out a black rag and handed it to me. Now I knew what this was all about. This was *darkness*. It was a game we had played several times. At first, he called it hide-n-seek. Of course he did. What child wouldn't want to play hide-n-seek? I sure did, even if it was down in a creepy basement with the lights off. From there it progressed to using a blindfold once I had learned to see movement in the dark, which I thought was the goal of the training. When I asked why I needed the blindfold, which, ironically, I was putting on while I asked; he reminded me of something he said often. Vampires are children of darkness. That is their world, and we are only visitors and prey. We must become as comfortable in the dark as they are and learn to see without our eyes.

Was I comfortable, yet? Not quite. I mean, I was without the blindfold, but there was something unnerving about the total blackout the blindfold created. It felt like I didn't have eyes, and here I was, standing in an old cemetery with headstones all around me, and a black blindfold taking my eyes away from me. What happened next was up to my grandfather. My job was just to stand here and try to sense what was coming. This was easier without the blindfold. Then I could see movement and prepare. With the blindfold, all I ever felt were the bruises from my training. I had to rely on my other senses, mostly my hearing. Speaking of my grandfather just tapped me hard on the shoulder as he ran past me.

I stepped back and lowered down into a half crouch, preparing myself to move out of the way for his next pass. I listened, hearing the leaves rustle overhead in the evening breeze. That was going to be a problem. If my grandfather slipped up and made a sound during his approach, I wouldn't be able to discern what was him against that background. It would all sound the same, unless my grandfather coughed or something, which I would never be that lucky.

The rustling of the leaves was a constant sound; almost deafening to someone searching the noise for a single sound. The crinkle of every leaf thundered against my eardrums as I strained. This was why I hated outdoor training. When we did this in a basement, I didn't have to deal with that. The quiet made it easier, but still difficult. I still missed hearing him in the quiet occasionally. As time went on, and my skill grew, I started winning more times than I lost. Once it seemed I had the upper hand, he started blasting loud music during our training sessions. I believe the first time he did that; I ended the day with nine bruises on my legs and arms. All from me bumping into things, disoriented. Luckily, I hadn't "earned" any yet in today's exercise. I already had that nasty one around my eye to cover up before school tomorrow.

There, in the constant roar of rustling leaves in my ears, I heard a pattern. A rhythm that wasn't random enough to be natural. It was to my left and getting louder. There was only one thing it could be. I waited patiently on the outside but coiled up like a spring on the inside. Once he was close enough, I would let that spring loose and leap out of his way.

I held my pose, so not to let him know I was on to him. I knew him well enough to know that if he found out I heard him, he would abort his charge, and then change in such a way I wouldn't ever hear him approaching again. The sound slowed but was nearby. How nearby? That was the question. I waited a few more steps, and because I didn't know how far away he was, I didn't let out the dramatic leap I wanted to. I simply stepped back and to the left, intending to just put more space between us, but my foot caught the hard edge of a headstone and put me on my ass.

"It's as important to be aware of your surroundings as it is to be aware of those surrounding you," he said from just above my head. I felt like swatting up at him, but I knew he would be gone before my hand arrived. All I could do was stand up and start again. Hoping not to trip over anything. I failed in that hope. I failed many times. Seven was the tally I came up with as I sat in the car, surveying the many bruises across my legs and back. It wasn't my worst training session, but it wasn't my best. Actually, I would grade it pretty good. Maybe a "B" or a "B-minus". I heard his approaches. I heard them all, which was a first. I just couldn't get out of his way without tumbling to the ground. But, better yet, my grandfather wasn't using the drive home as an opportunity to critique my performance. He never missed an opportunity to provide what he called "constructive critique" after a training session, unless I had done something well.

5

October 4th

Dear Diary,

    Ugh, my hand is the only part of me not throbbing this morning. Yesterday was a trip—literally. Spent most of it stumbling over ghosts or whatever. Some of them probably found it hilarious up there or down below, depending on where they are. Definitely going for long sleeves and pants today. Seriously, not enough doors to blame for the state of my legs.

    But hey, something clicked. I think I did a better job dodging him. It's happened before, a few good days of avoiding that mess. But this time felt different, like it was me, not just plain luck. I tried to get a couple of compliments, but nope, nada. Not surprised though, that was his style—everything his way, no exceptions. Not that he ever said it outright.

    I asked if I could tag along and watch. I mean, what better way to learn, right? He called me a liability but didn't exactly shut the idea down.

    Gotta get ready for school now. Actually, up earlier than usual, but I need time to address the shiner on my face before I walk in.

    Later

    Even though it was sweltering and humid outside, I wore jeans and a long sleeve shirt to school. It was all I had, and more importantly, it was what I needed to wear. It was bad enough I used a ton of coverup on the dark purple kiss the door left around my eye to only reduce it to a light gray spot. Nothing in this world would cover it. That was a given before I even started. But I didn't have the time, or enough makeup, to cover up all the bruises on both legs and both arms. My souvenirs from my stumbling around blindly during my training yesterday. It was bad enough I had a mark on my face that would draw attention, but if I walked in sporting all these marks, someone was going to think something, and my job was to be both memorable and forgettable. At least everyone already knew how I had gotten the one they could see. Most were there when it happened, and those that weren't heard it through the grapevine, I'm sure. My luck, there's a video on social media memorializing the moment.

I considered avoiding *that* door this morning, but thanks to the oppressive heat and how close it was, I decided to press my luck. The only other alternative was to park, walk back out of the parking lot through the fence, and all the way around to the front of the school. I would be nothing but a bag of sweat if I did that. So, being careful was the plan. I also opted to keep my hood down. There was no point in hiding anymore. If anyone was watching, then let them watch. They were probably watching because I was the new girl with the strange name—Thanks Uncle Mike, or to see if I was going to collide with the door again.

I glanced around as I walked down the same sidewalk I had yesterday. I think I was looking for Jamie, the only what I would call friendly face I had at this school so far. I didn't see her. There were plenty of familiar faces from yesterday, though. It seemed everyone had parked in the same spots and were all hanging out in the same groups before school they did yesterday. They were all there. Well, not all. I couldn't help glancing back to the spot where I saw the silver European sports car with the two brothers and their steel-blue eyes yesterday. They weren't there, and the spot was empty. Perhaps that was their spot. Just like the seat I sat in yesterday was Adrian's seat.

To be sure, I scanned around again for the car, which stood out among the rag-tag group of dented and faded used cars that make up student parking. That was almost an ill-fated look as my shoulder caught that same door as it swung open from the inside. As best I could, I turned, letting it glance off, and grabbed the door with my hand, holding it open for the group to come out. A few smirks adorned their faces, and I knew the tally was now door three and me a big fat zero. This one was my fault. At least I wasn't face down on the ground for the second day in a row.

I slipped in as soon as they all stepped out and headed to my locker. A quick change of books, swapping out the ones I brought home for homework with what I needed for my first two classes. I took a quick glance in the mirror at my eye and shook my head. It looked horrible, but there was nothing I could do about it now. Just as I was about to close the door, there was a light knock on the other side. I closed it and saw Jamie standing there decked out in school spirit. Green and yellow covered her from head to toe, well, except her face. I guess face paint was going too far. She even had green and yellow ribbons in her hair. Before I knew it, she had reached out and pinned a big "Go Dolphins, Beat Mustangs!" button on my hoodie. I resisted the urge to roll my eyes.

"You're coming to the game tonight, and you can't say no," she said cheerily.

"Yes, I can, and no, I'm not," I said, watching her bubble burst while giving my locker one last shove to close it all the way.

"No, you can't, and you're going," she tried again.

"Nah, I'll pass. Sports aren't my thing." I turned to head to English class, knowing she would follow me. The look I saw in her eye told me this wasn't over.

"It's not about the game. It's about hanging out with your friends. I haven't missed a game all year, and I can't tell you which ones we won or lost. That's not why I go."

A few feet away from Mr. Fletcher's door, I fired what I thought would end this brief discussion. "That's all right. I don't have any friends." I wasn't trying to be rude, but inside I heard my grandfather's voice doing the speech about attachments and being forgettable. To me, that always translated to distance, and that was what I had done everywhere we had been, except maybe the last place where I slipped up a little and let Lucas get close to me. Outside of that, I went to school, did the minimum needed outside of school, and stayed out of sight. Well, except for Lucas. He was the closest I had come to breaking my grandfather's rules. I wondered what he was doing right now. Mostly, I wondered if he had forgotten me yet. No, he hadn't, I answered myself. It had only been two days, but how long would it be before he did? A week? Two weeks?

"You have me," Jamie replied as I crossed Mr. Fletcher's threshold. "I'll pick you up. You can give me your address at lunch."

I thought about turning around again to decline the offer as politely as I could, and I actually did, but she had already disappeared into the sea of students all rushing to their first period class before the late bell. I was just a pebble standing there in the rushing river of bodies, trying to get into Mr. Fletcher's class. There was no point in standing here anymore. I headed inside, taking the same seat I had yesterday, where I sat anxiously waiting for Adrian Starling to arrive and remind me I was sitting in his seat, while I considered what Jamie said. I had a friend.

The rest of the class straggled in over the next few minutes, and I kept watch at the door for Adrian and his brother. Even after the late bell rang, I watched the door. Both had arrived late yesterday, but as the minutes clicked by and Mr. Fletcher started his lesson for the day, I realized they were not coming. Today must not be one of their test days, and I felt a slight letdown.

For the next three classes I worked out several ways to back out of going to the game tonight but when I sat down at the table with Jamie, Stephen, and Caroline and after I glanced past Stephen's mop of dark hair, I realized there wasn't a reason for me to not go. Like my grandfather said just yesterday when the topic of home schooling came up, I needed to learn how to live in the world and observe it. What better opportunity than a packed high school football game? When Jamie asked for my address, I gave her the address she could pick me up from. Of course, it was one several blocks away from where I lived at the moment. I still needed boundaries to follow my grandfather's rules.

Nerves fluttered inside my stomach on the drive home. I was about to tell my grandfather something that I hadn't before. At least not so soon after moving into a place. We had very specific rules about this sort of thing. Although I had permission and he expected me to socialize with friends, I had never done it so soon after relocating. There was a "get acquainted" period my grandfather always mentioned. How long that period was? Well, that was a detail he never included when he mentioned the period, and one I hadn't challenged before. I believe it depended on however long it took him to feel comfortable in an area. It wasn't like the minute we arrived, the vampires knew we were there and where to find us.

I pulled into the driveway behind my grandfather's car and walked in through the front door. Anticipation of more training waiting to fill my Friday night swelled inside. Why wouldn't it? That was usually what I did on Friday nights. More playing around in the darkness, or some combat training with a dummy. He hadn't yet opened up his bag of equipment and gone over the ins and outs of how to use each piece to kill a vampire. I wasn't ready, as he kept reminding me, and even reminding Uncle Mike when the topic came up.

"Grandfather, where are you?" I screamed down the hall, figuring I might as well treat this like a bandage and rip it off.

"I'm back in the study," his voice responded, and after a few beats, I heard the door close. Now we didn't really have a room set up as a study when we arrived. It was mostly a living room, family room, dining room, and three bedrooms with two baths, but just as he always did, my grandfather took the unused bedroom and made it his private office, which was off limits to me, always. The door stayed locked, and yes, I had tried the handle a few times in the past. I never saw inside of it, not even a glimpse. That didn't stop my imagination from running away from me, creating images of maps and papers stapled all over the walls with pieces of string connecting points. Way too many crime dramas at night, I guess.

I walked down the hall to meet him halfway. What is it they say about being direct and taking the initiative if you really want something? I wasn't sure I wanted this, but there was something about going to the game that I was warming to.

"I've been invited to the high school football game tonight at school. It's at seven o'clock, and I should be home by eleven. Jamie, the friend that helped me find my way around school yesterday, is picking me up. I gave her an address that is three blocks over." That should fill in all the questions he would have. Not that those answers would stop objections. I could hear his follow-ups before he even asked them. Or maybe it was me asking those questions. Had my grandfather's cautiousness rubbed off on me? That sent a shiver down my back, but I felt bad that it did. I was sure it was just a normal teenage response to realizing you were just like your parents. In my instance, it meant I was learning. Something I was sure would bring a smile to his face, or I hoped it would. He rarely, if ever, smiled.

He stopped in the hallway and appeared to think for a moment. I prepared myself for the flood of questions and stood still, waiting. "Okay. I have things to do tonight, anyway."

None of the questions echoing in my head made it to his lips, leaving me speechless. All I heard was his customary caution. "Just be safe. Watch your surroundings and be home right after."

"Yes sir," I said, but it came out more like a question, still in shock as he turned around and opened the door to his study, walked in and closed the door behind him.

That was too easy, and I found myself frozen there, waiting for him to come back out after realizing what he had just given me permission to do. Back in Portland, two lives ago, I asked just to go over to work with a classmate on a group project. A class assignment. Nothing social. An assignment that they would grade us on. We had been in our house for about a month and Sharon was only just around the corner. I spent the next half an hour sitting at the kitchen table answering questions, and he still refused to let me go. Instead of working on it in person, we did it over the phone. Not the best way to do it, but we still got an "A."

Hearing the silence, I realized he wasn't coming back out, and I accepted his agreement. That was when I realized there was a part of me that had hoped he would have said no. It would have been my out. I guess part of our lifestyle had made me part hermit. That side would just have to survive tonight. The other side of me screamed and shooed my hermit side back into the corner, and I headed upstairs to find something green or yellow to wear. If I had to bet, there was nothing in either shade up there. What I had seen of the clothes they had provided me were mostly darker colors. Which I understood. Someone named Raven probably wouldn't wear such bright colors. A quick check of my closet, and a rummage through my drawers confirmed my suspicion. The only thing I had was a simple white T-shirt. With my luck, our opponent tonight would have white as one of their team colors. It was the only choice if I didn't want to go in some dark gray, blue, red, or black shirt. None of those would work.

I changed and then ran down to the kitchen to fix a quick sandwich. My grandfather stayed in his study the whole time I was there, and even responded through the door with his standard, "Be careful," when I yelled, I was leaving. I locked the door behind me and rushed over to the address I had provided Jamie. It was a little early, but I needed to be there before she arrived. If she saw me walking, it would ruin the illusion, and I couldn't have her sit there honking or, worse yet, walking up to the house.

I gave a cautious look as I rounded the corner. No one was waiting yet, and I hurried to the curb in front of the simple two-story white wood-sided house at the address I gave her. It had a porch, but I didn't dare go up there and sit as if I was waiting for her. That would be way too risky. Waiting at the curb would have to be enough, and just my luck, there was an oak tree in a small little grassy area between the curb and sidewalk, and that gave me the perfect place to stand and lean while I waited, without looking too conspicuous.

My wait wasn't long. Jamie didn't tell me what she drove, but even if I hadn't seen her through the windshield of the pickup truck that had more exposed and rusted raw metal than original white paint, I would have still guessed that was her coming around the corner. It just screamed Jamie. The green and yellow streamers flying behind the truck from the tailgate didn't hurt.

She pulled up to the curb, and I didn't waste any time to reach out and open the passenger side door and hop in. First the loud creak of the door announced my entry, and then a squeak from the old bench seat echoed it. Neither of them was the loudest announcement of my entry.

"Get out!" Jamie screamed. "You aren't coming with me wearing that."

I searched her face for any signs she was joking, but she was dead serious. "I don't have anything green or yellow," I said with a shrug, hoping she would accept this and drive on. We were still parked next to the curb in front of my fake address.

"But why white?" she screeched.

"It's safe. It's neutral," I replied sheepishly, watching her cheeks turn several shades of red.

"B… B…But," she stuttered, as if she were in the presence of a mortal sin. Then it came. "The Mustang's colors are blue and white," she exclaimed, pointing at my outfit. I could see how this looked. I sat there wearing a white shirt and blue jeans, next to the green and yellow wearing unofficial president of school spirit.

"This is all I had that wasn't black." I replied, knowing that would not be good enough.

Jamie pulled out her cell phone and pounded away at the screen furiously. My own fingers twitched, sending a message on a phantom phone. Something I had done multiple times an hour before. I still hadn't received a new phone to replace the one I left on the counter where we had just left. Not that it mattered that much. I would only have one person to text with at the moment. Jamie dropped her phone on the seat beside her and put the truck in gear.

"We got you," she said with a smirk and sped off, not providing any insight into what she meant all the way to school. The ride wasn't silent, we just didn't cover that during it. Instead, Jamie brought me up to speed on every bit of high school gossip from the last six months. She gave quite a good report; one my grandfather would be proud of.

Jamie weaved wildly through the parade of people walking toward the school, and I feared for both their and our lives as she barely missed a few groups and several parked cars. Her tires chirped and the entire truck groaned when she swung it through the gate of the student parking lot, letting go of the wheel briefly to wave a yellow pass at the rent-a-cop perched on a chair at the opening. Even he lurched back defensively. She pulled into the first open spot she came to, and lunged over, grabbing my hand. I jerked back, slamming into the passenger door.

"Wait here!" Jamie commanding, staring into my eyes. "We can't let anyone see you wearing that. That would be the end of you at this school." Then out the driver's door she went, slamming it shut.

I waited and watched the parade of green and yellow go by each side of the truck. All on their way to the glow on the horizon. I hadn't ventured out that way yet in my first two days of school, but I had to assume that was where the stadium was. Just from the glow, it looked huge. Not like the rinky-dink field with a few sets of bleachers we had at my last one. Of course, no one, and I do mean no one, went to the games there. The only ones that did were those related to the players, or those with no other life, and the band kids, which had no other life. The "cool" kids wouldn't be caught dead at school after hours. With the mass of humanity heading that way, it seemed like this was the place to be on this night.

Two knocks on my window made my heart skip a beat. I turned. It was Jamie and Caroline. She was wearing more green and yellow than Jamie, and until now, I wasn't sure that was even possible. I pulled the handle to open the door, but Jamie slammed it shut, shaking her head.

"Roll the window down," she yelled through the glass.

I reached down and cranked it open, slowly. It squealed the entire way until it got stuck with about three inches left.

"What were you thinking?" Caroline asked.

Before I could answer, Jamie jumped in. "She didn't know." She added in a few "tsks" for good measure.

"Well, we can fix this." Caroline shoved a wad of green through the window. "Throw this over your shirt."

I untangled the mess she handed me and laid it on my lap. It was a green t-shirt with "Go Dolphins" on it in big yellow letters.

"Hurry up."

"All right. All right." I said, slipping the shirt on over my head, the best I could inside the cab of the truck. I only slammed my hand into the roof twice. The shirt was a little snug. It fit, but there was a problem. It was muggy outside. Make that stifling. Cool fall nights were something I guess people here only saw happening some place else on the Weather Channel. Wearing two shirts in this was out of the question. At least when I was wearing my hoodie or long sleeves during the day, we were inside air-conditioned classrooms. No such luck now, and I felt the sweat starting.

"I need to lose one shirt," I said through the window, while looking past both of them for a bathroom or something.

"Come on. You can change in the bathrooms inside the stadium," Jamie said, pulling open the door. This time, it was my turn to slam it.

"Turn around."

"What?" Caroline asked, confused, which I didn't understand. It was obvious what I was asking.

To help make it clear, I replied, "Turn around," and twirled my finger.

Both Jamie and Caroline turned reluctantly, and I laid down on the seat, slipping both shirts off and then putting the green one on in record time. I sat up and opened the door, bumping both of them in the back. They turned around, and I announced, "Okay, I'm ready."

"Okay, that works," Jamie said with a smile, while Caroline nodded her agreement. Then we joined the mass of people, heading toward the glow of lights in the distance, just like moths drawn to a flame. As we approached, the noise of the crowd and the bands grew, and I felt an unexpected level of excitement well up inside. The masses split between those that needed tickets and those that had student IDs. I fished inside my back pocket for mine, which was shiny new, done just today. This was the first time I had used it myself. I hadn't even looked at my picture. The person at the gate didn't either. He just waved us through, and we walked out on the track and the stadium opened up before me.

Good God! This thing was huge! These weren't just bleachers on either side of a field. These were concrete structures that scraped the night sky, but even more awe-inspiring was the horde of people that filled them. There wasn't an empty space anywhere. On one side was an army of green and yellow. The other side, blue and white, and I would have fit right in with how I left the house. That could have been a disaster. Thank God for Jamie and Caroline.

     I wanted to stand there a bit longer and take in the sight, but Jamie yanked me toward the sea of yellow and green as the band took the field for the pregame. I followed, not that I had much of a choice. She pulled me, and the mass of people behind us pushed. I was nothing more than a leaf caught in the current of a green and yellow stream. Up the ramp we went, and then I survived a tight-rope act along the level Jamie chose to sit on. I didn't see any space open for us, but as we approached the end, there seemed to be a parting of the sea, clearing a space for the three of us next to Stephen. He said something to all three of us, but it was too noisy for me to hear, so I just waved and said, "Hi" like the others did.

     We sat down on the hard concrete bleacher. Jamie and Caroline didn't let the noise deter their attempts to talk to one another. More school gossip, and I did my best to pay attention, even leaning forward and closer to them to hear. After a few moments of struggling to hear them, I tuned out the noise and heard what they were saying. A smile crept across my face and debated inside about whether to tell my grandfather or keep this accomplishment to myself. He would probably take credit for it; thanks to all the training we did with loud music blared. He may have been right, too.

     I'm not sure when the game started. We were so engrossed in our own conversation, or make that me listening to Jamie and Caroline talk about this person and that person or pointing out a cute boy in the crowd. The brief moment Jamie and Caroline stopped to join in the cheer for the Dolphin's first score of the night was my only cue it had started. That was the only interruption to our own little social gathering. There was a period when the noise quieted down, that was half-time, and then it started up again, with two more cheers in the third quarter. Caroline's obsession with Todd Wilks, the idiot from my English class, dominated the fourth quarter. I guess he was the starting linebacker or something, and really turned it up at the end of the game, making play after play, causing a raucous cheer from our stands. Jamie fueled her obsession with comments about how tight his uniform pants were. Something about a bump she kept pointing out. Stephen distanced himself from our group as the conversation went on, and it made me wonder. At first, I thought he and Caroline were kind of something based on how they sat together at lunch the last two days, but to Caroline, that didn't seem to be the case. Stephen may have had other ideas.

We won 17-10. A fact I only knew because I looked up at the scoreboard. Funny, I don't remember the other team scoring, but that was probably because no one on our side cheered. It didn't matter to me. Even if we lost, it wouldn't have diminished what I felt. For the first time in as long as I could remember, I felt like I was just a normal teen, doing what a normal teen girl would do, and it was wonderful.

With the game over, the surrounding crowd gathered their belongings, said goodbyes, and headed down the stairs. We were still talking, but we were standing now. Not because we were leaving, but because it made it easier for others to get past us. It also seemed it made it easier for others to find us. I saw a shadow fall over me from the row above us and turned around to see what it was at the same time as Jamie and Caroline. Jamie covered her mouth in surprise as the three of us looked up at heaven.

That was the only word to describe the vision of Adrian and Elijah standing over me, glowing. At first, I thought it was something supernatural. It was perfect, outlining his perfect hair, chiseled cheeks. Realizing it was from the field lights above him, didn't take away any of the awe from the vision.

Jamie and Caroline appeared just as dumbfounded as I was. The two brothers just stood there, looking down. They weren't looking down at us. They were looking down at me. Not that they didn't glance at the others for a brief moment here and there, but the stare of their steel-blue eyes always returned to me. I felt the intensity of their stare drilling a hole through me. I don't believe that was their intent, either. They just couldn't help it with those eyes.

"Am I in your seat again?" I asked, cringing as the question left my lips.

"No," Adrian said, kneeling down out of the field light, removing the glow from his profile, but not the awe of his presence. "Though these have a pretty good view of that end-zone, so half game, most of the action is happening in front of you."

Elijah hopped down in to the small gap between Jamie and me. Adrian gave him a scowl and grabbed his brother's shoulders, moving him over a few feet, before hopping down next to me.

"I saw you sitting here and remembered I hadn't properly introduced myself to you." He sat there, looking through my soul, and I felt an overwhelming and comforting urge to let him see it. "I'm Adrian Starling," he said, offering me his hand. I couldn't resist; I grasped it firmly. His touch was both commanding and tender, yet what truly struck me was the peculiar contrast of sensations. His skin felt cool against mine, yet the contact ignited a blazing inferno within me, leaving me on the verge of a gasp.

To cover, I said, "I know." It came out airy.

"So, my reputation precedes me, I see."

"You could say that," Stephen muttered, causing nothing more than a quick cut of Adrian's eyes.

"Stephen."

"Adrian."

"No, I heard your name in class," I said, pulling his attention back to me, our hands still touching. "What reputation are you referring to?" I asked, out of an abundance of curiosity driven by Stephen's reaction.

Adrian pulled his hand from mine, but he didn't yank it. As I lost grip of it, I felt anxious, and a desire to touch him again.

"Yes, Brother. What is that reputation you speak of?" taunted Elijah, leaning around his brother. "I'm Elijah Starling, but I am sure you already knew that."

These two were brothers, but they didn't have that much of a resemblance to each other. Adrian had that model jaw line. The type that belonged in a cologne ad in a magazine. His brother was the opposite. That friendly face of the boy next door. Unassuming, but not unattractive. They both were very attractive in different ways, and I felt a heat that was unfamiliar. What they both shared were the same steely blue eyes. I had never seen that color of blue in the natural world.

"What is your name?" Adrian asked, dismissing his brother's question with an annoyed look.

"Raven Cross."

Adrian reached up and rubbed his chin in thought. "Raven Cross?" he asked out loud that I presumed was just a question for himself. "Interesting name for such a tasty little morsel." The corner of his mouth curled up.

"Now, now, brother. Let's not live up to that reputation," Elijah warned. His voice trailing off and sounding almost pained as he looked down the bleachers at the track. Adrian turned his head, following his brother's gaze. The curl in the corner of Adrian's mouth turned, as did his entire expression. I looked down as well and met the death stare from their similarly eyed sister, Miranda Starling. She stood there with her arms crossed across her chest. Her lack of school spirit stood out against the sea of green and yellow around her. Even her brothers were in jeans and some form of school colors. She stood there in a white button-up shirt, black shirt, and heels with perfect hair and makeup, showing no effects from the muggy conditions.

"Well, Miss Cross. I will see you around school, I guess," Adrian said, looking blankly down at his sister. He and Elijah made their way down, but not without looking back in our direction a few times. He lingered at the bottom of the stairs until his brother pulled him down the rest of the way.

"What was all that about?" I asked.

"The ice queen calleth," Stephen remarked.

I didn't have the heart to tell him that wasn't *the thing* I was talking about. Seeing them leaving brought me back to earth and reminded me I needed to get going, too. My grandfather had given me the freedom to come to this game. I needed to be responsible and not be late. A habit I had developed in our last home.

It didn't take much to convince Jamie we needed to head home. Probably because everyone else had already left, and we stood there alone. We joined the end of the line leaving the stadium and easily missed the traffic leaving the parking lot. When we pulled out, I thought I saw a nice sleek gray car following us, but when I looked back, it was an old red Camaro.

Our gossiping continued through the entire drive home, or to my pseudo-home. I believe Jamie was attempting to bring me up to speed on everything in the school to help me fit in. How much she could tell me by the time we pulled up at the curb, I wasn't sure. It seemed like most of it, unless this place had more drama than the other schools I had attended. Surprisingly, absent from every story she told me were any mention of the Starlings. With how, well… odd they seemed, I expected them to be the center of much of it.

She pulled up to the curb in front of the white two-story with a porch at the address I had given her earlier. Which she found without me providing any directions, thank God. I may not have been much help. I hopped out as soon as her truck came to a stop, and closed the door behind me, with every intent of leaning back in through the window to say our goodbyes there. I needed her to pull off before I started my walk back home.

"Hey, why don't we go shopping tomorrow?" Jamie asked, beating my attempt to said bye.

"For?"

"Clothes, silly," she said with a giggle. "You need something green and yellow, and something you wouldn't die of heat stroke wearing. Those hoodies and long sleeves you keep wearing may have worked where you came from, but here they will just make you a sweaty mess."

"Oh," I responded. "I'm not sure. My grandfather might have plans for us." That was an absolute. Probably training, training, and more training. I wasn't even going to lie to myself. Shopping for clothes would be a hundred times more fun than any training, or so I thought. I had never been. I never needed to. They always provided my clothes.

"Well, here." She reached down to the floorboard and pulled her purse from under the bench seat. After rummaging around for a few moments, she pulled out a crinkled-up piece of paper and a pen. She scribbled on it and handed it over. "Ask him and text me what time I should pick you up. I'm sure you won't be busy all weekend."

I wouldn't be so sure, but I didn't tell her that. I had another disturbing and depressing reply. "I don't have a cell phone."

She dropped her purse down on the floorboard and then slapped her seat. "Well, dang girl. What kind of place did you move here from? Prison." she flashed an awkward smile, and I wondered if she considered that as an actual possibility. "Got a home phone?"

I nodded.

"Then call me old-fashion-like."

I almost laughed at that, but I held it in, and agreed to call her sometime tomorrow and let her know. That gave me enough time to come up with an excuse. I backed away from the window, hoping she would pull off, but my reflection in the passenger side mirror caused me to jump back to the truck's door, giving Jamie a jolt.

"Crap, I'm still wearing Caroline's shirt."

"No worries," Jamie said, waving me off with her hand. "Bring it tomorrow, or Monday."

"All right," I agreed and backed away, watching her drive off down the road and around the corner, before I headed in the opposite way and around that corner.

I made it home in just five minutes, looking around the whole time, though I doubted Uncle Mike would have set us up so close to the target. I had to consider there might be others here. Anything was a possibility. Not that I would know what to look for. That was something my grandfather hadn't covered yet.

I unlocked the front door, and stepped inside, looking around first before I locked the door behind me, another of my grandfather's rules. The house was dark except for the hallway and what looked to be the kitchen. I walked down the hall, thinking I would find my grandfather in the kitchen, when I noticed a light beneath the door to his study. He was here.

"Grandfather, I'm home," I yelled through the door, so he would know I was there.

"Good, so am I. Very productive night. Very productive. I will be in here for a bit, recording my observations," he yelled back.

"Care to give me a report?" I asked, half sarcastically, the other half curious. He never shared with me his targets. I wasn't sure why I thought this might be different. Maybe it was Mike's comments to him about getting me prepared.

"No. Not until you're ready."

Drat.

6

October 5th

Dear Diary,

So, guess what? I might have stumbled upon what might pass for having friends. I mean, Jamie and maybe Caroline—okay, scratch that, I'm not entirely sold on them yet. Friends? Eh, not really a concept I've had much experience with. It's like they just appeared out of nowhere, like a door slamming into your face. Classic.

Today marked my inaugural presence at a high school football game, and let me tell you, I barely witnessed a second of the actual game. But who needs sports when you've got a front-row seat to the epic soap opera that is this school? Move over reality TV, because this place could out-drama the Kardashians any day. It's like the who's-who of dating chaos and clandestine relationships. Seriously, there's more romantic intrigue here than all my previous schools put together. The gossip mill never sleeps.

I swear, it's a labyrinth of cliques and connections here. You could probably create multiple series just based on the tangled web of relationships and drama. And me? I'm here just trying to navigate this maze of teenage theatrics. Maybe this is all new to me, or maybe I've just been living under a rock at my other schools. Who knows? At least it's entertaining.

But, that wasn't even the strangest part of the night, not even close. Adrian and Elijah came to introduce themselves to me, officially. I guess our little interaction over my taking his seat wasn't enough. This *wasn't just two people saying hi. The whole interaction felt like a dream, right up until their sister woke us all up with her icy stare, but I don't know, as corny as it sounds, I'm not sure I have woken up yet, and I'm not sure I like that feeling.*

Later

At first, I didn't even want to bring up the shopping invite to my grandfather. We had the money, or so I thought we did. Money never seemed to be a problem. Anything we needed, we had. Then we left it all behind as we moved on to our next life. That wasn't it. It was the actual going part. Last night, every mall scene from every movie I had ever seen played in my head. Ah, no. The prospect of walking around in a large crowd of people I don't know, going from store to store to try on things I didn't want and wasn't going to buy, wasn't appealing, to say the least. I'd rather opt for training in the basement than go through that but, I needed a few other options to wear to school. Something I confirmed when I searched for something to wear this morning. Dang it. Who knew there were this many variations of the color gray? I was sure a few things in the purple and green families would fit in the world of Raven Cross.

Even though I had changed my mind, there was still a barrier left. The ultimate barrier. The great wall of my grandfather. He may object. Scratch that, he will object. It had been two days since my last training. We've never gone longer than that before, and that was usually when we were on the run.

I waited until we finished up breakfast and he headed back to his study. Again, just like last night when I asked him about the football game, he stood there and thought for a moment. I could see the internal debate in his head. Then he surprised me for the second time in two days. He said yes, with the only caveat being it would need to be later in the afternoon. I had training to do this morning. Big surprise there, but it was something I could live with. I just hoped I could walk after this training session. Those gravestones about did my shins in.

He instructed me to go upstairs and change, a luxury that I didn't always have, and informed me that he would be ready when I came back. He was. The door in the kitchen that led down to the basement was open for the first time since we arrived. I knew there wouldn't be a formal invitation. Those stopped after the first few weeks, then I settled into the routine. If the door was open, there was training scheduled. My version of Pavlov's bell.

I stepped through the door and down the stairs into a world of darkness. The darkness kept me from seeing what he had waiting for me, eliminating any chance I could prepare myself, defeating my grandfather's second rule, always expect the unexpected. "Your enemy will never announce their presence or their attack," he reminded me of often. Mostly when I used the excuse of not being ready when something put me on my ass.

It was mostly dark, but several pinpricks of light exploded through the covers on the window, that I believed my grandfather installed. I don't remember them when I came down and investigated during our first night. The dots of light were just bright enough to keep your eyes from adjusting to the darkness. It was disorienting to say the least. Just how my grandfather liked it.

At the bottom of the stairs, I saw the shape of a beam just above my head, and I reached up there for support as I leaned in for a quick look around. It was just more darkness and those blasted needles of light. Each time my eyes cross one of those, my irises raced to close, followed by a spritz of tears. My left foot reached forward and down for the floor. It found it and I stepped down. My right foot was about to join it when I saw a shadow about two inches from my face and then felt my back slam into the stairs. And so it began.

I stood back up, stepping away from the stairs before my grandfather could reset the dummy that hit me. I called him Henry, and I guess he traveled with us in the trunk, or my grandfather found another Henry. Over the last several years, Henry had given me more bruises than I could count. Henry had a brother, Bob, that wasn't so lucky. Duct tape held Bob together now. I had gotten the better of it every time. He was around here somewhere, but it would be a bit before he appeared.

I knew I needed to get into the middle of the floor, a tactic I had learned on my own. The middle was the farthest away from the shadows of the corners as I could get. Translation, the farthest from any hidden danger one could get. Maybe I should call that Maria's first rule. It was about time I started my own list.

There I stood in an aggressive stance, waiting, knowing he could see me. He was waiting, too. This was the game we played, which he explained was the same game he had observed in the real world. Vampires, most vampires, don't rush the attack. They waited for an opening, choosing not to expose themselves until right before the kill. My grandfather followed the same principles.

My head stayed on a swivel, jerking around at every sound I heard, or wisp of wind I felt. He was there. I could sense him. Where was the question? I turned around, searching the darkness, but never giving him my back for more than a second, no matter where he was. Out of the darkness, just as I turned away, came a fist on a pole. It glanced the back of my shoulder before I dropped to a knee, thrusting my hands up to defend the shot. I was slow, and my hands caught the pole as it pulled it back. As soon as it left my grasp, I was back up again, knowing he wouldn't waste any time. I was right. This time, I heard it before I felt it, and with a violent wave of my left hand, I deflected it away, knocking it from his grasp. It clattered on the floor. One down, but he had another one, and before I could turn my head back from the sound of the first clattering on the floor, the second fist on a stick caught me on the nose, sending me down to the ground.

A warmth trickled down my top lip, but I didn't take the time to wipe at it. This wasn't over. I rolled over and up into an aggressive squat, ready to jump, run, or whatever I needed to do. I saw something coming toward me. The only way to describe it was a mass of black moving in the darkness. I studied that mass, and then timed my move precisely, hooking my ankle around his. Sending my grandfather facedown to the concrete floor. He landed with an "Umph."

Without delay, I rolled up and straddled his back, grabbing the top of his head, pulling it back, and using my other hand to grip his chin. With a quick yank, I could have ripped a vampire's head off, but with my grandfather I didn't yank. That was reserved for Bob.

"You give?" I asked.

"No," my grandfather grunted from under me.

I slid off of him, and he rolled over. His hand reached up and wiped a trickle of blood from his nose and then pointed at mine. "Go get that cleaned up, and I'll reset."

I reached up and wiped my nose. While his was a trickle, mine was almost gushing, and I noticed the metallic taste in my mouth as soon as I saw my red stained hand. I squeezed it and held my head back as I headed up the stairs to the kitchen. A few drops still escaped. They probably landed on the floor. I grabbed a dish towel and wiped and squeezed, while taking a seat at the table.

"Oh, Maria, don't forget to call your friend back to tell her you can go tonight," my grandfather called up the stairs. "It'll be good for you."

"I will," I responded, muffled, after a few seconds. It took me a bit to recognize my real name. There had been so many, and I hear my own so seldom.

The nosebleed stopped after a few minutes, leaving the dish towel blood-soaked. I walked over to the sink and rinsed it out the best I could and then used it to clean up my face. Which probably just smeared red all around my lips and around my chin. There was no point in finding a mirror to look. This was going to happen again before we finished. After another rinsing of the rag, I went to the phone in the kitchen and did as my grandfather suggested. I pulled

Jamie's number out of my pocket, studying it for a moment before dialing it.

"Hello?" she answered.

"Hey, it's... Raven." I had to think for a second about which name I was using now. "If you're still up for it, I'd love to go shopping."

"Absolutely!" Jamie screamed through the phone. I held the receiver back until she was done. "What time?" Her voice asked from a distance.

I thought for a moment. It was just after ten now. I didn't know how long my grandfather planned for this to go on. We usually went for a few hours. Then I needed to clean up so I could be presentable. I already knew my nose was going to be swollen, and we were just beginning.

"How about four-ish?"

"That sounds awesome," she screamed before I could move the receiver away from my ear. "I'll pick you up. I've never picked up a celebrity before."

I slammed the phone back against my ear. Maybe a little too hard. "What are you talking about?" Now it was my turn to scream.

"You haven't seen it?" Jaime started, and then she began carrying on a conversation that I think was with herself. She was asking questions that she either answered herself. "I guess you haven't. How would you? You are new here. It's not like you would have friended anyone here on social media, or even followed the school. Are you even on social media? You haven't sent me a friend request yet. I would be first. Wouldn't I? Why haven't you? That's kind of messed up. I mean, we are supposed to be friends, aren't we?"

I finally stopped her before she continued any further. My mind was spinning just trying to keep up with everything, but there was one detail I latched hold of, and that was what I needed to ask about. "Whoa! Jamie, slow up. What haven't I seen?"

"The picture."

My mind flashed to the image of me out flat on the ground after my encounter with the door on my first day. Please God, tell me someone hadn't captured that in a picture and put it online somewhere. If I had my phone, I could probably find it, but again, I didn't. What a way to be memorialized. "Oh God," I gasped, and dropped my head. That moment will now live in infamy. It may be a short-lived infamy, but still haunting me the whole time we are here.

"The school photographer must have been walking around after the game last night and took a picture of Adrian and you sitting together. You and Adrian! No one has ever captured a picture of him or his brother before. They are a bit of an enigma. They come to school and then vanish. And, wow, the way he is looking at you in that picture. Everyone is commenting on it."

"Oh God," I uttered again, biting my bottom lip. "Can you show me when you pick me up?"

"I can tell you where to find it. It's a great picture. You really need to see it."

My head dropped with a sigh. In this day and age, what I was about to say would be hard for anyone to believe, and there would be questions. It was almost blasphemous. I knew it. I just needed to get it over with. "I don't have access to anything. I don't have a phone or a computer."

There was a moment of awkward silence on the other end of the line, and I was about to say something to see if she was still there when Jamie finally spoke. "What about your grandfather? Does he?"

"No." he did, but I wasn't allowed to use it. It was for official brotherhood business only.

"Weird. It's like you are living in the last century or something."

"Yep," I agreed, offering no further explanation. I hadn't asked my grandfather about a replacement phone yet. That didn't mean I wouldn't. Maybe this was the best opportunity. I was heading to a mall. They had to have a store there I could pick one up from.

"I guess... I will show the post to you when I pick you up then," she said, sounding disappointed. She was probably hoping I would look at it and squeal with her on the phone. No such luck. I had a bigger concern. Pictures. There was a reason I was sick on every school picture day for my entire life.

"Great, I can't wait," I said, feigning excitement. In truth, there was a feeling of dread. If my grandfather found out, there would be lectures and all outside of school activities would cease. It would be house arrest. Ugh. There was no reason for him to find out. "All right. I need to go. I will see you at four."

"See you then."

I let Jamie hang up first before I put the receiver back on the cradle, then I stood there for a few minutes. The worry about my grandfather finding out about the picture played with my mind. This has never been a problem before. When I thought about it, I wasn't sure what the problem really was. It wasn't like anyone that wasn't supposed to see it would, and if they did, who would recognize me? It was just a picture. A single picture. And, when I wasn't preoccupied with that worry, I imagined what it may look like. By the time I stepped away from the phone, that wondering grew into a fascination that I couldn't help.

"She's picking me up at four," I yelled down the stairwell to the basement.

"Okay," my grandfather yelled back up, and I tried to let the sound of his voice guide me on where he might be as I descended the stairs for round two.

7

October 6th

Dear Diary,

Maybe, just maybe, I was wrong... I couldn't help but wonder.. am I overthinking everything? It's just the usual teen drama, right? Jamie is, like, the drama queen of high school gossip, and she just blew it up like always. Drama is her thing, you know? And maybe, just maybe, my lack of experience in this area is making me read way too much into it. Ugh, I just need to chill and not do anything stupid. That pic? It's just a pic, duh! Plus... no sense in getting wrapped up in any of this. We won't be here long.

Oh, and brace yourself for this wild news—Hell Almost Froze over today. My grandfather actually almost complimented me! No "good job" or "great job," but we went two rounds without him giving me any extra instructions. His silence is as close to a compliment as I'll ever see. Not gonna lie, not everything went perfectly. I messed up a few things that, according to his past warnings, would have gotten me killed. But this time, it just cost me a few bruises. Now I gotta work some makeup magic to cover that up before stepping out. This is gonna take ages.

Later

My grandfather, Henry, myself, and even Bob—who will take my grandfather a few days to repair–went for another three hours. Not bad compared to some of my other training sessions which lasted all day and well into the night. The training was a bit more brutal than the others, and even involved some hands-on instruction from my grandfather about tactics vampires have used against him in close quarters. It was an odd treat that I rather appreciated. I felt my grandfather was still holding a lot back from me. Uncle Mike felt that way as well. He had brought it up a few times, and, just a few days ago, challenged my grandfather on it. Maybe I needed to push him a little more to help my progression through what I needed to know. That was probably what prompted me to ask what I had asked numerous times before, and yet to receive an answer. How will I know when I encountered or found a vampire?

It was a very basic question, and one I felt anyone in our position needed to know. I mean it was step one of the job, wasn't it? But yet, every time I asked, I received some blanket passe answer of "we will cover that later," or "don't worry about it." This time, I received something different. It was still vague, but it addressed the question. "You will know. You won't have to question it. You will just know." I asked him how, but he brushed that off.

So, I will just know? What exactly does that mean? I thought about it during the walk over to my fake address to meet Jamie. I sure hoped the answer to that wasn't something cheesy like they wear a sign or a certain outfit. Do they all dress like the characters in the classic monster films? I can see it now. I will encounter my first vampire and he will pop up out of a coffin wearing a bowtie and a black cape lined with red velvet. If that happens, I'd die laughing long before they did me in. Killed by Leslie Neilsen from *Dead and Loving It*. That will be my end.

Those thoughts left my mind when I saw Jamie's truck round the corner. Seeing it brought anticipation forward, pushing all other thoughts from my mind. I caught myself bouncing on my toes standing on the curb and did my best to hold it back. I failed, and practically bounced in through the passenger door as soon as I opened it. Jamie was already holding her phone out for me as soon as I landed on the bench seat next to her. There it was, THE PICTURE. It was just a random shot taken of us from the bottom of the bleachers looking up at us, but it was also so much more, and I couldn't stop the grin that crept across my face.

"Look at all the likes and comments on that thing," squealed Jamie. It echoed around the cabin, rattling my ear drums. There was no holding the phone away from my ear this time. She was right on top of me. I looked below the picture and held back my gasp. 1,103 likes. I didn't know there were that many students in the school. There were over 300 comments. I grabbed the phone and scrolled through the comments as Jamie pulled away. Some comments were on the rare capture of Adrian in a photograph. I guess the guy was camera shy or something, not that he had a reason to be. The camera seemed to adore him. Heat flashed in my cheeks as I read the other comments. After every few comments, I scrolled back up to look at the picture, and then back to the comments. Back to the picture. Back to the comments. Up and down until my eyes had whiplash, and I felt a headache start behind them. By the tenth trip up and down, all I could think was holy crap. The way that man was looking at me. His eyes were caressing my soul, and while everyone else saw it and commented on it, I had something they didn't. I felt it, and just sitting here looking at the picture, that overwhelming sense of calm and submission that overcame me and would have let his eyes do a lot more than just caress my soul, came back. It was intoxicating, even now, and my body melted back into the seat, and my hand dropped to my lap with the phone.

"Pure magic," commented Jamie.

"It's just a picture," I said, trying to dismiss what I saw, and even more so trying to pull myself from what I felt. It was an odd feeling. Not at all unpleasurable. It was the opposite, which made it harder to understand. I didn't know Adrian. We had spoken, what? Once, just once, when I took his seat in class. That was it. Oh my god, this can't be happening. I wasn't even sure what this was.

"Girl, it is so much more. You are the envy of every girl in school."

I turned and looked out the window, ignoring what she said on the outside. On the inside, I knew what she meant, and I hated it. So much for being memorable and forgettable. Now my name was going to be in the gossip circles.

"Come on, you can't say Adrian isn't easy on the eyes," Jamie said, glancing over at me in disbelief.

"He's not bad," I replied with the understatement of the century. He was everything television, and the movies told you the ideal teenage male should look like. He was… perfection.

"Not bad?" she asked, surprised. "His brother is not bad. Adrian is a god."

"Hey, don't sell Elijah short. He is kind of cute, too." I said, deflecting the best I could. Both brothers were rather cute in their own right, but Jamie was right. Adrian was a god, but Elijah had the boy next door that you ran upstairs to your window to stare across at his window in hope of a glimpse, look.

"So, you noticed."

Crap, I got caught in my attempt to get out of it. There must be another offramp away from the discussion. The topic made me uncomfortable, but not for obvious reasons. Admitting it was my only way out. I nodded, grinned, and dipped my head.

Jamie cackled from the driver's seat as we pulled into the mall parking lot and parked not far away from the front door. "Let's go get you something to wear that is more presentable for Adrian to see you in."

"Now wait…" I started, but Jamie escaped out the driver's side door before I could finish. I threw open the passenger door, hopping out. The truck rocked back and forth, groaning with each exit. "Now wait a minute," I finished, slamming the door, and giving as stern of a look as I could muster while inside I was all a glow from the picture.

"I'm just joking." Jamie marched around the truck and looped her arm around my own, bumping a new bruise from today's activities. "Let's go get you something more colorful than that."

We walked like that in through the door, and under the quick blast of cold air from the overhead vent. A shiver went through me, but it was short-lived. Within the next step, any remnants of the cold air blast were gone, and we were just one of the mass of people that rushed from store to store. Jamie was my guide. Most of the stores she pulled me into I didn't recognize the names of. Not surprising, this was my first time.

Inside each store, we did the same, a quick walkthrough looking at the racks. I selected a thing or two, and Jamie followed behind me selecting more, and then lead me to the fitting room, where she slammed the door behind me and shoved what she had gathered for me over the door, before taking the room next door for her own.

Jamie was going for color. I had rationalized that muted tones of red, green, yellow, and maybe blue would work. There was an image to uphold, by the way. No broody teen wears a hot pink shirt. Jamie obviously didn't get the memo. What she threw over the door were not muted colors; they were straight out bold neon shades. One of the yellow shirts appeared to glow all on its own, hanging there over the door. None of these selections matched what I imagined as acceptable for Raven Cross. Now Maria Foster would love them, and I even tried them on long enough to admire them in the mirror, tossing my newly blonde hair as I spun around, wondering if Adrian would like this color on me.

"Raven, what do you think?" Jamie called from the next changing room.

"I'm not sure these are me," I responded, pulling myself back to reality, and trying on a bright green tank top that made my eyes pop. This was me, all right. Just not the me I could show. But again, the same question popped into my head. I sat back on the bench in the dressing room and wondered where this was all coming from. This wasn't like me, but that picture kept flashing in my head. Had I become smitten? Just the thought of that made me giggle at myself. This was so unlike me. I collected myself and went back to trying on the horde of tops she threw at me.

"Come on. Live a little. You can't hide behind gray and black hoodies all the time."

I wanted to agree with her, but I couldn't. Even as I danced in front of the mirror in a red top. "I'm not hiding," I said, cringing as I said that very word. "It's what I like." I shimmied out of the red top and slid back on the black hoodie I wore with a look of surrender staring back at me from the mirror. With the clothes I brought in, and what Jamie threw over the door at me, across my arm, I walked out and waited for Jamie.

"Girl… you need some color," Jamie declared again. I didn't disagree, and this time I said nothing. I just stood there outside her door, taking a last glance at what was destined to be re-racked.

Jamie's door opened, and she stepped out with two stacks of clothes. One over each arm. "These are going back," she stated, holding out her left arm. "These are keepers." This time holding out her right arm. She gave me a once over, and I prepared myself for the assault. "Nothing?" she asked.

I shrugged.

"All right." Jamie marched over to the return rack and hung up the stack that was over her left arm. I followed her to do the same, but she spun around quickly and grabbed my arm. "I can see this make-over to get that west coast counterculture out of you is going to take some doing. Why don't we start small?" She took the stack of clothes from my arm and flipped through them, selecting the glow in the dark yellow shirt, and then putting the rest on the rack. After they were all securely on the rack, she turned, holding up a shirt that was as blinding as the sun, smiling just as brightly. "How about we start with this one? It's school colors, so it checks that need off the list."

My head kicked back. She had me there. That thing was bright, like obnoxiously bright. Even if I wasn't going for the grudge emo look, that wouldn't be me. I wasn't that out there with my choices, but I made one more pass over what she just hung up and nothing else was our school colors. If I had that, I could avoid a repeat of last night's poor choices. Of course, I might blind the other sideline, but hey, it would be a home field advantage, right?

    I silently conceded but held up a finger to ask her to wait. Then I reached past her into the clothes that she had re-hung and grabbed a milder, less offensive, green shirt. It was close to the school's shade, and it would fit what I needed.

    "Wow, living on the edge there," Jamie teased with a huge grin.

    I stood there staring back at her until she stopped and turned around. I followed her up to the cashier and stood in the rather sizable line. That was something else I had been spared from experiencing in my rather sheltered existence. It was one I was fine having to not experience it often. The whole waiting made me fidgety, and I messed with all the little displays of jewelry, lip gloss, and candy as we waited, only sliding forward at a pace that would make a snail laugh.

    Almost to the front, I watched Jamie swipe her card, punch in a few numbers, and then wait for the clerk to remove the three shirts off the hangers and place in the bag. While she did that, the receipt printed, and waited, flowing in the air on the register. It didn't take long until I figured out what the cause of the slowdown was. Jamie only had three shirts. Just three T-shirts. Things that will probably be all balled up on the floor of her room, anyway. Well, that is not fair. I didn't know if Jamie was a slob or not. She might be the type that hangs them all up in her closet, ordered by shade. Even so, it seemed like a waste to take several minutes per shirt to straighten it out, put it out flat on the counter, and then slowly fold it before shoving it in a bag where all that hard work will be undone.

    When it was my turn, the clerk started her same routine, until I interrupted it. I handed her cash out of the envelope my grandfather handed me before I left. The dim-witted clerk stared upon the twenty-dollar bill as if it frightened her. All she had to do was reach in and hand me back three ones, a dime, and two pennies. She finished her folding of both of my shirts, but with attention divided between her task and the sight of the twenty, she lacked the precision and care the other customers' items had received. She shoved them in the bag and then took the twenty with two fingers, pressing a key on the register screen that, if I had to guess, rarely got touched. The register drawer opened with a slam, and she placed the twenty inside and, against my expectations, handed me the correct change. I shoved it back in the envelope and then put that back in my pocket.

Jamie grabbed my arm and walked me out of the store in a hurry. Outside, she walked to the center where there was a bench and turned me around, looking concerned. I believed she hadn't seen actual cash before, either.

"Raven, don't you have a wallet?" she whispered just above the noise.

I did, and it was back home on top of my dresser, with my past life, in our last home. "I do," I replied with a nod.

"Then why the envelope?" she asked, concerned and stressed. "You can't go around flashing wads of cash like that. Someone could grab that envelope and be gone before you even knew it."

I hated to tell her the likelihood of that happening was next to nil. If someone tried, I would know they were there to try before they even knew they were going to try. My grandfather had sharply honed my instincts of anticipation. But of course, I couldn't tell her that, so I played along. "You're right," I said, shoving it deeper into my pocket.

"You need to protect that. Keep it safe," she said, relaxing. "I can only imagine how many hours of babysitting it took to earn that."

"I didn't babysit," I said before I realized I shouldn't have answered at all.

"Okay then," Jamie said. "Then your parents are a little more generous with your allowance than mine. We have a few more shops to hit."

Jamie backed out into the crowd and joined the procession on that side. I followed, and as I did, for the second time in just a few minutes, my mouth opened, and something came out that I hadn't completely planned out. "My parents are dead."

She jerked to a stop, causing a few minor rear-enders by the shoppers following to close behind us. They grumbled as they twisted their bodies to pass by.

"Look. It's no big deal," I said, trying to dismiss the sympathy I saw growing in her eyes. "It happened years ago when I was five. I live with my grandfather now."

It didn't work. She reached out and grabbed my hand. "Raven, I am so sorry. I didn't know."

"It's no big deal," I assured her again. "It happened so long ago. I don't really remember much about them. Life has just been me and my grandfather, and he's been great." I did my best to force a realistic smile, realizing all the while how tragic that sounded. Her eyes dropped toward the tile floor, and I knew she did too. "Come on. We have shopping to do." It was my turn to grab her arm and lead her forward. "What store is next?"

For the next hour, we went through five more stories. I bought two more shirts, a hair clip, and a pair of black stud earrings with a fake purple jewel in the center. They were perfect for both Maria and Raven. I was officially shopping for two people. The whole time Jamie was over helpful and complimentary. Even when I put on a horrendous burnt orange shirt and lime green skirt outfit, she told me, "That looks great!"

After the sixth store, she, and the chorus of smells singing to my stomach, enticed me over to the food court. Another American teenage institution I had yet to experience. It was a madhouse.

Ignore the overload of options and mouthwatering smells in every breath. It was a devilish obstacle course that not even my grandfather could dream up. People walked in every direction. Unlike the main mall concourse, which appeared to follow the rules of the road, one side went one way, and the other side went the opposite direction. The food court was like ants on speed. Everyone came from every direction and then changed on a dime to go some place else. Tables were like prime real estate in the game monopoly. If one opened up, mobs of people raced to it.

I didn't know what to choose. There were way too many choices. I could have stood there for hours, studying the menus, but the crowd didn't give you that chance. At best, you had a couple of seconds before they ran you over, leaving you with picking a place based on the name alone. Some were obvious, like Hot-Wok and Pizza, but what do they serve at Buns and Things? I wasn't sure I wanted to know what "things" were. I gave up and just followed Jamie around, not even looking at where she stopped until it was my time to order. Scared to slow up the line by looking up at the menu, I just said, "I'll have what she's having."

"Oh, how *When Harry Met Sally* of you," Jamie squealed. "I absolutely love that movie."

I wasn't going to admit I didn't know what she was talking about.

Luckily Jamie had good taste in food. Chicken Alfredo and garlic bread. You couldn't go wrong with that. Once we got our drink at the self-service fountain next to the register, it was time to find a table, but it was our lucky day. The table in front of us opened up. It was almost as if fate had intervened. All that was missing were the golden rays shining down from above. We sat down before anyone else saw it, and then it started.

In between bites, it was gossiping time. I thought I had heard it all last night. To my surprise, there was more, and even updates on what she had told me about last night. As she explained, I wasn't on social media, so I didn't have a constant feed flowing in front of my eyes like she did. Which reminded me, I needed to remedy that. While she updated me on someone named Sara Nichols and her on again off again relationship with two guys, both of whom were clueless about the other, I searched the mall behind her for a store selling cell phones. One of the standard cell company's stores and kiosks wouldn't do. They would want an account, with long-term commitment, and all that. I needed a pay as you go phone. A disposable one that you just buy it off-the-shelf, take it out of the package, and make a call.

Through a forest of green ferns, I saw it. A kiosk selling cell phone cases, chargers, screen protectors, and go-phones. Perfect. From here, I could see the variety of phones and picked out which type I wanted. Then something, make that someone, walked right through my view. My eyes followed his features until I lost them behind the forest of planters. My head jerked left, to the end of the planter, and then waited for him to reappear. When he didn't, I searched back and forth on both sides of the planter as the seconds passed, but Adrian never reappeared. Where did he go? I knew I saw him. I wasn't imagining things, was I? I looked again, this time craning my neck up to see over the planter the best I could. He still wasn't there. Maybe I did imagine him, but why?

"Earth to Raven. Earth to Raven." Jamie waved her hand in front of my face.

"Sorry," I stammered, bringing myself back to the table and our food and quickly shoveling a forkful of pasta into my mouth with a few glances for Adrian.

"You all right?"

"Yep," I mumbled with a mouth full of food. After a quick swallow, I added. "Just looking at the cell phone store over there. I need one."

"You sure do. No self-respecting teenage girl can live without a phone. Let's get you one after we finish."

I nodded, and returned my attention to my food, but with every bite, my eyes did a quick scan for Adrian.

"Who's your grandfather's plan with?"

"Plan?" I asked, shoveling another bite into my mouth, while my eyes darted around, hoping to see Adrian emerge from the ferns. Perhaps I had imagined him.

"Cell phone plan. You need his plan details so we can add your phone to it."

I shook my head, twirling my fork to gather more noodles. "I'm just getting a go-phone. He doesn't have a cell phone." Which was a lie. He had one, but he only used it for his "official" business. It was rarely outside of his bag.

"Odd," Jamie remarked.

That was me, the oddity. I knew it, but that didn't stop me from having to play along. Ignoring the feeling that it would lead to probing and questions and being looked at as even odder. I had to blend in. "Odd how?"

"Well," Jamie said, scrunching her face up. "There are a lot of things odd about you, I'm sorry to say."

I leaned back and let my mouth drop open, feigning shock the best I could. "Like what? What makes me so weird?"

"Well," Jamie started, planting her fork in what remained of her pasta like a flag. "How you dress is a little odd. Not having a phone is really odd. Walking around with a big envelope of money is both odd and dangerous. It's like you are from a different time. Plus, you moved here with your grandfather. People that age don't usually move around much. They retire and stay put, or move to Florida to die. Some shit like that. Come to think of it, you never told me why you guys moved here. Why did you leave San Diego and move all the way across the country to our little corner of the south?"

I had been waiting for someone to ask that question. Normally, a teacher took the honor of asking it on my first day, but no one one did this time. They didn't seem that interested. So now, on my fourth day here, someone had finally asked, and I gave my standard answer, with a slight modification to address something Jamie had already brought up. "Well, not all grandparents are retired. Mine isn't. He is an engineering consultant, and his latest project is here in Savannah." The engineering consultant cover story is one we had always used. I always found it rather odd that there was that level of specificity to his occupation, and it was always the same. I often wondered if that was his occupation before all this, if there was a time before all this. Maybe he had some practical knowledge in that area that would help solidify the story if he were ever asked.

"Well then, that is something else odd. Who would want to work at that age? When I am 65, I am going to be retired on a beach somewhere with a fruity drink in my hand."

"Well, that's not my grandfather. He's a workaholic of sorts and will probably work until the day he dies." There was way too much truth in that statement. "And the thing about the phones is simple. I broke mine. If you haven't noticed, I'm a complete klutz. Last time that happened, he told me that was the last one he would buy. This one is on me, and with the move and all, I just haven't had time. As for how I dress," I stopped and shook the bag of clothes we just spent the last hour buying.

"Well, it's a start," Jamie agreed with a laugh.

We finished our pasta and threw away our trash on the way around the planters and the crowds, weaving our way to the cell phone kiosk. Jamie made it clear that was our next stop, and I didn't fight it. Actually, I had already decided that was our next stop before she said anything.

I knew which one I was going for. The same smart phone I had before. The same smart phone I had picked up the last few times. And, while Jamie looked through the various models and colors, I picked out a simple black smartphone and a protective case. The lack of flair drew a look from Jamie, which I dismissed with a shrug. The cashier opened the packaging and went through the activation sequence and then asked me if I wanted him to put it in the case. I could do it. I had many times. But he already had everything opened, so I agreed with a polite, "Please."

I watched the screen as he did. The activation progress bar hit the end, and the phone rebooted. It was done, but the clerk didn't hand it to me until the customary test call they all made, just to be sure everything worked. The kiosk's phone rang, and the clerk hung up the call and held my phone out for me while he started helping the next customer. I reached forward to take it, but another hand reached over my head and swiped it from his grasp. I attempted to do the same, but missed, and then spun around ready to chase the cellphone thief. But there was no chase necessary. My heart fluttered as Adrian stood there typing furiously on my phone.

"Now your phone is ready," he said, offering it to me.

I took it with a snatch and looked at the screen. The text message screen was up, and he had sent a simple "*Hi*" to another number.

"Yours?" I asked, holding the screen up for him to see.

"In case you get bored and need someone to talk to," Adrian said with a smile.

I felt that sensation again to let him look right into my soul with those steel-blue eyes that sparkled under the lights. They were striking against his perfect complexion, his perfect smile, his perfect hair, his perfect everything. He was just perfect. So perfect that I could barely speak and managed just an airy, "Thanks."

"Doing some shopping?" Adrian asked, reaching down for the bag I carried. His hand touched mine, and a cool spark leaped from his skin and through mine.

"I'm trying to get her to wear some colors," Jamie explained from behind me. Her voice sounded miles away.

"Why? I like her style," Adrian responded while looking deep into my eyes. That clinched it. I would now wear black and dark-colored hoodies every day. "I do think she needs to lay off the hoodies, though. She doesn't need to hide." His hand reached up and brushed my bangs away from my eyes, brushing my cheek. That settled that. No more hoodies.

"Brother, we should probably get going," Elijah said, sliding in next to him. "Hi, Raven." Until that moment, I hadn't even noticed Elijah standing there.

"True. Can we walk you ladies out?" Adrian asked, and for the first time he looked over my shoulder at Jamie, and I heard a soft squeal. "If you two are leaving."

"We are," Jamie exclaimed, and I looked behind her and found her grinning, giving me a very non-discreet thumbs up. Then that was what they did. They walked us out, with hordes of familiar and unfamiliar eyes watching us.

"We didn't finish our introduction last night before we were rudely interrupted," Adrian said.

"You have to ignore Miranda. Our sister's bark is usually worse than her bite. She is a bit protective," Elijah added.

"Is she your older sister?" I asked, assuming that was so.

"In a manner of speaking, she is. Though I doubt that matters. She assumes roles she hasn't earned yet. Our protector is one," Adrian looked back at his brother with a curt look. "So, Raven. Where are you from?"

"San Diego."

"California? Interesting. You and your family looking for the quiet of small-town life?"

"Can't get much smaller than right here," Elijah remarked.

"It's just me and my grandfather. He moved here for work." Then I turned the tables and asked him basically the same question. Hoping to take the spotlight off of me for just a moment so I could catch my breath. At the moment, it seemed to escape me. "What about you? Are you from here?"

Adrian laughed and pushed open the door, and the four of us walked out into the cool night air. "Sort of. We have moved around all over, following our father's work, but all roads seem to bring us back here from time to time. Probably because our family has lived here for centuries."

"Speaking of family." Elijah punched his brother in the back of the shoulder and pointed toward the curb where Miranda stood, looking very prim and properly dressed in a navy-blue suit. She was waiting next to the same gray European car and tapping the toe of one of her high heels on the sidewalk. I swear I could hear it from here.

Adrian turned to me, and said, "I'm afraid this will have to be continued." He pointed down at the phone in my hand as he and Elijah backed away. With every step that mindless bliss, that calm comfort, that electricity I felt when he was near drained away.

Once they reached the car, there was a quick exchange of words between the brothers and their sister. From here, it looked like a lecture. Then she jumped into the passenger's seat. Elijah slipped into the back, and Adrian sat in the driver's seat, but not before giving a quick wave in my direction.

"Come on, love puppy. Let's go find my truck." Jamie grabbed my arm and yanked me from where I stood frozen.

Jamie was non-stop on the way home. Adrian this. Elijah that. She even got in a few remarks about Miranda, which weren't as flattering as the brothers. All I could do was stare at the phone and the simple text he sent himself. I took care to add his number to my contacts, out of fear I would lose the message if I turned the phone off or something tragic happened. There was no backup to the cloud for me. No traces of my existence at all. That was the rule.

She dropped me off at the usual place, and I almost slipped up and started walking toward the corner before she pulled far enough away not to see me. My head was a bit in the clouds. To be honest, the rest of me was too. The walk back home was a bounce filled trek. Not even one of my sneak outs to go see Lucas made me feel like this.

As soon as I walked in the door, my grandfather emerged from his office at the end of the hall and walked into the kitchen. He probably had some late-night surveillance planned and was loading up on the coffee. I followed him in, seeing what remained of dinner on the table. He looked at me, and then at the bags I carried. I didn't show my grandfather what all I bought on my shopping trip with Jamie. His concern was not what was in the bag. Where the hands on the clock were, that was what concerned him. Late was not the word to describe what the time was. It was still a few minutes before nine, and two hours earlier than I came home last night. What mattered was I was later than he expected. In his mind, as he explained, we were going to just run into a few stores and come right home. Not walk the full length of the place–twice, eat dinner, talk, and whatever that was we did with Adrian and Elijah.

He cast a disappointed look in my direction and then at the table where a plate of food sat uneaten. It didn't take Sherlock Holmes to understand what that was about. Other than lunch at school, we had eaten every meal together since I was five. This was a first. With a gruff huff, he asked, "Did you get a phone?"

"Yes. Disposable as always, and I-"

He interrupted me, and we both finished my statement together, "used the Raven Cross id for the registration."

"Okay, good. That will be good enough to fool their systems for a while, and that is all you need."

"No traces," I added, walking to the table to cover the plate with some foil before I put it in the refrigerator. Just because I already ate, didn't mean I wouldn't be hungry later. Maybe a midnight snack. Something told me I wouldn't be sleeping a lot tonight. Energy surged through my body. There was a little bounce in my step that, surprisingly, went unnoticed by my grandfather. He rarely missed anything.

"I have good news," my grandfather announced, exiting the kitchen and reaching for his office's door. "We won't be here much longer. I'm almost done."

My bounce disappeared before the door closed with a slam. Normally, I wouldn't care one way or the other if we moved along. We did it so often. It was just part of life. Live a little, move, and repeat. Just the rhythm of life, at least my life. This time was different.

I put my covered dinner in the refrigerator and headed up to my room, collapsing on the bed. I wasn't tired. I just didn't know what else to do. My hand mindlessly reached for the television remote and clicked it on, just for background sound. I didn't care what was on. I laid there for a bit, or more than a bit, and did something I hadn't ever done before. I searched my thoughts, not sure why I was feeling the way I was. Letdown was a new sensation. Especially the letdown of possibly never seeing someone again. That thought played over and over in my mind. Once my grandfather was done, I would never see Adrian again. That thought hit me with a deep, cold jab that was unfamiliar and extremely unpleasant. And what was my reaction? To lay there on my bed as stiff as a corpse.

That was what I did. I lay there through three sitcom re-runs and half of a movie of the week. What caused me to finally move? The urge of nature? No, the urge of a technology obsessed society. I had forgotten to plug in my new cell phone. That was a sin that needed to be corrected immediately. I got up and put my phone on top of my nightstand. Then I rummaged around in the bag of purchased clothing for the original packaging holding the charger. I found it and unraveled the cord while I searched for a socket close enough to plug in to. There was one just behind the nightstand, perfect. All I had to do was slide it out a bit, and I had plenty of room to plug it in. The little chime I heard told me it was doing its job, and I went back to pretending to be a lump on a log on the bed, but I had already been that for an hour or more. My thoughts were still swimming, and I felt there was only one way to remedy this. So, I reached over and opened the drawer in the nightstand and pulled out the simple leather-bound book, took the pencil from the loop of ribbon attached to the cover, and started another entry.

8

October 7th

Dear Diary,

This is absolutely the first OMG moment of my life, at least in a good way. There I said it. I was fighting myself to even think that way, but I wrote it, I might as well scream it out the window, but I won't. Save the neighbors at this late hour. All I can think now is --- what the hell is this? I mean I have seen this before, but only in those cheesy rom coms, but not in real life... and I seriously doubt life imitated art, or even the other way around. Wait... maybe I am being punked. I've seen movies and shows like that. The popular clique becomes friends with the new student and then crushes them. I did make a clumsy entrance. That must be...

My phone chimed, and I jumped. I knew what that sound was. I had heard it a lot before on my old phone. I just wasn't expecting it, and sat there for a moment with my diary still open, wondering, did I want to check the message? I quickly decided to ignore it and turned back to my diary entry, but just a few seconds later it chimed a second time, and again I debated whether to get up and check it or sit here and finish my diary entry and then try to get some sleep. But whoever that was, probably Jamie since only two people had my number and I doubted the other was writing to me at this hour, had already written twice, and I thought I knew Jamie pretty well. She wouldn't stop until I responded. From what I had seen of her, she was a habitual texter. I figured I would check really quick, let her know I was going to bed, then finish my entry and call it a night. I slung my arm blindly at the nightstand, hoping to hit the phone on the first try. It did I and held it up to my eyes. Seeing the name next to the message changed my entire plan. My body leaped up, and I sat on the edge of my bed with the phone in my hand, shaking. That diary entry would go unfinished. Priorities. I was sure my diary would understand. I'm not even using it for the right type of entries yet.

"Hi, Raven."

"It was great seeing you tonight."

It was just eight words, but it meant so much more. I must have read and re-read them twenty or thirty times before I realized I should probably respond, but what would I say? My thumbs positioned themselves in their very natural spots over the keyboard. They knew where every letter was all on their own. What they were waiting on were the words my mind wanted them to create with those letters. I was mush. The more I started mapping out witty replies in my head, the more irritated I became with how useless my brain had become. I was in full-on analysis paralysis. Every phrase I thought of, I second guessed after thinking of all the ways he might read it, no matter how ridiculous my interpretation of his reaction was. Inside, the clock was ticking. I had to say something. My thumbs developed the ability to think on their own. A simply marvelous feat of evolution. They typed out a simple response that as soon as it displayed on the screen, I died a million deaths.

"You too."

Oh Jesus. I wasn't going for a Shakespearean sonnet, but I didn't want it to be so campy. My head collapsed into my left hand, while my right hand held the phone with the offending message still displayed on the screen. The next chime sent a shudder down my spine. My mind had already guessed it would just be a simple good night. Whether or not to reply with the same bounced in my head as I raised the phone to my eyes.

"I never imagined you a mall rat ☐" At that moment, I felt like I was on the bow of the Titanic and we miraculously missed the iceberg. Feeling a resurgence of energy from my near-death-by-

embarrassment experience, at least in the terms of teenage life, which was a new sensation for me, I typed out a reply. This one didn't torment me as much as the last one. It was almost…acceptable.

"*Jamie thought I needed a little color in my life.*"

"*Don't let her change you. You are perfect just the way you are,*" flashed on my screen, faster than seemed possible.

"*I won't,*" I replied, having a hard time tearing my attention away from the word—perfect. My cheeks felt warm, and I was flustered as I tried to complete my response, but my thoughts drifted to his cool touch, and wondered if it could help with what I felt burning inside.

"Whoa, where did that come from?" I whispered to myself and took a deep breath and finished the reply.

"*I needed something that matched the school colors. I couldn't show up to another Friday night game in the other team's colors. Jamie bailed me out last night. LOL.*"

"*Yea, in some circles, that's a sin. Are you planning to attend more games?*"

I wanted to reply, "I will if you are", but I couldn't make myself type that, so I replied with a simple, "*Maybe. You?*"

"*Last night was my first. It's not really my thing. That might have to change if you attend more.*"

It might change if I…? That was an interesting phrase. Slow down, girl. I was reading way too much into it; I was sure of that. It was a question I couldn't come right out and answer, but there was an avenue. "*So, if it's 'not your thing'… why were you there?*"

"*Elijah was there and called me and told me he saw something interesting. Our sister was picking him up after the game, so I had her go early and rode with her so I could see too.*"

"*What was interesting?*" typed my thumbs before I thought about it.

"*You.*"

The phone fell from my hands, clattering on the floor. I made no attempt to catch it. My body was a frozen statue sitting there on the side of the bed with my mouth gaping open. The perfect opening for any of the millions of mosquitoes flying around our house to fly right into and make themselves right at home. It took a few moments for me to gather myself, which were surprisingly quiet, absent of any messages.

There was a simple and logical response. My only hesitation about sending it was out of fear of the answer. I didn't know what the answer would be. I just knew there were variations of the possible responses that I wouldn't like. I typed the message, and hit send, before turning the phone over and placing it down on my bed.

"*Why me?*"

My hands, now free, found their way up to my mouth, where I engaged in my grandfather's least favorite of all my habits, picking at my teeth with my thumbnail. I couldn't hear the clicking that always annoyed him over the droning of the TV in the background. We were now into infomercials. The pitch man was doing his best to convince all of us viewers that this was the greatest thing since sliced bread, but wait, there's more. I didn't hear what else came with the deal. Another chime interrupted his pitch. My hand reached out and hovered over the phone for a moment before grasping it and turning it over. There on the screen was a rather brief explanation.

"*You are new, and I hadn't introduced myself to you.* "

My free hand reached up and covered my face. Who was I hiding from? I wasn't sure. I was the only person here in the room. That didn't stop me from feeling silly about my overreaction.

"*Oh, so you do for all new students?*" I asked, feeling rather calm and more than silly. There was no hiding the phone this time. I sat there waiting for the reply.

"*No. Just you.*"

The phone slipped in my grasp, but this time I caught it. "*Why just me?*" my breathing grew more rapid with each word I typed.

"*You're different ☐.*"

Why do I feel like he just gave me a back-handed compliment? Maybe it was the word different, or that damn smiley. I put the phone down beside me and fell back on the bed, staring right at the ceiling. My breathing calmed, and there was only a light hammer of my heartbeat in my ears. I wanted to leave it with just that and be different, but I couldn't because it wasn't solely that. If it was just that, it would have ended at the game. What happened at the mall just cemented that this wasn't as simple as that. Again, my hand reached over and grabbed the phone, and typed out a response. Call it a clarification that I thought was witty.

"*Dark and mysterious different, or clumsy and geeky different?*"

I kept my phone held above my face this time and waited for the reply. This one was taking a little longer than the others had, and I felt the strain on my shoulders. A throbbing marked each second that passed, and then my arms gave up completely and I let my elbows collapse down to the bed, propping the phone on my stomach so I could still look down and see it.

"That's a complicated question. You're just different. Everyone in the school stays away from us. You didn't. Anyone else sitting in my seat would have moved when I arrived. You didn't."

I let out an exhale, feeling a quirky and curious expression creep across my face. *"Why? Are you the king?"*

"Not exactly. I think it's our family name. We've lived here since the city was founded, but you probably know all about us."

"I don't."

I closed the chat window on my phone and brought up the web browser and did a quick search–Starling Family Savannah, Georgia. The results filled the screen. Everything from news stories about charity dinners hosted by who I could only guess were Adrian and Elijah's parents. To social media posts of the extravagant parties hosted at what I could only call a mansion. This thing was enormous, and made of brown stone on the outside, and dark wood walls and red velvet covered furniture on the inside. Most of the pictures are from the annual Starling Foundation Christmas party. There I found the perfect family picture. Mother, Father, Adrian, Elijah, and Miranda dressed in tuxedos and black cocktail dresses in front of the largest Christmas tree I had ever seen. If there were a picture in the dictionary for the word magical, this would be it. Okay, maybe people feel intimidated by them. I kind of did now.

"Does it change what you think of us now?"

"No," I replied, swapping windows to check out more of the pictures.

"Oh please. Don't act like you aren't Googling my family right now. Just do me a favor. Don't believe what you read or see. Okay?"

"Okay," I agreed, and then switched back to a story I had just started reading about them at the Cannes Film Festival last year. It was one of the few pictures I saw Miranda smiling in. I am sure that

red dress she wore came with a label with the name of a famous French designer on it.

My phone chimed, announcing the arrival of another message, but I was too busy looking through all the pictures of Adrian looking like the cover off the GQ magazine in everything from a tuxedo to just a casual pullover shirt, hanging with every A-lister I could mention, and many more I couldn't. I saw one picture of him with a girl about his age, who was rather stunning, with flowing blonde hair and sparkling blue eyes that jumped through the screen. Not to mention the body that, well, I wasn't even going to try to compete with it. I thought I had a good body, but she looked like a masterpiece sculpted by a master artist. I looked again and even laughed, wondering if maybe a master artist had really carved her. Someone with scalpels and silicon. Probably a sixteenth birthday gift. All I wanted was a driver's license for mine.

My phone chimed, and knowing this was the second one I hadn't read yet, I flipped over and checked.

"We're just regular people."

Sure, they were. Nothing I saw even whispered normal. Everyone summers with the Princess of Monaco.

"In fact, let me show you. My parents are holding a charity dinner tomorrow night downtown at the Hyatt. Come with me."

A flush of heat raced to my cheeks, and I sat up, my legs dangled off the edge of the bed. I started typing my reply but found my fingers stuttering just like my mouth would have if he had asked me that in person. Maybe even worse. The reply eventually made it to the screen, and it was more of a question. *"Why me? Is this more of your new student introduction?"*

"No, it's because you are dark, mysterious, and a bit clumsy. I'll have the hotel pad the doors… lol."

"Plus, I find you very attractive and would like to know more about you. What better chance?"

"I won't take no for an answer."

All I could do was stare at the screen; heat rushed to my cheeks like a raging inferno while my heartbeat pounded in my ears. I leaned back on the bed, feeling lightheaded. The phone chimed multiple times in rapid succession.

"And don't worry about what to wear."

"Miranda has several dresses she is planning to choose from."

"You can have your pick of the rest. I believe you are both the same size."

"Just give me your address, and I'll have our driver pick you up an hour early, so you have time to get ready."

How could I refuse?

9

October 8th

Dear Diary,

It is now 3:17 am... WOW! I had no clue it was that late. Have I really spent the last 4 hours researching my date for tomorrow? I mean tonight; I guess.. and yes, yes, I have, and I am scared. I mean good GOD! I was joking about him being some kind of royalty. They might as well be. They came over here on their own private galleon in 1627, first living in Virginia and then heeding a call from Oglethorpe for rich families to help him establish the colony of Georgia and practically founded Savannah. Their family was credited with financing most of the early settlers and business, dealing in an import and export business with the Caribbean nations, and the Spanish as they settled Florida to the south. There are three roads: a road, a street, and an avenue, named after them and the children's ward at the hospital is named after them too. Thanks to several sizable donations made on behalf of the Starling Foundation. A three-hundred-year-old foundation started by his family with no particular cause, they seem to help everyone, and everyone helps them. The list of people who have attended any of their annual galas or donated to the foundation is a who's who of anyone. Celebrities, business leaders, actual royalty, and a pope... an honest to God actual pope, there's even a black-and-white picture of someone in a tuxedo, probably Adrian's grandfather, standing there shaking hands with the pope, pointy white hat and all.

That's not even the worst of it. I thought I recognized a few of the people in the pictures I saw online earlier. Seems, according to a UK gossip rag, that Adrian and Princess Sarah of Monaco were rumored to be an item last summer, and Elijah was seen canoodling with her cousin, Lauren, the Duchess of Glasbury. What does canoodling even mean? I might google that later, but I might have more to google too. Before that, Adrian was rumored to be dating Sharon Lars, the teen pop star, but according to another gossip site, he was also seeing Michelle Balore, the movie star who was a few years older than he was. That story was rather scandalous. Each story had a picture, too. Jesus. Why the hell did he invite me? They are classy and gorgeous, and I am just... me. Maybe I can find a reason to get out of it. This isn't exactly keeping a low profile, that's my out.

Later

"What the hell have I gotten myself into?" That was the question I repeated to myself while pacing along the curb outside my claimed address. There was a slight limp in my pacing, thanks to the hours of physical training by my grandfather. He had ratcheted up the intensity and changed up the training a tad. Probably thanks to Uncle Mike's lecture. I must have stabbed that dummy a few dozen times, which ironically was the about the same number of times I kicked my shins on the stairs or other obstacles my grandfather had put in my way.

What made our session today even more unique was the academic work, a first. After we were done with the physical, and I was a sore and sweaty mess, he sat me down in the kitchen and pulled out a small chalkboard from his office and placed it on the table for what I liked to call "Vampires 101". First up in the lesson, what is a vampire? As he wrote that out, I almost laughed, but I held it inside. Not that I really knew what one was. His manner of presentation was rather cheesy.

"First," he said, "Vampires are not immortal. You can kill them, and they can die. They extend their life and stop aging by replenishing their body with the blood of others. They suck a bit of life from each of their victims to stop the progression of time. The ultimate parasite is what they are. This gives them extraordinary immunity and healing abilities. For example. If you or I cut our finger, it would take time for that cut to heal. If we get cut deep enough, we will need a doctor to stitch us up. But not them. If they get cut, their wounds heal almost instantly. Stab or cut them deep enough, and they will need to feed on a healthy living person. Once they do, the wound will close instantly. It is true. I have seen it with my own eyes. I cut a hand off one of them before," he said, dragging his finger across his other wrist. "The wound started healing right before my eyes. A few days later, I found him again. The wound had completely healed, and he was as strong as ever. That brings us to the next point: strength and speed. Yes, they are faster and stronger than us. That is why we have to train to expect their every move. Again, because they continually feed on fresh blood sources, it, in the best of terms, without going into the biological explanations, recharges their batteries. They never sleep, but that doesn't mean they don't become tired or become weak. Denying them feeding will cause them to weaken and, if denied for long enough, they will die. I have, in the past, starved some out of existence. A tactic that takes a lot of patience but avoids conflict when you're not likely to survive."

With that, he looked across the table at me while placing the piece of chalk down.

"And?" I asked.

"That's it. That is the first lesson. We will cover the second one another time." He pushed up from his chair, tucked the chalk board under his arm, and turned for his office. And that was how, and where, today's lesson ended, leaving me only few minutes to relax before I started getting ready for tonight.

Before he disappeared into his office, I asked him about going out to the charity dinner tonight. Something I expected him to balk at. That was my out. If anything, I expected a few additional questions, being this was a guy asking me, and it sure sounded like a date. Nope. Nothing. Nada. Just a, "Don't be too late." My grandfather wouldn't win an award for being a model parent. As far as he knew, he may have just given me permission to go out with a serial killer. Hell, as far as I know, that was what this was. I didn't know much about him. Most of what I knew I had read online.

With butterflies holding a convention in my stomach, I stood and waited for a driver. Adrian didn't provide any description or name of the driver. Instead, he said I would know when he arrived. He was right. As soon as the black four-door Mercedes rounded the corner, I knew it. The reflection of the leaves played in the body lines of the car. It pulled up to the curb, and a man in a black suit and tie, with white hair, got out of the driver's seat, and walked around the car to my side.

"Raven Cross?" he asked with a hint of an accent.

"Yes," I said.

In a single smooth movement, he opened the back passenger side door, holding it open until I sat down, then he closed it and walked back around to the driver's door while I sat alone in the posh tan leather interior that smelled dealer fresh. The driver entered and started up the car, pulling off without another word. I sat there watching the old southern buildings speed by. Savannah had a beauty I had not seen much of yet. I hadn't ventured out far away from home or school. The closer we drove toward the waterfront, where the Hyatt was, the more historic the buildings were. We passed parks and squares with plagues on poles, probably describing the significance of the location. I made a note to come explore some of these one day.

At the waterfront, we turned along the river, pulling up to the front of the Hyatt. This was the end of my ride, and I reached over and gave the door handle a yank. It didn't open. The door was locked, and I couldn't find any buttons to unlock it from the inside. I gave it another yank just as the door opened. The driver stood outside, holding it open for me.

"Go up to room 416," he said, offering me his hand to help me out of the car.

I accepted it and stepped clear of the car. The door shut behind me, and I watched as he hurried back around to the driver's seat and pulled away, leaving me standing there in front of the entrance. I guessed it was too late to second guess my decision now. I walked in through the marble lobby to the elevators. As I stood there waiting for the elevator to open, I heard dishes clanging and conversations down at the far end of the hall. A sign stood outside the ballroom, "Starling Foundation Fall Ball." A ball? First off, I didn't know people still had balls. That was something that always seemed very fairy tale-ish from several centuries ago. Second, he told me this was just a charity dinner.

The elevator door opened, and I stepped in and pressed the button for the fourth floor while I tried to even imagine what a modern-day ball would be like. Every image that came to mind was something right out of Cinderella, and that couldn't be realistic, could it? The doors opened, and I stepped off, looking at the sign on the wall directing me to the right for the rooms numbered 400-420. Four doors down, on the left I found one with the gold numbers 416 on it.

I knocked, and it opened.

"Miss Cross?" asked a pleasant-looking woman dressed in a dark suit, wearing bright red lipstick, with her hair pulled back in a tight bun.

"Yes."

"Come right in. My name is Stephanie."

I did, and she reached behind me, closing the door.

"Master Starling will be up to get you in twenty minutes," she said, leading me through the elegant suite's sitting room, pulling open a set of double doors, leading us into the bedroom.

"Mistress Starling has made her selection. You can choose any of the remaining three to wear tonight and to keep. The rest will go back to the store." She spun around on her heels and gave me a quick once over, while I tried to process the word—keep. "There is a full array of makeup over there," she pointed to a makeup table with a mirror. "But I would recommend going light. You have such a natural glow about you. It'd be a shame to cover that up. Let me know if you require any help. That is what I am here for." She walked back out of the room, closing the double doors behind her.

Now who was living a fairy tale? I stood there in the middle of one of the most glamorous rooms I had ever seen. Marble floors. Dark wood walls, an entire wall of mirrors, and a rack of the most spectacular gowns I had ever seen anywhere. Was I dreaming? I walked over to the rack and slowly examined the dresses, touching each of them. Yep, they were real. Each dress had a bag of matching shoes hanging from its hangers. I looked at the first dress, just curious. Surprise, they were my size. That was either a lucky coincidence or a very disturbing detail. The beauty of the first dress puts that thought out of my mind. It was a blue sequined full length off-the-shoulder dress. I snatched it from the rack, and then I saw the next dress and put it back. The white full length off-the-shoulder dress was truly magical to look at. The skirt had fabric bunched around it that looked like waves rolling down its length. I pulled it off the rack to look at it closer and noticed there was a short train hanging from the back of the skirt. This was it. There was no need to look at the rest of them, but that didn't stop me from looking. The last one on the rack was a green one. Green was not one of my favorite colors, but the dress was stunning, and I considered it for a moment before walking the white one over to the bed, dancing circles around the room as I did.

I laid it down carefully on the bed, not wanting to wrinkle it or mess it up, and proceeded to explore the room. This was, without a doubt, the most magnificent room I had ever been in. We frequented hotels every time we were on the move, but those were budgeted, out of the way places. I bet this place put a mint on your pillow. If you found something brown on your pillow in some places we stayed in, it was probably a roach. My hand brushed the comforter on the bed, and I about cried. I now knew what a cloud felt like, but I wasn't going to stop there. I turned and fell straight back onto the bed. My whole body let out a sigh as the comforter and mattress molded itself to me with just the right balance of warm comfort and firm support. I wondered if it would offend Adrian if I skipped the ball and just stayed here and took a nap.

After forcing myself to put an end to that bliss, I stood up, got undressed, and before I slid the dress over my head, I held it in front of me and gazed into the mirror. This was an image I never in my life thought I would see. Me, in a dress like this. A shudder came over me, and I laid the magnificent dress back down on the bed. I couldn't wear it. It was too glamorous, too perfect for me. I wasn't anything like those other women I saw Adrian with. I was just plain Jane, me.

There was a knock on the door, causing me to jump. "Miss Cross, are you almost ready? Master Starling will be here in ten minutes."

"Crap," I whispered, and hurried to get ready. When I sat down at the makeup table I instantly realized my mistake. This white dress would catch and show everything. Even the smallest speck of powder that fell while I was applying it to my face would be noticeable. Taking the dress off was a momentary consideration, but as I lifted it up, I realized I might brush my face putting it back on. No matter what I did, I was doomed and needed help.

I walked over and opened the double doors and found her standing there in the center of the room. Was she standing there the whole time waiting for me? I guessed so. "Um, I could use some help with my makeup. I'm afraid of messing up this gown." I spun around, and the train followed me.

"Of course, I have just the thing." She marched through the door and right over to the makeup table. With two firm hands on my shoulder, she instructed me to have a seat. I couldn't resist. One hand left my shoulders and opened the table's side drawer, pulling out a black fabric cape and affixed it around my neck. Both of her hands repositioned themselves on the sides of my head, jerking it back and forth as she studied my face in the mirror.

"Miss Cross, as I said earlier, you don't need a lot. There is a natural glow to your features. Might I suggest just some lipstick," she said, leaning over, her back straight as a board, checking the assortments of tubes on the table. "Might I suggest this? It's very roaring 20s, which is all the style now." She had a tube of bright red lipstick in her hand, and I puckered up, letting her do the honors. I doubted she would have allowed it any other way.

"What about my hair?" I asked, using my own hands to hold it up.

"Nothing," she said, running her hands through it. "You do nothing. This short messy style is a modern day take on Eton Crop. It's perfect."

A knock at the door gave us both a startle. She checked her watch. "Just in time. That will be Master Starling. He is never late." She marched toward the door. Her heels clicking on the floor. I stood up and followed her slowly, only making it as far as the center of the room before she opened the door.

"Master Starling, your guest is ready." She opened the door wide open, and Adrian walked in right off the cover of a magazine. His hair was a perfect flowing mane, eyes piercing as always, and a smile that rivaled the sun. A tailored black tuxedo clung to his muscular but thin build. I had seen several pictures of him at the beach in Europe during my brief research. It was obvious he didn't eat many carbs. The urge to gasp came over me, but I held it in. He didn't. His gasp escaped as soon as we locked eyes. To see if I could elicit another response, I did a quick twirl there in the center of the room. The dress followed my body, flowing effortlessly. I even thought I saw a bit of a shimmer from the fabric.

"You… are… breath taking," Adrian said breathlessly with a hand extended toward me. I took it and followed him out the door.

"Miss Cross. Miss Cross. Don't forget your clutch." Stephanie ran out the door and into the hall, holding a white clutch that matched the dress. "I already put your phone in it. I'll pack your clothes and have them waiting for you at the end of the night. You don't need to worry about a thing. Enjoy the evening." She handed me the clutch, and before I could thank her for everything, Adrian stepped in.

"Thanks Stephanie."

"You're welcome, Master Starling. Enjoy your evening."

We walked down the hallway to the elevator and stood there, waiting for the door to open. "You really look breathtaking," Adrian whispered, giving my hand a little squeeze.

"Thanks," I responded, trying not to let my face explode from smiling so hard. The door opened, and he led me in and pressed the button for the lobby. The doors closed, and I saw our reflection in the elevator doors. Mine in one door, his in another. Another fairy tale image to add to the list of others from the night, and I had to turn my head before Adrian saw the starry-eyed look I had on my face. It was altogether possible it was too late. Who knew how long it had been there?

His hand squeezed mine again. "Don't be nervous. This is just a family dinner." The door opened, and we walked down the hall toward the sign I saw earlier. We turned right into the door, and Adrian added, "And about a hundred of their closest friends. That's how many seats they sold."

He wasn't kidding. It was wall to wall people. Some sitting and talking at the tables scattered throughout the room. Some standing and talking anywhere there was room. A large group chose the area around the ornate ice carving of a swan sitting on top of a jack-o'-lantern. Perhaps the table full of food was the draw, more than the swan. I wasn't sure, that swan looked pretty spectacular.

We walked in and I headed straight ahead, but felt Adrian's hand pull me to the right, putting us in a line with others, and I realized what this was, and it added another fairy tale moment to the list. If this was what I thought it was, I had only seen this in movies involving royal families. This was a receiving line. Everyone stood in line, waiting their turn to greet, and to be greeted by the party's host. That was when it hit me. We were about to meet his parents.

I pulled my hand back from Adrian. Not because I didn't want to hold his hand anymore. I did. I loved the cool feeling of his hand. Mine was betraying me and had become sweaty. He let it go with little fight. We crept forward, waiting for our turn. I peered ahead a few times, looking for his parents, but struggled to see pass the crowd. All I knew was we were getting closer, and I needed to solve the problem developing on my hands, but I had a severe shortage of options. There was really only one, and it was almost sacrilege, but with no other options, I grimaced and wiped my clammy palms on this magnificent dress. Just in time too, the group in front of us moved up, and Adrian reached forward and took the hands of a woman that couldn't be more than ten years older than us, and then leaned in and kissed her on the cheek. "You look radiant tonight, Mother."

Mother? I was thinking older sister, or some aunt who was more of a cousin, but mother? I had realized the genes were strong in this family. Every inch of her looked radiant in the red form hugging dress. It seemed Stephanie may have helped her pick her shade of lipstick, which was quite the contrast sandwiched between her ivory skin and raven hair.

"And this must be Raven," she said, turning to me.

"Yes Mother," Adrian, grabbed my hand, sweat and all, and presented me to her. "This is Raven Cross. Raven, this is my mother, Katherine Starling."

"It is so nice to meet you, my dear. You are all my son has talked about for the last few days." She turned and smirked at Adrian, and I saw just a hint of a squirm in his movements as he attempted to break our embrace and move the line along. "You are just as gorgeous as he described."

"Thank you. It is so very nice to meet you," I replied.

"Dad," coughed Adrian. His mother released my hands with a smile. "This is Raven Cross. Raven, this is my father, Michael Starling."

Once again, I felt startled. The man standing before me didn't look any older than mid-thirties, if that. They both shared the same model-like sharp lines and cutting blue eyes. The only difference, his dark hair was shorter than his son's youthful rebellion.

"So, this is the mystery girl that got my son to his first high school football game. I can't tell you how long I have tried. It is so great to meet you." He reached out and shook my hand, and I felt a familiar cool sensation. That must be a family trait. All I knew was it had a calming effect.

"It is great to meet you as well," I replied, being cordial and unsure if I should bow or something.

Adrian put his arm around me and guided me down the line, letting those behind him have their time with his parents. That time was probably why they spent whatever exorbitant amount to attend this dinner. That and the cause it was supporting, whatever it was. Adrian hadn't mentioned it.

"Of course, you know my brother." Adrian said as he presented me to Elijah.

"I might say, brother, this is a unique way to get out of having to stand here like the rest of us," Elijah grinned at his brother before turning to me. "What, no hoodie?"

"It's upstairs," I said, leaning in toward him.

"If my brother gets on your nerves, don't hesitate to give him a hard shot in the ribs. That's what I always do."

"I'll remember that."

"Don't mind my little brother. He knows what would happen if he gave me his best shot." Adrian grabbed my elbow, leering at his brother as he pulled me away, but if he thought he was leading me to safety, he was mistaken. I guess we couldn't skip that last member of the receiving line. That might appear rude.

"And you know my sister, Miranda," Adrian said, but he tugged at my elbow to keep me moving. She glared at me with her steely blue eyes. They were piercing, haunting, and threatening. I felt violated by them, physically and spiritually.

Her ruby red lips parted, and said a very curt, "We've met."

Elijah snickered, pointing at the two of us. I didn't see what about our icy introduction was funny. Then I heard Adrian snicker too. I looked up at him and felt my heart sink. Was I now part of some sick joke? Miranda's eyes dropped and raced up and down me. She was about to deliver the punchline, I knew it, and steadied myself. When she looked up, she was not laughing. There wasn't even a smile.

"I guess I should have told Stephanie to remove that choice, if you picked the other, sis," Adrian turned around, trying to hide a huge, humorous grin.

"Well, we know which one is the white queen, and which one is the black queen, don't we?" Elijah remarked and pointed at our dresses. I looked down at mine and then looked at Miranda's. Now I got the joke, and I wasn't the punch line. We kind of both were. We were mirror images of each other. I guessed there was a white and black version of the same dress. She had selected the black one, which matched her dark hair. I selected the white one, which matched mine. That was not why I picked it. We both even wore the same shade of lipstick. Stephanie's influence, I thought. Now I had to fight back a grin at seeing her furrowed brow and down-turned corners of her mouth.

"We should move along." Adrian grabbed my elbow again and urged me forward. I couldn't help but give Miranda a little finger wave bye as we walked on and entered the room with the rest of the attendees.

Our first stop was the table at the very front of the hall, our table. Labels marked where each of us would sit. Seeing my name, written there in calligraphy on a name card next to one with Adrian's name, threatened to crack my face. I put my clutch down on the table next to my name card.

"How about some food?" offered Adrian, and then he walked me back to the center table with the ice sculpture. Every type of hors d'oeuvres you could imagine filled the table. Fruit trays, vegetable trays, cheese trays, little quiches, and things I didn't even recognize.

"This is the best part of these dinners, if you ask me," Adrian whispered into my ear from behind and handed a plate forward to me. "The main course isn't bad, but after that, it only goes downhill."

"The desert can't be that bad," I remarked.

He laughed, and I wondered what was funny. Adrian moved up close behind me. The coolness of his breath tickled my neck, rattling me slightly as I tried to use tongs to grab one of the mini quiches.

"It's not that bad, but that is where it ends. Raven, look around. This room is full of stuffed suits. Old retired money, that is just here for either the picture opportunity with my family as some kind of status symbol, or for a few moments with my father to pitch some kind of foolhardy business idea. We won't have a silent moment to just enjoy. Just a parade of person after person motivated by greed and self-gratification. There isn't a single interesting person here, except you." I felt him back away and wanted to reach back and pull him closer. As we reached the end of the line, I did as he suggested and looked around. He was right. Only a few were under retirement age, and they hovered around the door where Adrian's father and mother were still receiving the last few stragglers to arrive.

"But this is all for charity, right?" I asked, walking next to him back to the table.

"Yes," Adrian responded, tossing a cube of cheese into his mouth. "Don't get me wrong. This is all for a great cause. The proceeds from the insane per-plate ticket price and the after-dinner auction fund several worthwhile programs in the area hospitals, but I doubt that motivated anyone to attend. So, it's a tradeoff," he looked around the room with a sigh, "We torture ourselves for the evening and suck what we need from them in return, all for the greater good, charity."

"That's rather cynical," I said, while Adrian pulled the chair out for me at our table. I sat first and then he sat next to me.

"Perhaps, or just experience. We do this almost every other month. So, I speak from experience."

"What mischief are you into now, brother?" Elijah slapped his brother on the back before taking the seat next to him with his own plate of food.

"The usual."

"Raven, this is the part of the night where my brother will go around the room, pointing out people and telling you their backstory and purpose for being here. It's something of a sport for him."

"Not just me. You do it too."

"True." Elijah tossed a grape in his mouth, and while chewing he asked, "Where shall we start?"

Adrian searched around the room. His eyes settled on a group, and an evil smile appeared on his face. "Just to the left of the sculpture, blue bow tie and receding hairline."

I watched as Elijah's eyes zeroed in, and then I followed each of their gazes to a group of six standing there, talking.

"The one with snow on the peak, or a bald mountain?" Elijah asked.

"I said receding, not bald."

"All right." Elijah tossed another grape into his mouth. "Go for it."

"First, that woman is not his wife." Adrian turned his attention to another cube of cheese.

"Adrian, don't allow yourself to be fooled so easily. It could be one of those May December things."

"It's not that. He's wearing a wedding band, and she isn't. No woman in these social standings would go out without a sizable rock on her hand, and if he was widowed or divorced, he wouldn't wear his. He's just sloppy and forgot to take it off. His wife probably thinks he is at a business function, and that leaves only one option–"

"He's here to pitch an idea to our father."

"Right. A picture would be evidence of his little tryst, risking it being discovered if published online or in the paper."

"That was an easy one. Pick someone else, harder this time," Elijah challenged his brother.

For the next twenty minutes, Elijah and Adrian played that game. They never disagreed on anyone. I rather enjoyed it. There was a playfulness between the two brothers that was humorous. It cut through some of the mystique they had at school. Maybe Adrian was right. They were just normal people. What I didn't enjoy was their attempt to recruit an out of the ranks spectator and into a player in their little game. They tried more than a few times, asking my opinion. I ignored them until neither would play without me, so I had to give in. It looked fun. Why not? Of course, I would have liked to have picked my target. Instead, Elijah picked him for me. A man younger than most in attendance, probably in his forties, in a classic black tuxedo with a black cummerbund and bow tie. He was alone, and he wasn't wearing a wedding band. I really wished I could have picked one. I would have gone for someone more geriatric. Those seemed easier.

"This isn't easy," I moaned.

"It's easier than you think," Adrian replied, stone faced, looking right at me. The heat of his gaze made me nervous.

"He could be either. Maybe someone looking to be seen to further his career, or he has…" I stopped and watched for a second. There was something I just picked up on, and I need to confirm my thought. There it was again. He kept looking around, almost nervously. That had to be it. "I got it now. He's here to pitch an idea to your father. See how he is nervously looking around? The pressure of his pitch is eating at him."

Elijah chuckled. "Not bad, but wrong."

Adrian ducked his head, hiding a devious smile behind his hands until he looked up, laughing as well. "Neither. He's the auctioneer. He is scanning the room trying to gauge who the major players will be. Sorry," he looked at me sheepishly, as if he begged for my forgiveness. "My family uses the same one all the time."

I wanted to slug him in the arm, but I resisted, finding a little humor and comfort in the moment. It felt almost as if they had accepted me. Of course, the question of why they had, and why I was even here, still loomed large, but that would have to wait for a more private setting. I looked around the room again, trying my hand quietly at the game. Some were easy to peg, and others were not so much. Of course, everything was all a guess, but I felt Adrian was probably right on point about the ones he picked. It seemed everyone I picked could go either way. I kept searching for an easy prey so I could show off, but I didn't see anyone. There was an interesting grouping standing against the opposite wall, and I couldn't ask about what I saw.

"Who is that over there with Miranda? A boyfriend?"

My timing was wonderful. Both brothers had just taken sips from their water glasses, and both choked on them. Elijah coughed and gagged. Adrian grabbed a napkin as some of the water leaked through his lips as he struggled to swallow it.

"Hell no," Elijah croaked. "That is just some fool trying to crack the uncrackable nut."

"So, she isn't interested in him?"

"Have you met our sister?" Elijah asked.

"Fair point." That didn't stop me from wondering. She still had a bit of the frozen bitch showing, but she was engaging and talking. I didn't know she had that side to her. "If she isn't interested, then why-"

"Why is she taking the time to talk to him?" Adrian completed my thought. "She is just preparing herself to step up and take the reins as the head of the family one day. That is all. She doesn't have it in her to be warm and engage with anyone. It's all about appearances."

"Well, that appearance is cold," I said without thinking.

"You're not wrong, and don't think that underneath what you see is a warm, soft person. She is what you see, but she loves us, and we love her."

"I meant nothing by it," I said, offering an apology, while trying to shrink down to nothing but an invisible speck in the universe. This wonderful man had invited me to this wonderful dinner, and was giving me an evening most girls only dream of, and what have I done? I insulted his sister. Not the smoothest of moves. Not by a long shot.

"Don't worry about it. We get it. We live it."

"I'm going to make another pass through the table before the main course arrives. Anyone want anything?" Elijah offered as he stood up.

"I'm good."

"The key to understanding Miranda is understanding one single fact. She believes anyone who tries to get to know our family is after one thing. That makes her very protective of the whole family."

"What does it take to make her understand that someone just wants to get to know your family?"

Adrian chuckled and sat back in his chair. "I'll let you know when she does," he said with a smirk. "So, are you saying you just want to get to know us?"

"Well now," now it was my turn to lean back in the chair. "You tell me. You're the one who invited me."

"I did, didn't I?"

He opened the door and gave me the chance to ask the question that had pressed against me since last night. I'll admit, I was more than a little afraid of the answer. What I had to remind myself of was the answer was *the answer*, whether or not he ever spoke it. Never hearing it wouldn't change it. "So, why did you?"

"Would you believe I wanted to genuinely get to know you?" Adrian flashed a smile back at me.

Touche. I had to give it to him. That was a rather clever response. But I had an even more clever question for him. "Why?" Smack, the ball was back in his court.

He looked up at the ceiling, his hands running down his face. "Why? Why indeed? Why is the world round? It is, by the way. Why is the sky blue? Why is water wet? Why do I want to get to know you?" His hands pulled his face back down, and he looked right at me. "Because I like you. I know you are going to ask me why again, and I honestly can't answer that. Call it biology if you want. There was something about you that first day I saw you. Was it an attraction? Absolutely, but it was more than that. There was just something about you. I can't put my finger on it. It's as simple as that. I knew then I wanted to get to know you. I know how people at school talk about us, so I knew you wouldn't come to me, so I came to you."

Well, there I had it. A warmth rushed to my cheeks as his gaze made me squirm. I felt speechless, and this was absolutely the worst time for that. There was an awkward silence between us, and I hated those. They weren't called awkward for nothing. I had to say something, but that was going to be a challenge as I was biting my lip. "Okay." That was all I could manage, and I did so, drawing no blood from my lip. My hands wrestled with themselves on top of the table, and Adrian noticed. His eyes left my face for just a moment and looked down at them. That just intensified their battle.

"I'm just not like the others," I whimpered, looking away from him.

"Oh." Adrian all but chuckled and leaned back in his chair. "You've been using Google, I see."

"Maybe a little."

Adrian reached over and caressed my cheek, gently turning my head until our eyes met. "Don't believe everything you see, Raven. Those are just pictures. Remember what I said about most people here? Everyone wants something, an exchange of favors.

Some want something from my father, and other times, my father wants something from them. For a nice handsome donation, sure I'll escort someone to a movie premiere. At no time did I choose any of them, but I chose you." His gaze lit a fire inside, and I felt my face move closer to his. The coolness of his breath licked at my lips.

"Your main course," a red coat wearing steward announced, while reaching over and placing the plate down in front of me. I sprang back in my chair and looked up.

"Thank you."

He returned a quirky, uneven smile.

"Master Starling." Then the man placed a plate down in front of Adrian before walking around to Elijah.

I looked down at my plate, steak, carrots and some kind of fancy looking rice dish. Everything smelled wonderful. A quick glance at the table and I realized I was the only one eating the meat. Adrian and Elijah and what I had to assume were the plates for his parents and his sister were just uncooked long green beans, broccoli, and other vegetables.

"I didn't know you were vegetarian," I commented, not really meaning anything by it, just hoped to end the awkward silence. Just small talk.

"We aren't," Adrian replied. "They can't fix meat how I like it, so I don't even bother."

Well, that made complete sense. I guess. We ate, and talked, ate, and then talked some more. About the time I was telling them my life story, the one I was given, his parents came and sat. Adrian's father asked about my grandfather and his work. He accepted the simple answer of engineering consultant. I was thankful he didn't ask where. I didn't have that detail prepared. When someone asked in the past, we made up company names, but with how connected Mr. Starling was, he might see through it, and if we picked a real company, he might know someone in the ownership there. That was all our cover story needed to unravel right before my eyes.

We got into our likes and dislikes. After hearing a few of the bands and movies Adrian liked, I went off script and gave him several that Maria Foster liked. We had very similar tastes, mostly. I would describe Adrian's taste in both as eclectic. There was a variety of good modern-day choices mixed in with several eye raising older classics. Few teenagers are going to list a Fred Astaire and Ginger Roger's movie in their top five all-time favorites, but I let it go. Everyone has the right to their own taste.

After dinner, a three-piece jazz band with a vocalist took the stage, and many people, including his parents, headed to the floor. Elijah did as well, and I watched as he walked right up to some mid-thirties blonde socialite and whisked her away from her husband and out to the dance floor with a single word. Miranda disappeared, but I didn't really care where to. All I knew was that left Adian and me alone at the table. In our own little world, doing exactly what he had stated he wanted to do. We were getting to know each other. While we talked, his hand toyed with mine. At times, he merely brushed mine. Probably testing the waters to see how I would react to contact. Which was stupid. He had held my hand before, and very recently. This was something else. Something less casual and it felt more intimate. A single finger made its way on top of my hand, with a slow progression to where we are now, holding hands. Again, his cool touch soothed me, and to my surprise, my hands stayed dry.

Without warning, he yanked me up to my feet and pulled me to the dance floor. One of the most frightening experiences of my life. I didn't know the first thing about dancing. I never had. Not even by myself to a song on the radio. Even if I had, it wouldn't have helped. This was a slow, classic song. Not the rock I listened to on the radio. The lyrics were about taking someone to the moon, and it was smooth. I let Adrian drape my arms around his neck and did the only thing I could. I let him lead. I had nothing to do but follow him, if

I could keep my mind focused on that and not how close our bodies were.

When the music stopped, Adrian whispered into my ear, "Sorry, I just had to have one dance before the music stopped."

I didn't complain. Everything was perfect in fairytale land. His hand pressed firmly in the small of my back, urging me even closer and closer. His head tilted toward me, and my insides jumped. Was this it? I could feel his cool breath on my cheek. Slowly, it made its way to my lips. I felt it, so softly, and I tilted my head to match his, and closed my eyes to prepare for what I knew was coming. Even without looking, I knew he was becoming closer with every moment, or was it me moving closer? The slight pressure in the small of my back stopped, and we stayed there, swaying to the smooth beat of our own music. Then the pressure released, and I knew something was wrong. He stopped, and so did the music.

Adrian let go and turned around. Miranda stood there, arms crossed, scowling right at me.

"Brother, a word."

"Not now Miranda."

Adrian attempted to turn his back to his sister, but she grabbed his shoulder and rather easily turned him back to face her. "Now," she insisted, her tone cutting.

"Give me just a moment." His jaw twitched as he left the dance floor, just as the band started up again, leaving me standing there in the way of the other couples dancing.

I started back for the table, watching Adrian follow Miranda to the far corner of the conference room, but a hand grabbed mine from behind. With a yank, I spun around and was face to face with Elijah.

"This is not a song that should be wasted. Shall we?"

I neither agreed nor declined. We just danced while I watched a brother and sister in a very heated conversation. Miranda did a lot of pointing, while Adrian stood there with his hands in his pockets. Adrian turned away from her a few times, with frustration dripping from his face, only to turn back and yell his response.

"Just ignore them," Elijah whispered into my ear. "Brothers and sisters fight. It's just nature. But let me say, you do that dress more justice than she does. You bring it to life."

"Thanks," I said, only half aware of the compliment, and that he had pulled me in closer. "What are they fighting about?"

"Who knows with those two. Adrian probably inhaled the wrong way or something. It could be anything." Elijah applied light pressure to the right side of my back and attempted to turn me away from the view. I resisted. "Just ignore those two and enjoy the dance, Raven." He attempted again, and I gave in, turning and just listening to the song, only to be interrupted a few moments later when Elijah was ripped from my grasp.

"Brother, I'm sure you don't mind my cutting in." Adrian stood there leering at his brother. There was no fight between the brothers. Elijah backed away, bowing gracefully.

10

October 9th

Dear Diary,

    Wow, where do I even begin? Last night was like something out of a dream, a fairy tale dream that unfolded right before my eyes, and I was in it. I still can't believe it all happened, and as I sit here with the morning sun casting its gentle glow through my window… see everything sounds like a fairy tale to me right now… LOL… I can't help but relive the magical moments of the night before… but it is morning and I've been up all night, and I have school, this might be where my chariot turns into a pumpkin.

    So, Adrian wanted to get to know me. That was why he invited me. Why? He couldn't say, but I'm not too sure I really care at the moment. It probably also explains why we spent all night texting back and forth after his driver dropped me off just a little before 11 last night. The good news, I don't feel tired, the bad news… this high will wear off, and I will. Which class is the only question left.

    There are other questions. I still want to know why Adrian wanted to get to know me. Yes, he said attraction, and I was different, blah blah blah… Those are cliché answers. I've seen the other girls he's been around. Lord knows they are all prettier than me… and I am sure I'm not the only one that hasn't bowed at his feet before… but I will admit to myself, maybe I really don't want the answers, and just maybe I was reading too much into this, I mean he had a chance to kiss me and didn't. Talk about confusing and mixed signals. After that, he bought me this very expensive Jade bracelet at the auction and insisted I wear it to school today. That thing is more expensive than my damn car. I'm a fool for even considering doing it. Maybe I am a fool in a lot of ways here... such as staying up all night on a school night. I am going to pay for this sometime today.

Later

I pulled into the school parking lot and parked in the spot that seemed to be selected for me. Jamie stood there, flagging me down and pointing out the spot. Before I even put the car in park, she was at the door. A flood of questions shot out of her mouth, muffled by the window. I looked out, feigning not being able to hear, frustrating her, causing several groans in between the squeals. One thing was for sure, this girl squealed a lot.

After a few more times of pointing at my ears and mouthing, "I can't hear you," I finally gave up and opened the door. Jamie backed up, but her mouth never stopped moving. I believe she started over with her first question. "Why didn't you text me back? I wanted to hear all about it."

"I fell asleep." I lied.

Her text arrived in the middle of my deep conversation with Adrian about losing my parents, and I ignored it. It was something we hadn't talked about at the ball, and I was glad for that. I doubted I could have opened up to him face to face the way I had in the text. The separation and lack of a face looking back at me as I descended into an emotional and sobbing mess made it easier. It's also possible I opened up to him like that because no one had ever asked how I felt when I realized they had died. It was such an odd and specific question about the moment your life was ripped apart, the moment everything changed. It's an understatement to use the words traumatic or tragic to describe that moment. It's so much worse. A part of you died with your parents, and you never get it back, while the rest of you tried to cling to life, but you are just moments from losing your grasp. What was weird about the conversation though, his replies made it seem like he understood, but how could he? His family was the front of a greeting card perfect.

"You slept? There is no way in the world I could have slept after a night like that." I wouldn't admit it, but I knew the feeling. Jamie reached and took my hand in both of hers. "You… have… to… tell… me… everything."

I retrieved my hand from her grasp and reached into my car, grabbing my books, and closing the door. As I walked into school, Jamie followed me like a lost puppy dog, begging the whole way.

"Please, you have to," she asked in several ways before grabbing me by the shoulder, spinning me around like a top. "Do you really understand how big this is?" She looked at me like her face was about to explode.

"It was just dinner," I said, downplaying the whole thing, trying to avoid a day full of this.

"Just a dinner? Raven, news flash. You are the shit now. Look around. The food chain changed, and you are at the top. The social pecking order now starts with you. Seriously, look around," she motioned her hand toward the parking lot, and I did exactly what she asked. I looked. My heart thumped loudly twice, before accelerating to a full-on jack hammer, accompanied by several rapid breaths before I realized what was happening. I pulled things down a few levels before the world spun out of control. It had been over a week since I hit the ground in the parking lot. I wanted to keep that streak going.

With every set of eyes in the parking lot watching me, for a completely different reason than when this had happened in the past, I grabbed Jamie's hand and yanked her down the sidewalk and inside, taking care of the door. Inside, the school was no different. There were people lining the hallway and standing by their lockers. They all turned and watched as we walked down the center to our lockers. Jamie followed me to mine first.

"Is it that big of a deal?"

Jamie's cheeks puffed out, and her face turned red. All she was missing was a cartoon steam whistle above her head. "Yes!" She looked around at the crowd still watching us, and then leaned in closer, as if that gave us any privacy. There were at least forty people or more hanging on everything we did. "This is huge. You know who their family is. It's like they are royalty."

She reached down, rummaging through her bookbag, yanking out her phone and flashing it up to my face. There I was, in that white gown, looking like a princess standing next to Adrian. Then a finger appeared in front of the phone screen, swiping furiously. Picture after picture of me floated by on her phone as social media posts.

"I get it, but why is everyone looking at me?"

"That's simple, silly," Jamie said, dropping the phone and leaning in close enough we could use my locker's door for privacy. "You're the one."

"The one what?" I whispered back.

"The one he picked," she whispered back with a starry-eyed look. "Adrian Starling hasn't ever given any of us the time of day, but you… he let you in and he picked you."

Her words and expression swirled in my head, and I leaned back against the locker, feeling the danger of being pulled into her world. Hell, who am I kidding? I had been there since last night, and it was wonderful. My only problem was my brain. It didn't happen all the time, but it happened often enough to shock me back to reality. It was the little reminder that this couldn't last forever. I wasn't talking about some teenage drama and breakup. The ultimate destination of most high school relationships, no matter how much they promised each other to stay together forever, and I caught myself thinking about forever a few times last night. Maybe it was my lack of sleep. I wish I could chalk it up to that. It would make it easier. This was the nagging truth to our existence here. It was only temporary, and when my grandfather was done, we would move on. That was a fact that was as inevitable as death, which was rather poetic since Raven Cross would die.

Before that, I had class, and I reached up and closed my locker. Jamie grabbed my arm again, pulling the sleeve of my hoodie up away from my wrist.

"What is that?" she asked, her eyes locked on the bracelet of gold and green.

I yanked my arm free and pushed the sleeve down to cover the bracelet. "A gift," I mumbled, walking to first period. The first few steps were alone, as I traveled down the center of the wall, with students on either side watching my every step. I felt the urge to turn around and tell them all to get to class, but the first bell would do that all on its own in a few minutes. Maybe I could take advantage of this and get to class without having to fight through the crowd. It would be nice to walk through without being bumped around like a ball in a pinball game.

My solo journey was short-lived. Jamie was again on my arm, asking, "From who?" I really didn't believe she needed me to answer. The who was quite obvious. "Was it Adrian?" she asked for confirmation.

"Yes. He bought it at the auction last night."

I heard a gasp, followed by a gulp. "How much did it cost?" Jamie squeaked.

"Breathe before you pass out," I cautioned. "I don't really remember." Oh, I remembered. There was no doubt about that, but I wasn't going to say. It wasn't proper to speak of such things. Not to mention, I didn't believe I could say the amount without passing out myself.

"I hate to break it to you, but it wasn't just a dinner." Jamie nudged my side with her arm.

I walked into Mr. Fletcher's room; gave in and agreed. "I know."

Who knew a day would come that I was happy for English class? Not that I hated English. It was actually my favorite subject, but today it was my extra favorite. It gave me a break from all the attention from Jamie and others… well, check that. It gave me a break from Jamie. The silent attention from everyone else continued as I walked into the class and back to my claimed seat. The one Adrian used to call his own.

It was right out of the eeriest haunted house in the world. Every head in the room followed my path back to my seat. Even Mr. Fletcher watched me. Maybe it was just my imagination, but then again, maybe it wasn't. I sat down and returned their stare. Every head jerked around to the front, and casual conversations resumed. But, even then, they didn't ignore me. There were quick glances back in my direction, and everyone who entered took their turn. It was freaking me out a bit. Okay, more than a bit. I pulled out my notebook, opened it, and wrote the date at the top of the page, tracing it over and over again to avoid having to look up. I heard someone enter, and a murmur spread through the room. Then there was a squeal, and I heard footsteps approaching.

"You? Of all people. Why you?" That southern belle draw was all too familiar even though I had only heard it once before, Other than the day she called me door girl, she hadn't talked to me. Now everyone believes that cute little southern drawl is as syrupy as the sweet tea the south is so famous for, but this one was nothing but vinegar.

I looked up from my notebook, and there stood Gracie holding out her phone with a very familiar picture on it.

"Babe, why do you care?" Scott asked, annoyed, from the first row. His body language exacerbated as he turned and looked forward, slamming his books on his desk.

"Just why?" She asked me again, shoving the phone closer.

It was like she believed I had some grand answer for her, that I was just withholding to be mean. The truth was now, just as it was all night and the morning, I didn't know. So, I gave her the only answer I could, a sheepish shrug.

"Is that it? Just a shrug?" She shrugged her shoulders with a violent jerk.

"Ummm, yea." I looked around her at what I presumed was her boy friend sitting at the front of the room. He had his back to us, but you could see the agitation in his body language. "Why do you care? Don't you already have a boyfriend?" I pointed pass her to the front where Scott threw his hands up, and let them crash down to the surface of his desk.

That lit the fuse. Her jaw twitched as she ripped her phone from my view and turned and stormed back to her seat, leaving me to assume there used to be something between her and Adrian, a question to add to the pile of things to consider later. This one wasn't all that important. As she stomped back to her desk, the rest of the stares and glares followed her, finally leaving me alone, with my numerous thoughts and question in the back of the room. Not a pleasant thought, but it was something I needed. I had to find some answers.

Why did I underestimate Jamie's reaction to all this? I wasn't sure. With everything I had learned about her, I should have expected it. She went nuts over just a casual picture. Not that she wasn't wrong. Oh, I knew she wasn't wrong. This wasn't just a dinner. This wasn't just an invite-an-interesting-person-to-dinner-to-get-to-know-her. Even if he stopped short of making the night a true dream–damn, why didn't he follow through and kiss me, we were so close–I knew this was so much more, and I wasn't sure how to handle it, and while the rest of the class diagrammed sentences on the board with Mr. Fletcher, I did my best to appear engaged while considering that problem. What to do about it?

There were two answers, *the answer*, and *the answer I could dream about*. *The answer* was to do nothing. Let things happen. Go around and be as normal as possible, and then one day disappear, hoping everyone forgot about me soon. I was good at that, though I hadn't ever felt this close to anyone before. So much for keeping with my grandfather's "no attachments" rule. This was how it had to be, and I knew it. I knew it would hurt when we left, which, according to my grandfather, would be soon. It had hurt before. There was no denying that. It always did. Some hurt more than others. Hell, in some ways, I still missed Lucas. This time would be different. That was clear in both my head and my heart. This one would hurt more and last longer than any time in the past, ever. That was why I really liked *the answer I could dream about*, though it wasn't practical. I would leave. I would run off alone, or maybe with Adrian. Just considering it made my heart flutter, while feeling silly at the same time. I had just met Adrian. What did I really know about him? He could be a monster.

I paid little attention in English, or any of my classes. Moments from last night played back in my head, blocking out the lessons. It was more the emotions than the images. By the time lunch rolled around, my mind was all consumed, no matter how much I tried to refocus it. I guess I could also blame the lack of sleep a little as well. It wasn't helping. Either way, it seemed I had finally descended into the same crazed state that Jamie occupied, which melted away any resistance I had to answering questions Jamie and Caroline asked during lunch. Stephen sat next to me, mimicking every reaction, drawing a few terse looks from my two hysterical friends. None of the looks appeared to deter him. Instead, they appeared to inspire him to dig into his drama background just a tad more, making them cheesier. I couldn't help it, and had to sneak in a laugh or two, turning my head and hiding behind my hand.

Stephen was in the middle of one such mocking, complete with an over-exaggerated snort, when he went dead silent. I turned, expecting to find him distorting his face or some other silent but physical reaction, and I found one, but not the one I expected. With wide eyes, he stared above my head. Almost as if against his will, his body rose, and moved back one seat, his hands sliding his lunch back with him. A figure stepped around me, and Adrian plopped down in the now vacated seat, wearing a very uncharacteristic pair of black jeans and a black hoodie. I felt my mouth drop wide open, a look mirrored by Jamie and Caroline.

Fortunately, I caught mine after just a few seconds, and managed the best smile I could at the moment. My pulse raced as Adrian reached over, grabbing my hand. My fingers attempted to interlace with his, but his danced around mine. It seemed holding my hand wasn't his intention. They raced up my wrist, pushing up my sleeve, exposing the bright jade bracelet.

"Good, you wore it." Adrian said, as his fingers traced it around my wrists. "It's too beautiful to sit at home in a box."

"You're here," I croaked out. "Is there a test today?" I wondered if I had just daydreamed my way through a test in one of my earlier classes.

"No." His hand left the jewel adorned item and finally found mine. "My father is always telling me I should spend more time at school."

Elijah sat down across from Adrian. "Please, you're all he has talked about all night." Adrian released my hand long enough to pay his brother back for that comment with a punch that thudded against his shoulder. Elijah didn't wince. He laughed.

"Well, um," I started, trying to compose myself while my mind adjusted to what was just dropped on me. "Nice black hoodie."

"Thank you. I thought I would try a different style for a bit."

"So, what were you all talking about when we interrupted?" Elijah asked, looking up and down the table at everyone. It was only then that I realized the entire cafeteria was silent, and all eyes were on us.

We never went back to the original topic for obvious reasons. Instead, the topic dipped and dodged through other topics of a teenager's high school world until it naturally settled on to our drama class. Something we all had in common, but it seemed the brothers had a bit more "Drama" in them than the rest of us. They were talking about the Winter Show, which I guess was a thing, and auditions were normally in mid-November. Each person took a shot at trying to predict what the play would be this year. The details were a tightly guarded secret until they made the official post online and on the bulletin board outside of the classroom. The guesses thrown out at the table were anything from any of Shakespeare's works to *A Streetcar Named Desire*. Some even suggested seasonal plays like *A Christmas Tale* or an original adaptation of *It's a Wonderful Life*, but the group quickly dismissed that idea. I guess two years ago, several seniors tried to adapt a classic movie to a play, and it was a disaster. It was probably their choice of movie that doomed them from the start. *Gentlemen Prefer Blondes* doesn't scream theater play for me.

As we worked through each suggestion, the Starling brothers provided us with a preview performance. Elijah's speech as Biff Lomax confronting his father about living up to his expectations in *Death of a Salesman* earned him some applause from several of the neighboring tables. It didn't help that he stood up and acted it out while stomping around our table as if each of us sitting at it were his Willy Lomax. Even more amazing than their performance was how they knew the lines from every play. Adrian stopped his performance mid-line and sat down. Life drained from his face as he looked pass me, Elijah did the same, but he sat back with his armed crossed.

I turned my head and looked, and after my encounter this morning, I felt a similar sensation. Gracie Jones approached, with Scott fixed to her side as always. Those two were practically Siamese twins except when he was out on the football field, but even then she wasn't far, being the head cheerleader and all had her right down there on the field.

"Look, it's a table of drama freaks."

Jamie and Caroline both rolled their eyes. I diverted my eyes from her and stared at Adrian's beautiful face. I had much preferred it when that girl left me alone like she mostly had, but right now, nothing she could say could get to me. I was in my own world. I just wished Adrian was there with me. He was agitated.

"You're in our class too," Elijah pointed out, leaning back in his chair rather smugly.

"I am going to be an actress," she announced.

"Maybe in some crappy dinner theater somewhere," Elijah countered. "Your delivery is about as emotionally flat as you were before your daddy gave you your sweet sixteen gift."

Gracie squealed while the table when quiet. Scott lunged at the table, and I jumped out of my chair to avoid the fray. I thought he was going to come across the table at Elijah, but Adrian sprang up, stopping him with a hand to the chest. "As much as I would like to see you and my brother go at it again. I don't think it is wise for you," he warned.

Scott backed away slowly and threw his arm around his girlfriend. Probably to comfort her wounded pride. Her face was several shades of red. As they walked away, Adrian took his seat, and I reached over and grabbed his hand. He was as cool feeling as ever.

"Do you really have to stir the pot?" he asked his brother.

"Someone had to," he responded with that same smug smile he had had on his face for the last few minutes.

"No, they didn't."

"Isn't it rather odd that you have become the diplomatic one?" Now Elijah appeared to be taunting his brother.

"Elijah and Scott had a little issue with each other last year," Jamie leaned over and whispered into my ear. "Scott thought Elijah was trying to steal Gracie. Elijah put him through a locker door. Her father bought the school a new row of lockers to replace the damaged one."

I couldn't believe what I was hearing. Elijah always appeared to be the calmer one of the brothers. Not that I didn't doubt Scott deserved it. I knew his type. Braun over brain, in every instance.

"Okay, then." I commented, confused. That didn't make sense. If it was Elijah, why was she so upset about the picture? Elijah wasn't even in that. I had to ask. It was my turn to whisper into Jamie's ear. "Did Gracie and Adrian ever date?"

My answer didn't come from Jamie, it came from the horse's mouth himself, accompanied by some loud uncontrolled laughter form his brother. "Hell no." Adrian jerked with that response.

"She thinks every guys is hers." Elijah said through his laughter.

"Its not that funny brother," Adrian warned.

"Actually it is," replied Elijah, the laughter subsiding. "You and her. Complete opposites." Elijah sat up and leaned forward against the table. "Raven, just ignore her. Gracie is the type that believes she is God's gift to men, and can't accept when someone doesn't want her. She believed her and my brother were destined because of her family and our family. She has practically thrown herself at my brother, and most guys in this school from time to time. Fact of the matter is, I'm not sure why Scott puts up with it."

"So they are dating?"

"If you call it that," interjected Caroline. "Gracie gives him the honor of being her arm decoration."

Elijah pointed right at Caroline with one hand, and at his nose with the other. "Exactly."

"And yes," Jamie leaned in and whispered again. "In case you were wondering, Gracie's dad bought her plastic surgery for her sweet sixteen."

I gasped and felt Adrian's fingers tighten around my hand.

We walked to, and into, drama class hand in hand, again earning a ton of stares. Gracie wasn't one of them. It appeared she was still stinging. I had become used to the sensation, but that didn't mean I liked it. We only let go of one another after we took our seat in class. Well, that is we let go of one another physically. Our eyes stayed glued to one another, only pulling away in small bits to make note of what we were doing today in class. It was *lines* day, and one by one pairs of students had to walk up and perform a set of lines they had prepared outside of class, and Mrs. Prentice and the rest of the class provided critique. Jamie and I obviously had elected to work with one another, and our day was Wednesday. I was wondering if it was too late to change. Adrian would make a perfect partner, even if that meant Jamie would have to scramble to find someone. I was sure she would understand.

Drama was our last class together for the day, but as we left class, he promised me that wouldn't be the last time I would see him today. He said he would meet me by my car this afternoon in the parking lot.

The more the day marched on, the harder I found it to focus. It had to be the lack of sleep. Even my thoughts about Adrian were wandering all over the place. They were good places, but they were still wandering from place to place. I even wrote his name in the middle of the instructions for my physics homework assignment.

"Read pages 90-103, and then properly show the derivation of Newton's first law using Adrian kinematic equations."

When the dismissal bell rang, I rushed to my locker, trying to avoid Jamie and others. I wasn't trying to be mean, but I had someone waiting for me at my car, and I could text her later. We talked practically most of the day as it was. My mind was so tired, or preoccupied, I struggled to figure out which books I needed to take home. I pulled world history out twice before putting it back both times. I considered pulling out my notebook to see which I had homework in and what I didn't when I felt someone standing on the other side of my locker's door, and felt bad for wanting to ditch her earlier. Now she was standing there as my savior.

"Hey Jamie, do we have homework in world history and…" I pulled the locker door closed and froze in the icy stare of Miranda Starling. For someone dressed like a fashion model, tight black leather pants, white form hugging top, and hair that looks like she just left the salon, her expression sure cast an evil spell. Noticing how others shuffled clear of where she was, I realized she had the secret that I had wanted all day.

"Hi," I wheezed.

"Look," she spat. "I want to give you one warning, and I want you to listen to it good. Stay away from my brother. You are the wrong type for him." She turned and walked away.

Her words echoed in my ears, but her message had already reached my brain, and it had cleared the fog that was there before.

"What exactly does that mean?" I screamed, stopping everyone around us in their tracks. I believe I knew what she meant, but I wanted her to say it. I wanted her to say it in front of everyone, as if that would tarnish her. Not that anyone would care. She wasn't very "popular". People cleared the hall when she walked by.

"You heard me," Miranda said, turning around.

"I'm not good enough? From the wrong side of the tracks? Is that what this is all about? I don't fit in your world?" I was on a roll and had more to throw at her, but a breath of fresh air blew in and grabbed my arm before I followed Miranda down the hall.

"Let it go. My sister's bark is worse than her bite," Elijah said, leering at his sister.

"Oh, she wouldn't like my bite. I can assure you of that."

"Miranda!"

"And dear, this isn't about what you think it is, and trust me, you wouldn't like our world."

"Miranda!" Elijah warned again, his grip on my arm squeezed almost painfully.

She turned and walked down the hall, while Elijah pulled me back the few steps I took toward her. "Just let her go. Raven, just let it all go." He urged, finally releasing my arm, and then rummaging through my locker. "No history homework, but you do have pre-calc." Then he shut my locker, carrying my books.

"What's her problem?" I asked, still seething.

"She is just protective of us, like we told you last night. Just ignore her."

I wanted to, but I couldn't. Her words cut, and those cuts were stinging. "And what did she mean? I wouldn't like your world?"

"Oh, nothing." His voice quivered as he opened the door leading out to the parking lot and continued to urge me out of the school as fast as he could. "She believes our lifestyle is both a blessing and a curse. It's just her. Ignore her."

Adrian was right where he promised to be, waiting for me beside my car, but seeing me and his brother emerge from the school together appeared to surprise him, and he met us halfway.

"Brother?" he asked, watching us with a curious gaze as we approached. Once he reached us, he took my hand, as if to claim me from his brother. Adrian gave a quick jerk of his head, and Elijah rolled his eyes, stepping a few steps away from me.

"She had a little run in with our sister."

"About what?" I felt Adrian's hand tremble.

"Nothing. She was just being protective, as always. Nothing new. I told her our sister's bark is worse than her bite."

Adrian tensed up, squeezing my hand. The constant smile on his face turned into a straight-line grimace.

"Relax. It's handled. I will talk to her when I get home," Elijah assured him.

"We both will," Adrian seethed.

"I can't wait." Elijah smirked, handed me my books, and opened my car door for me.

"I think I should give you a ride home," Adrian offered, his grip loosening.

"Nope, I have my car. Why don't I give you a ride home?" I pulled Adrian closer as I leaned back against the back fender, trying to put what had just happened with his sister out of my mind, and being as coy as I could.

He took one look at my car and said, "Not in that thing. We might have to fix that."

"Fix what?" I asked, hoping he didn't mean what I think it meant. The jade bracelet felt heavier on my wrist. He leaned in, and this seemed familiar. It was like the moment last night. His breath again cool on my cheek in the sweltering heat of the afternoon. We were so close, and I tilted my head to match his. All he had to do was lean in just another few inches. We were almost there, but again he stopped, and inside my body screamed, and I leaned to meet him, but he zigged when I zagged, and he hugged me, pulling me close, and a wave of comfort cascaded across my skin.

11

October 10th

Dear Diary

>Today was... interesting

"Raven, are you ready?"

"Just a minute."

>Let me rephrase that. Today was fascinating in every sense of the word. I couldn't stop thinking of Adrian all day, no matter what I tried. Then, wouldn't you know, if thinking about him wasn't enough, he surprised me at lunch. He had no reason to even be there, except... and dare I even think it... I feel so silly doing it... that reason was me. And it's far beyond he finds me interesting and wants to get to know me. I doubt he would come into school on a day he didn't have to if it were just that, or talk about me all night, like Elijah said. He kind of sounded like me. LOL. How ironic. Mr. Cool actually seems obsessed with little old me. And speaking of cool, if I had any questions at all about it, his ice princess of a sister put the exclamation point right in it.

"Come on, Maria."

"Just another minute."

>She practically threatened me. I wonder if she knows who she is dealing with! HA. HA. Miranda is going to be a problem if

there is a future…. I really should stop those thoughts. I'm only making it worse for me, but I can't. There is just something that feels, dare I even say it, perfect. Like this is some kind of match made in heaven, and that is the life I'm supposed to live. Not the one my grandfather selected for me. Maybe there was a way out of this life, and just be normal. Maybe I could ask my grandfather about it! That might take more nerves than I would need for my first hunt. In the meantime, I have training beckoning me.

Later

My phone chimed right as I closed my diary. With a quick glance down at its screen, I saw Adrian's name on the notification. I wanted to read it, and then respond to it. Which would lead to more reading and more responding, and my grandfather had already called me twice. He even used my real name once. I was one more warning until he would be knocking on my door. I would respond as soon as we were done, but I knew there wouldn't be any staying up all night again. I was exhausted, and he had to be too.

I dragged myself downstairs, knowing this was going to be a rough session. Physically, I wasn't anywhere close to where I needed to be for training, and mentally, I was even worse. Distractions are your enemy's openings. A great proverb from my grandfather. It should probably be one of his rules. At this moment in my life, distractions had the door wide open for my enemies to walk right in and pummel me. This was going to be a session of pain and there was a part of me that knew I had it coming. Maybe that was the voice of my grandfather, planted in my head, whispering all his many virtues. Something like always stay vigilant, or any of the other dozens of rules and mottos he had. The man was a walking inspirational phrase of the day calendar. I didn't doubt that there was a portion of his voice in my subconscious, reminding me over and over what I needed to do, and even more important, who I needed to become.

At the bottom of the stairs, I was relieved to find my grandfather sitting at the kitchen table with objects placed on it, and most importantly, the door to the basement was closed. My chair was already pulled out across from him, and I walked over and sat down, allowing my eyes to take in the objects in front of me. I had always had my suspicions about what was in his bag. Movies, books, and several cheesy investigative shows had covered all the angles of what vampires might be afraid of, and what tools a vampire hunter might use. That didn't diminish the impact of seeing the bag sitting on the table open, and its contents spread out across the table. This was the moment I had been waiting for. No more dodging things in the darkness for years on end. Now we were getting some place.

"Maria, these are the sacred tools of our profession. I gave you the first tool for your own bag, back on your birthday." His hand reached over and grabbed a tattered black leather-bound book with papers hanging out of it. I had a much newer one upstairs in my room. "This is your diary. It's your everything. Every hunt is an investigation, and with every investigation, you have notes. Locations. Times. People. Behaviors. You will document everything and then analyze it for patterns. Those patterns will help you find where they are, and sometimes tell you the best time to take your shot, and how. Without this, you are just swinging in the darkness." He held his diary for me. My hand reached for it, stopping short of grabbing it. I waited for a nod of permission. This was an object of *the bag*, and my grandfather had been very clear for the moment I first saw his bag, those objects were off-limits.

He gave me the nod, and I took it. "Open it. Go on," he urged.

There was no waiting for a nod this time. I had it opened before I put it down on the table. Scribbles and drawings filled the pages that faced me. A date sat affixed on the top of each page. These were from July nine years ago. I thought back, wondering where we were then. There had been so many places. The timelines for each ran together. A quick glance at the drawing, and I remembered Pheonix. The drawing was a map of our old neighborhood. The school I went to was right there on the top corner of it, with a big star on a lot three blocks away.

"Let me see that page," he said, reaching over and spinning the book around. "Pheonix. This page here has a map of the area the vampire lived, which was our own neighborhood, and then below it, the complete documentation of his comings and goings over a period of two weeks."

He turned it back around and what he said popped off the page. All the little scribbles fell into place. It was line after line of times and notes. Each time, followed by a note. The note was followed by another time. The first was the time he left. The note was where he went. This particular vampire went to the liquor store every day at 7:00 pm and not a minute earlier or later, and then followed by the time he returned home. Most stalkers didn't have as complete a set of notes on their target as my grandfather did.

"That list gave me everything I needed. Turn the page." His finger motioned for me to flip it over. The same list was on each page, just for different days. "Flip it one more time, I think," he looked over with curiosity. I flipped the page, and he declared, "There!" A finger pounded the center of the page. A similar table of times and events was present, but he had circled several sets together and placed other notes around the circles. "Each group was what I identified as moments of opportunities, and the notes documented where I would take my chance. It was only through my meticulous observations that I identified those patterns of behavior. That one was an easy one. He was a creature of habit and did the same thing every day. Others I have had to correlate events across days to find the pattern. I hope you understand how important this is. Without this," his hand waved over the table, "none of this other stuff matters."

He picked the book up, put it back into his bag, and turned his attention to the other objects. His finger pointed to the one furthest to the right. "That is a vial of holy water. It's not just tap water," he cautioned, holding his finger up. "It is actual water consecrated by a priest that works with us. When you run low, call Mike, and he will send more. Holy water is mostly for your own protection. Splashing it on a vampire's flesh will burn like a son of a bitch, but it won't kill them. It will give you time to get away."

"Will it hurt if I get any on me?" I asked, out of genuine curiosity.

"Nah, to you, it will feel just like regular water."

"Then what is so special about it?"

"A priest blesses it, that is all, but it is very useful against any unclean souls."

"Like vampires?" I asked.

"Vampires. Those possessed by demons. Any being that has an unclean soul," he explained, as if it were common knowledge, and maybe it was in this world. I knew a few people from some of our past lives that had unclean minds. I wondered if that would work there too, but I didn't ask.

"Next up is another defensive tool, but," my grandfather glared across the table at me. "Do not, let me repeat, do not rely on this one for anything other than a distraction." He reached down and took the top off of a simple black wooden box. The box contained white crystals that resembled something very common. I doubt that was really it. This had to be some kind of complex chemical agent specifically blended to fight vampires. "Salt," he said, reaching in and grabbing a pinch between two fingers and letting it fall from a few inches above the box. "We use it to cleanse a room because it is said to block spirits, demons, and vampires. More times than I can count, I have drawn a line on the floor with just normal table salt, and watched a vampire not cross it. But I need to warn you, it is mostly just a legend. I really don't know if there is any truth to it. I don't know if it will cause them any actual pain or discomfort. If it will work at all depends on if they know the legends or not. If they do, this should only buy you the time you need to escape. Got it?"

I nodded and looked across the table for cloves of garlic. There were none.

His hand moved to a black velvet drawstring bag. With a single hand, he pulled the string open and allowed the contents, six small iron crucifixes, to slide out onto the table with a thud. "These will be yours one day." He picked one up and held it between two of his fingers. "Press these into their flesh and it will burn. They will become confused, and their mind will be yours. You can command them with the word of God. These are my favorite. I use them to set up for this."

The last item on the table was one I already knew. Anyone who had ever watched a movie about vampires and vampire hunters knew what those were. I just didn't expect to see bloodstains on the tips of his wooden stakes. He picked one up in his hand and stabbed the top of the table with the pointy end. "Thrust one of these puppies into the heart, and it's all over. It's the easiest way to kill a vampire. Got it?"

I nodded.

He picked it up and pointed the stained tip at me. "Do not miss. You won't get a second chance. "

"But," I started, remembering something from our other training.

He pointed the tip back at me and gave it a cautionary wave. "Yes, you can kill them by pulling their heads off, but remember. They are faster and stronger than you or I. You won't be able to do that. Trust me on that. Try that, and you will be dead before your hand even touches them. The stake is the way to go, but only after you have distracted them or incapacitated them using one of the other ways. I cannot stress enough how fast they are."

"Okay, I get it. They are fast." He made it seem like they would be nothing more than blurs in the room unless I found a way to knock them out, and then I could attack them. If that was the truth, then most of the defensive training he put me through over the last decade was worthless. That rubbed me the wrong way. "So, this is pretty much useless." I sighed.

I heard a huff from the opposite side of the table, and my grandfather rose from his seat, gathering all the stakes and putting them back into his bag. Next were the crosses, and I sensed my sigh had disappointed him. "I'm sorry."

"About what?" he asked, putting the top back on the box of salt.

"Saying this is useless. I'm sorry."

"You're not wrong," my grandfather replied with a wave of his hand. He gathered the box of salt and the vial of holy water and put them both in the bag. "I'm actually glad you see it that way. The worst thing would be for you to be overconfident. You need to be wary, even afraid. That would be the best mindset for you to have when you face off against one."

"Then I'm confused." I truly was and felt my head dipping toward the table in either frustration or exhaustion. It could have been either. My forehead reached the table with a light thud. "If they are faster and stronger than us, how can we win?"

"Now that is the question, isn't it? Look at me." he thumped himself in the chest. "I'm an out of shape old man. I can barely run twenty feet, but I have thirty-eight kills to my name, and best of all, I am still alive. How is that so?" His hand rose, and a single finger tapped the side of his head. "Training and study. The same training I have given you. You have been taught to sense even the slightest movement in a room full of distractions. To think of preservation of your life first. These are just natural instincts in you now, that your body and mind will execute in a perfect concert without you even being aware they are doing it. That is the point of everything we have done, and that is what makes you more equipped than anyone else to take on such a lethal opponent. I have one last skill to give you." My grandfather walked over to the sink and grabbed a small glass and then filled it with a few drops of water. Next, he yanked open a drawer, pulling out a clear plastic sandwich bag. His other hand reached above to the cabinet positioned over the stove and retrieved the salt. I had a feeling I knew where this was going, and I was right. He poured a little of the salt in the bag and sealed it with the zipper. "Now, I need to show you how to deploy these implements in coordination with all I have taught you." With that, he reached over and swung open the basement door, and I knew what that meant.

12

I sat in English tapping my fingers on the top of my desk, hoping beyond hope that there was a test today in one of Adrian's classes. I didn't mean to fall asleep before texting him back last night. After a training session that went well into the early morning hours, compounding on to my existing exhaustion, I didn't stand a chance. I laid down on my bed holding my phone, planning to respond to his text from earlier, but as soon as my body hit the softness of my mattress, that was all she wrote. I didn't even write a diary entry. The first night I had missed since my grandfather gave it to me. When I woke up, with drool running down my cheek, I found there were thirty-two messages from Adrian waiting on me. They were asking if I was all right, then asking if he had done something wrong, and why I was ignoring him, but those weren't the ones that burned at me most when I finally woke up. It was the one that asked, are *we* okay?

We? I didn't know we were *a we* yet. Were we Radrian, or maybe Adriven? I could use my real name, Adria, that had a better ring than the others. But seriously, was there *a we*?

I sent him a message as soon as I woke up and then stared at the phone's screen for the next hour. A reply never arrived. The first notification on my phone was the low battery alarm. I had the volume up to its maximum while I took my shower, just in case, but there was nothing. It went off while I walked down to my car, and I almost dropped my books trying to get to it. It wasn't Adrian. It was Jamie asking me how my night was. I didn't see a need to answer, since I was going to see her in a few minutes, anyway.

The temptation to send him another message, maybe some great apology for not responding last night, burned in my fingers, but I held off. I didn't want to seem too eager or make that too desperate. Of course, one might believe he had already beaten me to that. He did send thirty-two messages while I slept. I felt a small smile try to form at that thought.

When the bell rang, I put my phone in my pocket and then switched to staring at the door. The first day I saw him, he and Elijah had walked in late, and Mr. Fletcher's reaction told me that wasn't an abnormal occurrence. Five minutes passed, then ten, and then fifteen. By the time we were halfway through the class, the realization he wasn't coming had settled in. Even with how damp that wet blanket was, it didn't snuff out all hope. There was still lunch. He could still surprise me, just like yesterday.

When lunch finally arrived, I rushed to the cafeteria like I was starving, even though no one in the world was hungry enough to hurry for school cafeteria food. He wasn't there. Though few were. I had beaten most everyone to the line. I grabbed something edible; a prepackaged sandwich and an apple before heading to our usual table. Grabbing a seat against the wall gave me the perfect vantage point across our table, and across the cafeteria, where I saw him sitting the first day. Even as students filed in, I didn't change my focus. Adrian was a creature of habit. He had a dedicated seat in each of his classes. Why wouldn't he have a dedicated table? Hell, no one else sat there.

After drama class, I gave up on the thought of seeing him today, which wore away at the hesitation I felt about texting him again. My hand even moved toward my pocket more than a few times. My desire to not appear desperate stopped me, but even that was waning. The only defense I had left was turning my attention to the classes themselves. Something I should have done earlier. I couldn't tell you anything we discussed in those classes, or even who ran lines in drama.

The bell rang after the last class, signifying both the end of the school day and my willpower. My hand jolted into my pocket and pulled out my phone; my fingers were unlocking the screen before it cleared the denim. They even typed and sent the message before I thought about it. It was a simple two-word message, and after fighting all day to avoid sending him one and seeming desperate, I turned around and did that with a simple, *"I'm sorry."*

    I threw my head back as I walked to my locker. I even threw a few books into my locker out of frustration, and then forced my phone down, deep into my pocket. The deeper, the better. I had to resist compounding things with another message, and I wasn't sure I wanted to hear it if he responded.

    "What's wrong?" Jamie asked from the other side of the locker door.

    I had to think fast. Yes, I could tell her and seem like any other obsessed teenage girl, but I didn't want to be one of those. Just like I didn't want to appear desperate. I had failed at one. I wasn't about to fail again. "Too much damn homework."

    "I hear you, but we have a week for the English paper."

    "True," I agreed, slamming my locker door closed and not remembering anything about the assignment of an English paper. Just like each day, Jamie followed me out to the parking lot, and just like the last few days, people parted, clearing a path as I walked through the hallway and out the door. My skin no longer crawled at the feeling of their stares.

    "So, what are you doing tonight? Want to come over and hang out, or can I come hang out with you? Maybe listen to some music or watch a movie."

    "I can't," I said with a quick shake of the head. "Too much homework." It wasn't a lie. My grandfather had lesson two in what I called Vampire 101 planned for me once I got home.

"Not even for a few minutes?" Jamie practically begged, and I felt a little guilty about my decline. "I need your help to pick out a dress for homecoming. It's this Friday. I bought two, and don't know which one to wear."

"It's this Friday? How about tomorrow or Thursday?" I offered, not wanting to seem like a rotten friend.

"Tomorrow. Thursday would be too late to go get something else if you hate them both."

"Okay, that works. Tomorrow." That gave me enough time to clear things with my grandfather. I didn't see why putting what I assumed would be lesson three off a day would be the end of the world.

"You can show me what you are wearing, too." Jamie suggested.

"Well," I stuttered, looking around and realizing I had missed the hundreds of posters plastered all over the school. One even hung on the door I ran into on my first day. It was a bright yellow poster with green letters, almost day glow, and impossible to miss as I pushed the door open. Where had my head been? Oh yeah, there.

"You haven't bought a dress yet?"

"I," I stuttered again because of the embarrassment of what I was about to admit. "I didn't know about homecoming."

"Raven? Come on? Adrian hasn't asked?"

"No."

Her jaw dropped, and I sensed a series of uncomfortable questions coming, but the refuge of my car was only a few feet away. All I had to do was use homework as an excuse to hurry home, and I could escape this, but I couldn't help but admit she brought up an interesting point. Why hadn't Adrian asked me yet? I thought there was a *we*.

"I'm sure he will. We need to get you a dress."

I stepped off the sidewalk and reached for the safety of my door. All the while, the urge to grab my phone and see if Adrian had responded pulled at me. Perhaps there was a message about homecoming waiting for me. A yank of my hand opened the door just as a silver sports car screeched to a stop behind mine.

"Get in. I want to show you something," Adrian said through the passenger window. He threw the passenger door open, and I shut mine, and all but sprinted to his door.

As I sat down and pulled the door close, I heard Jamie asked, "What about homework?" I owed her an apology later, but that would be later, and all that mattered to me at the moment was the here and now.

"Sorry, I stopped replying last night. I fell asleep."

"I figured," Adrian said, smiling and sitting there wearing jeans and another black hoodie with the hood pulled up. I see I was wearing off on him. "Buckle up." He didn't give me a lot of time after the warning before he slammed on the accelerator, slinging back in the seat as we left with a chirp of his tires.

"Where are we going?"

"Just enjoy the ride." Adrian whipped us around a corner at high speed just as the light turned from yellow to red. I sat back in the smooth leather seat and did as he suggested and sat there enjoying the ride. We were heading east, and as the city melted away, the coastline opened up ahead of us. This was the first time I had seen the Atlantic Ocean. What surprised me was the color. It was quite darker than the Pacific. Maybe that wasn't fair. It was extremely overcast, but despite that, it was beautiful, with sparkles dancing along the top of the water. We drove for half an hour, and I found myself mesmerized by the beauty of the coast the whole time. The rolling of the waves, capped with white foam was hypnotic, and I felt the same feeling of a perfect moment coming over me, just as I had at the charity ball. I turned my head to look at Adrian and glimpsed a building up ahead. This wasn't any building. It was the only building out here for miles, and from here it looked marvelous perched out on a point. He pulled off the road into a long and curved driveway leading out to that house on the point. The wrought-iron gates opened as soon as he pulled up, and then he drove right up the brick driveway to the front door of this very modern beach house that appeared to be made completely of glass.

Adrian walked around and opened my door, extending a hand to help me get out.

"Where are we?"

"My family's beach house. We have had one on this very property for one hundred and fifty years, but as you probably noticed, it doesn't look that old. We had the old house torn down and rebuilt about five years ago."

"It's beautiful," I said, trying to open my eyes as wide as I could to take it all in.

"Oh, just wait."

He grabbed my hand and pulled in through the front door. I was right. Tinted glass covered every exterior wall, providing an amazing view from everywhere. Everywhere you looked was another spectacular view, with the ocean to the east and south, and a river to the north. "The views are–"

"More beautiful now that you are here." Adrian's arms wrapped around me from behind, and I melted back into him. I felt a coolness from his chest, but that didn't bother me. It was comforting. "I wanted to bring you out here."

"To show off?" I asked with a smirk, which he couldn't see from where he stood.

"To share. We are very selective about who we let in our lives, and while my parents have brought a few people out here for meetings or social evenings. I've never had anyone I wanted to share this view with… until now."

My head dipped, hoping to block him from seeing the goofy look on my face, but the windows we stood in front of gave back a perfect reflection.

"This view is beautiful, but it doesn't hold a candle to you."

This time, I dipped my head further, hoping my hair would fall over my face, providing me with a veil of secrecy. It did, but two firm hands spun me around, and my hair whipped back over my shoulders.

"Sunday night, you asked me why? That is a question I can't answer. It's a question no one has been able to answer throughout the ages, and as long as I have lived, and as long as you will live, neither of us will be able to answer it either. All I know is you are special, and you captured me from the first moment I saw you. If I can't even explain how I feel, how could I answer why?"

His words melted me, and with both arms enveloping me, he leaned down once more, and his breath became a tantalizing whisper against my skin. Why something so cool feeling could ignite me, I didn't know, but I didn't care. Instinctively, I leaned towards him, though a part of me feared his retreat, just as he had done before. But when he hesitated, regret for the missed opportunity clouded my mind. I refused to let it linger. Summoning the courage to be myself, my true self, I took the lead and closed the remaining distance between us. At first, his lips resisted, but with gentle, teasing kisses, then he took the hint.

Adrian's kiss wasn't merely a kiss; it was a consuming force that left me breathless. His touch was commanding yet tender, pulling me closer until there was no escape, nor did I desire one. I yearned to be even nearer.

As our lips parted, he effortlessly lifted me into his arms, and I inhaled deeply, eagerly awaiting his next move. And he did not disappoint. His lips found the sensitive curve of my neck, sending shivers down my spine as he traced the line of my collarbone. A fleeting touch of his teeth sent tingles through my body before he returned to claim my lips once more.

Adrian eased back, and I found myself on top of him, tangled together in a dance of desire. Amidst the shifting of our bodies, he skillfully guided us to a luxurious black leather sofa. A smooth maneuver, indeed. But I was not to be outdone. With determination, I pushed him down, breaking free from his embrace, and straddled him, feeling his hands find their place on my waist.

"Is anyone else coming?"

"No," he hissed. "We are all alone."

"Good," I replied, yanking my shirt over my head.

***

I woke up, with the reflection of the moon dancing on the rolling waves, and my cell phone vibrating like mad in my jeans on the floor. I searched for a clock, but didn't see one, and rolled off the sofa to the floor and made my way to my jeans and my phone. It was just after nine. Which meant we had been here for just over five hours. That wasn't the most shocking fact at the moment. The thirty-five text messages and eight missed calls were. Most of the text were from Jamie, but a few of them, and all the calls, were from my grandfather.

Most of the text were of the *"where are you?"* and *"are you okay?"* variety. The voicemails were probably more frantic versions of the same. I didn't need to listen to them to know that. To put him at ease, I typed out a quick, "*I'm fine. Out with friends. Be home soon.*" After I hit the send button, I shoved the phone back into the pocket of my jeans, and then slid them on while gathering the rest of my clothes.

I sat down on the sofa, hoping not to wake Adrian yet, but that was when I realized he wasn't asleep. His hand reached up and stroked my back, and I felt the urge to fall back down on the sofa into his arms, but I couldn't.

"You need to go, don't you?" Adrian asked.

I turned and looked him right in his steely blue eyes and marble-like chest and nodded while biting my lip to keep my mouth from giving another answer. Adrian sat up and wrapped his arms around me. He was going to pull me back down with him, and I was helpless to stop him, not that I wanted to. I wanted it. Then he let go of me and got up, gathering his clothes off the floor. I just sat there and watched.

We left without words. There wasn't much left to say that our bodies hadn't, and we both shared the same stupid grin the whole ride home. My hand held on to his when he wasn't shifting gears, and he followed my directions back to my pretend home, where he pulled up to the curb just before ten o'clock. The door opened, and I stepped out reluctantly. There was a strong desire to not leave this dream world and return to the real world, but all dreams end, and you have to wake up.

"Raven," he called as I started to close the door. My heart jumped at hearing his voice say my name. It was the sweetest sound in the world. "Friday is homecoming. Would you do me the honor?"

Did he really just ask if I would do him the honor? I leaned back into the car and gave him my reply that I felt would be just as adorable as how he asked. "Do you really need to ask?" Then I reached and grabbed him behind the neck and pulled him in and gave him the answer as a kiss.

The walk back to my actual house had a bit of déjà vu to it. I knew my grandfather would be sitting up, waiting to lecture me, and I should have called him or texted him and told him I was out and would be home later. That would have been courteous and may have saved me a bit of what I was about to walk into. With a deep breath of preparation, I unlocked and opened the front door.

The light from the kitchen washed the hallway, and the family room just to my left remained dark. That didn't stop me from making a quick sweep of the room. My grandfather had a habit of sitting in a dark and empty room like that to teach me a lesson. Not finding him told me this wasn't one of those times. I proceeded slowly down the hall, ready for him to jump out at me, but again, he didn't. He waited for me at the kitchen table. There was no cold dinner waiting. He had already put that up. The bag that was there yesterday was not there. The table was actually clean.

"I'm sorry," I said, hoping he would quickly accept my apology and leave it at that.

"It's fine. You have a life to live, and it helps you blend in, but don't get too comfortable. Things are progressing quickly, and I should be done here by next week or the week after, and not a moment too soon." He slid a newspaper across the table to me. It spun around, stopping just in front of me. The headline, "Fifth person missing this year in Westland Park Area."

"Vampires?"

"Yes, Maria." He reached across the table and retrieved the paper. "This is one of the clues you look for to know if there is one in the area. There's at least one here, and I have tracked them down to where they live. In a few days, I will end their reign of terror over this city."

"You mean kill them?" I asked him to clarify. I didn't want any big dramatic statements, just a yes or no.

"Yes, kill them. Then we move on to our next job, and you can leave Raven Cross behind."

My grandfather didn't know it, but he had just dumped the world's largest ice bath over my head. The glow from earlier faded away, leaving me with a shudder as my soul struggled to adapt to the void it had caused.

"Come have a seat. We have a lot to go over, and we can't waste an opportunity." He pointed over to my waiting chair. I felt numb as my feet slid across the floor. With every step, every good memory I had created over the last two weeks, make that just the last three days, dissipated, and I felt stupid. I had let myself ignore the truth of who I was, and my existence here, and I had fallen too hard into that dream world of being normal.

"Since it is late, we will keep this purely academic," I heard my grandfather said as I slowly took my seat.

"So, what is the one detail you are most curious about?"

The weight of reality pulled me low in the seat. I knew my grandfather had asked me a question. His expression told he had, but I couldn't hear it over that loud sucking sound of the black hole in my soul sucking the remaining life right out of me.

"Maria?"

This time, I at least looked up at him, but I still didn't know what he was asking. I thought this was going to be another academic lecture, probably lesson two in Vampire 101. Not a round of twenty questions. "What?"

"The question I asked, what is the one detail you are most curious about?"

Well, that was anything but a direct question. There were so many ways this could go. I took a second and tried to predict where he was going with this, instead of asking what I really wanted to know. Maybe he wanted to have some kind of existential topic, versus anything practical. In that category, there was only one question. "Why?"

My grandfather jerked back in his chair, startled. "No, not that. What I thought you would ask was, once you arrive in a town, how do you find your target?" His finger pointed to the headline on the paper. "That is what I wanted to cover tonight. That is the next step."

"Oh," I commented, sounding uninterested as I leaned against the table. My lack of enthusiasm didn't dampen my grandfather's spirit as he launched into tonight's lecture.

"When we are sent to a new town, all we know is there is a coven of vampires that are active in the area. It's up to me to find them. That is my first step. The key to finding them is understanding how they live. They don't have a sign over their head. Or go around flaunting things. Instead, they are private creatures. They live in the shadows, not wanting to attract attention to their existence and behavior. So, searching for them directly will never work. You need to track behaviors. Use news reports of mysterious attacks. Listen to local myths and rumors, no matter how outrageous. Combine all that data in your diary. Once you have enough, you will notice a pattern, and can localize it down to a few areas of town. Vampires like to operate in familiar areas… Raven!"

My body jerked upright in the seat. I didn't remember when in my grandfather's lecture it had happened, but I had dozed off.

"Are you listening?" my grandfather asked.

I nodded, feeling my eyes already growing heavy, and again shifted in my seat, hoping to rouse myself awake.

"This is important. You need to pay attention."

He looked into my eyes as they continued to grow heavy again. There was nothing I could do. It may have been better if my training was of more of the physical type tonight, movement would keep me awake. Here I was, comfortably sitting here, listening to him, and the longer he talked, the further I sank toward sleep. I knew he could see my fight to keep my eyes open. How could he miss it?

"Like I was saying. Vampires stick to areas they know. This means the news stories of the attacks, the rumors, myths, legends, all of those pieces of details will be localized to their area, or areas. Use a map. Stick pins. Draw circles. The pattern will pop. Then go hang out in those areas. Watch and listen. See who frequents those areas, but in a way that is hard to notice, and trust your instincts. You'll know when you find them."

My fading from the world of the conscious slowed for just a moment. He had hit on a point I had wondered about, and asked about, many times before. "How will I know?" I asked, hoped for a better explanation, or any explanation. This was a question he had avoided more times than I could remember.

"You just will," he explained, … not!

That was the worst explanation ever. It's kind of like a parent telling you "because I said so" and expecting you to just accept it. Where are the dang facts, the dang details? All the stuff I needed to know in order to learn this. Was he still holding stuff back from me? There was more than just a slight interest now, and I was now wide awake. "But how?" I asked. "How will I know the difference between a vampire walking through their hunting grounds, and just a local to the neighborhood that is always there, but likes his privacy? There are thousands of reasons a person would frequent an area, want to remain private, and not be a vampire. How will I know?"

"I know. It sounds stupid, but you will know. Now, it's not some kind of superpower or anything like that. There's no tingle up the back of your leg." My grandfather let out a little laugh, which I found odd considering the seriousness of the moment. "You're right, there are dozens of reasons someone could frequent an area and try to remain private. Dozens and dozens of reasons, but when you see a vampire do it, you'll know. A normal person doesn't look like a lion walking along the local watering hole for food. That's the difference. It's the look in their eye. It's how they watch their surroundings. A normal person just passes through. A vampire will watch those passing through. They will size them up and pick one out and follow them. That's the person that will show up as a headline in the morning newspaper as missing."

"They only go out to hunt?" I asked, realizing how much my grandfather's description made them sound like an animal.

"Mostly," he said, sitting back from the table. "Even when they aren't, they can't help but to note the prey available that stands around their watering hole. That is what you will notice."

"Okay," I said, still wondering if I would recognize it as easily as he made it seem. In my mind, there was a lot of wiggle room in this description. Maybe someone was just watching people because that's what they like to do. Hell, I do that. Someone might mistake me for a vampire because I am constantly making note of everyone, as my grandfather called him. "Have you ever made a mistake?"

His head nodded up and down as he replied, "Yes, a few times."

"So…" a cold chill ran down my spine as my mind filled in the blanks, "you have killed…"

"Oh no!" my grandfather blurted out, cutting off my question. "Absolutely not. I have followed someone back to their home to realize they weren't what I was looking for. I never attack on the first instinct, and neither should you," he warned with a point of his finger. "Follow them first, and make sure."

"And how do you make sure? Ask them?" I asked, but upon hearing my grandfather's explanation, I regretted my little sarcastic comment.

"I watch them attack their victim, then you know for sure."

Now a real chill ran down my spine and froze me to my core. "You watch them kill?" I asked, struggling to force each word through my throat, while wondering if I could stand there and watch that too?

"Yes, I do, but," he leaned forward, and his voice dripped with concern. Probably a response to my expression. "What you need to realize, there is nothing you nor I could do to save their victim, and know that they killed makes it easier for me to kill. I consider all the lives I will save with my one act."

That didn't help. I mean, I understood his point, but that didn't stop my stomach from turning at the thought of watching someone die. The room spun a little, and I pushed back from the table. "I need to go lay down. I'm very tired." That was the best excuse I could come up with at the moment. I couldn't tell him the truth, that I was about to vomit.

"That's fine. You've had a long day. We can pick up tomorrow," he said as I walked past him and stepped into the hall.

"About that. I'll be a little late again, but probably not as late." I said, standing there, holding onto the door frame for support.

"Oh?"

"Jamie wants to show me her homecoming dress, and I guess I need to get one, too. It's this Friday."

"All right. As long as you aren't too late. I have something else I need to cover with you before we wrap up here. You'll be helping me at our next stop. Mike's orders."

13

October 12th

Dear Diary,

So I will just know? That's the best answer he can give me? Please. I've had all this great training and when it comes down to knowing who a vampire is and who isn't a vampire, he tells me I will just know. Maybe it was time to call Uncle Mike for some advice. Well at least he's talking about it. After years of avoiding the question, he is finally talking about it. Wait, I have an idea. How about a trap using blood for bait? Maybe that is something I try when I am running the show. Now that's a funny thought.

But wait, there is more. I am now officially grateful for a diary… There is no way I could tell this to Jamie, but I have to tell someone… I had a movie moment. I'm talking about one of those, the guy picks you up and carries you off to some magical place before making love to you, just adding another chapter to the fairytale that is becoming mine and Adrian's story, and wow what a story. The place, the time, the him… so perfect. I pinched myself before I sat down to write this to make sure I wasn't dreaming. I didn't pinch myself too hard. I didn't want to wake up if I was… Of course, one day I am going to have to wake up and all this will be just a distant dream… or do I?

Laters

"You ready?" Jamie asked, bouncing and about to explode as she stood next to my locker. Hopefully, she didn't. It would make a horrible mess of my locker.

I don't think that was really a question where I had a choice of answers. This was all Jamie had from the moment she picked me up this morning until this very moment. Wall to wall, homecoming this and her dress that. Of all days for me to need a ride to school. Thanks to my after-school activity yesterday, my car had been locked up all night in the school parking lot. By the time school ended, I felt a little homecoming nauseous, but I was a good friend, and I would not bail on her. I couldn't, really. Now that I was going, I needed her help. Our first stop after school? The mall to pick out my dress, and then to her house so I could help her choose which of the two dresses she bought was the best. Once she realized I was going, she spent the last few periods texting me pictures of dresses she thought I might like. It was a big no on each of them. One was so hideous; it had a huge bow on the hip. I just had to send it to Adrian. His reply? *"We can arrive in different cars."* It didn't hurt my feelings. I would have been the same way.

"Yep. Let me grab my books from my locker and I will meet you outside."

"It's fine. I'll wait, and we can walk together."

Great, there goes my hope for a little peace and quiet. That was the one thing I hadn't had a lot of in the last twenty-four hours. After the trip to the beach house, I felt like my brain had been on overload for at least the last two days. I was feeling something I hadn't ever felt before. Everywhere we had been, I knew our limits, or make that my limits. My existence there was only temporary. I had friends before. I had even felt close to some, but never like this. This was different. My grandfather's words about us being done here soon hit me hard. Now, the idea of leaving all this behind was… well, unacceptable, to use a clinical term. I couldn't leave. To even try to leave would leave the only piece of me that felt alive behind.

I felt a little like Adrian when he tried to explain to me how he felt last night. I couldn't. There were no words. It wasn't that they escaped me at the moment, they just flat didn't exist. There were no logical phrases to explain it. It was just a need. I needed Adrian in my life. Just like I needed oxygen to live, I needed Adrian. To rob me of that would kill me, and because of that, I couldn't leave. Now the question was, what could I do about it? That was the question that robbed my brain of any peace.

"Raven, are you coming?"

"Ah, yep," I stammered, standing there staring at the books in my locker for who knew how long. I didn't even remember opening my locker, let alone putting my books in it. What I needed tonight was just a guess. My brain had shorted out. Not that it mattered. Grades were the least of my concerns. Especially if we were leaving here in a week. Oh, I needed to scratch that thought from my mind. "What do we need?"

Jamie pulled back my locker's door, and reached in, grabbing my history and math books, and then placed them in my arms. "These, I'll write down the assignments for you once we get to my place."

"Thanks." I slammed the locker door shut, and we headed out to the parking lot.

"So what color are you thinking of for your dress?"

And here we go again. We hadn't made it two feet until she started again, and I resisted the urge to sigh. We made it to our cars before I gave in and answered. It wasn't an actual answer. It was just, "not sure yet." I wasn't. I just knew what colors I didn't want. With it being so last minute, I just hoped there were a few to select from.

"Hand me your phone?"

I blindly handed it over to Jamie and watched as she typed something in.

"This will get you to my place. Think you can follow it?" She handed it back, showing the map from school back to her home.

"I think I can do that." It was only two rights, one left, and another two rights away.

"Good…" Jamie started to answer, but the screeching of the tires of a familiar silver European sedan car coming to a stop behind my car cut her off.

Just like yesterday, the passenger door flew open, and Adrian said, "Get in."

My body stepped forward before my brain cut in. I couldn't. No matter how badly I wanted to, and I wanted to. I wanted to more than anything.

"I can't, not tonight," I said, in complete disbelief that I uttered the words. My hand reached back for my car's door and pulled myself back the few steps my offending body had taken.

The driver's door opened, and Adrian rushed around the car to my side. "What do you mean, you can't?" There was an edge to his tone.

"I can't," I replied, looking at his chest. His eyes were off limits to me. "I need to go get a dress… for homecoming. I have nothing to wear."

"I can have a dress picked out for you." Adrian's hand grabbed my shoulder.

"Well, maybe I want to pick one out on my own?" My eyes slid up for just a second and met his. "Plus, I need to help Jamie.

She has two dresses and wants my help to decide which is the best one for her to wear."

Adrian didn't even look over at Jamie, who was standing with her car door open in the spot next to mine. "Then how about after?"

"I can't," I muttered, hating having to tell him no twice, so close together. "I promised my grandfather something."

There was not a third offer from Adrian. Instead, he stood there. His face writhed, then he marched back to his car.

I looked at him through the passenger window, meeting his eyes for only the second time. I didn't like what I saw. There was hurt. "I'll call you later."

There was no response before he started up his car and sped off like a bat out of hell.

"What was that all about?"

I didn't want to say it, but I was pretty sure I didn't need a dress to homecoming now. "Nothing, let's go." I opened my driver's side door and collapsed down into the seat, slamming the door behind me. It rattled along with my nerves, and I sat there, trying to pull myself together while I waited for Jamie to leave first. I needed to follow her. In my current state, that little voice coming through the phone telling me where to turn was just a voice in the distance behind all the noise in my head.

I somehow managed to follow Jamie without incident and waited outside alone, leaning against her truck while she went inside to put her books down. I was in no shape to do a big meet and greet with her parents. Maybe when we got back from the mall, but I didn't see that as being likely either. My cell phone was a constant fixture in my hand. I had already sent several messages to Adrian. Who cared about looking desperate? I sure the hell didn't anymore. The first message was an apology. The second was trying to explain that

I had plans yesterday with both Jamie and my grandfather, and I blew both off to go with him. I thought that would make it seem like I picked him above all others. Which I had. It just didn't seem that way now. The third message was a simple question, *"understand?"* I sure hoped he did. Though his lack of response had me worried. I even called him. What my grandfather called old-fashioned communication. It rang twice before going to voice mail. No automatic voicemail picking up like he was on the phone. No ringing a bunch and then go to voicemail when he didn't answer. Someone swiped, deferring me to voicemail, and that action broke me enough to decide not to try calling again. The lack of responses to my text didn't sting as bad as knowing he sent me to voicemail.

When Jamie was finally done, we piled into her truck and headed out. Luckily for me, she did all the talking while I checked my phone half a million times. It would appear I underestimated Jamie. Not only did she have two dresses to choose from, but she also had two dates. Brandon Hall from drama was one of them. He was kind of unmemorable. Probably more like how I should be. There, but not memorable. I had a feeling I was making way too many memories for anyone to forget me, but did I really want them to? I had been so brainwashed into one way of thinking; I had to keep reminding myself that I was about to flip the script.

Jamie told me about both of her dates, or options of dates, as I liked to think about it. Neither were familiar to me, even though as she told me I had sat in class with one of them for the last 2 weeks. After two more attempts to describe Brand, sandy blonde hair, glasses, and dimples, I still wasn't sure I remembered him. The other, a football player, Scott Straus. Now he just has a name that makes you think jock. She said we weren't in any classes together and giggled when she talked about him. I think she really liked him. When we parked at the mall, she whipped out her phone and showed me a picture of him. Not the All-American hunk with no-neck I was imagining. He was our punter, and maybe 120 pounds soaking wet, even in all his pads and helmet. I said nothing, though my mind was already rolling jokes around. I wonder who they let punt when the wind blows. Jamie hadn't mentioned it yet, but why did I have a feeling the topic of which one to choose would come up later.

We went in and straight to the one and only formal dress shop in the mall. Jamie said there were a few stores down on the river walk, but you had to have Starling money to shop there. Blaire's Bridal was more reasonable. Seemed we weren't the only ones that knew that secret. The store had a large crowd. I think every high school girl in Savannah was coming in and out of their doors. Signs welcoming each of us were on the glass front. Our homecoming was this Friday, but Windsor Forrest and Alfred E. Beach were both next week.

"Let's see if we can find you something presentable in this mess." Jamie shoved through the first rack of formal dresses with huge puffs on the shoulders. "Any ideas on color and style?"

I squished my face and shook my head. "Definitely not those."

Jamie sighed and looked up at the ceiling. "Well, that's a start." She looked me up and down and then cocked her head to the side. "You're a traditional black, white, and maybe blue type of girl, I think, and a size three?" she guessed, but didn't wait for an answer. "You check that side. I am going to do a search over here." So, the epic search began.

It was as close to hand-to-hand combat that I had been in outside of my grandfather's training. Elbows and hands were flying everywhere, each quickly followed by an apology. I avoided each, but that was me. I had been trained to. Most others weren't that lucky. A few girls were going to be sporting bruises on their shoulders above those strapless numbers they were buying. I wondered if they needed any tips on coverup. That was something I was an expert on.

Three racks in, and nothing had caught my eye. Mostly, the color was the problem. I was not a peach person, and the amount of peach dresses left on the rack hinted that few others were. That was more of a springtime color. Why they had them here… well, maybe I understood. This was also a bridal shop, bridesmaids. They wear the most hideous dresses out there. That would also explain the puffy shoulders and all the peach and sea-foam green options. When I finally reached a rack with a little more color variety, I hurried to those of the darker shades. The first dress, a long black strapless body-hugging number. I felt my eyes sparkle when I saw it, and there was only one reason my hand yanked it down and threw it over my arm. I wasn't much into tight clothing to flaunt anything, but if I had screwed things up with Adrian, this would pull him back.

With the winning dress in hand, I worked my way over to the other side of the store to find my ride. Jamie met me in the middle, holding up a familiar long black, body hugging, black dress. "Adrian will have a heart attack if you wear this."

I held up the one I was holding, and we both burst out laughing while Jamie put her identical dress back.

We walked out back to her truck, with my dress thrown over my shoulder. My heart skipped a beat when I saw Adrian and Elijah there, leaning against Jamie's truck.

"Hide your dress. He can't see it!"

I didn't know if this was something about tradition or not, but I did as she asked and shoved as much of it under my hoodie as I could. God, it was going to wrinkle.

"Had a feeling you would be here." Adrian said, as he stepped forward and grabbed my face, taking command of my soul, and kissing me right on the lips as if nothing had happened earlier.

"Lucky guess. I told you we were getting me a dress."

"You didn't need to do that." His arm reached into the bed of Jamie's truck and pulled out a white box with a red ribbon on it. "This is what you are going to wear."

Adrian held the box out toward me, but I didn't take it. Instead, I gave him a cockeyed smile. "I already have a dress." I tapped the bump under my hoodie.

"Not like this," Adrian retorted, shoving the box closer.

Jamie hovered over the box with a little bounce in her legs. "You can say that again. Is it real?" she asked Adrian.

"Yep, bought this afternoon."

"Raven," Jamie said, turning to face me. Her hands grabbed mine, causing me to let go of my dress, allowing a portion to slide out from under my hoodie. "That's a Jackie DeLane. Those are custom made designer dresses. She has her own shop downtown. Maybe you should…"

Maybe I should, yep. I probably should, but I felt a rebellious bone in my body scream to push back for my independence. All my life, I had been told what to do. This was a new me. A me that was taking control of my life in every way. "Nah. I have my dress. Picked it out myself." I shoved what slid free back into its hiding place.

Adrian spun around, slapping the truck with a bang. I swear I even saw a small dent that instantly blended in with all the others. Then he spun back around while tearing the top off the box, ripping the red ribbon in half in a blink of an eye. I had to admit, his strength impressed me. "No, you're wearing this, and that's that."

What I saw was hard to argue with. This thing was gorgeous. White beaded. It looked like it was strapless but full length. This was more of a beauty pageant gown than a homecoming dress, but that didn't stop me from imagining what I would look like wearing it. That very image put the one I had under my hoodie to shame. There was no comparison, but I wasn't about to give up that easily.

"Why exactly is that that?" I asked, while doing my best not to look at the dress.

"Because I said so." Adrian stepped forward, holding the box and dress under his arm. "This is what you are going to wear, end of story. You will be the envy of everyone there."

Well, I couldn't disagree with him there on multiple levels, but that didn't mean I enjoyed having my choice taken from me. "Maybe I prefer the one I bought. I can make my own decision."

"Raven, you're crazy," spouted Jamie.

She may have been right, but I held up my hand to block any new rebuttals from her. This was no longer about the dress. This was about earlier when he got upset because I wouldn't come with him. This was about picking out the dress for me without even talking to me. If I even think back to it, this was having dresses already picked out for me for the ball. This is about establishing boundaries of our, dare I say it, relationship.

"I can make my own decision." My eyes glanced down at the dress I was about to turn down. I swallowed down the pound of regret I felt in my throat. "It's a beautiful dress, but I think I will wear the one I just bought."

"No, you are wearing this one," demanded Adrian. His eyes took on a hard edge.

"Why? Why can't I wear the one I want to?"

"Because you're mine." Adrian tried to smile.

"I'm what?" I asked, feeling a little anger boil up inside. "Am I some kind of possession of yours?" What had just started to boil didn't take long to boil over completely and make a mess. "I'm no one's property. You need to get it through your head." I took a step forward and placed a finger firmly on Adrian's chest. "Just because we had sex doesn't mean you own me."

Adrian stared right at me. I could see the rage bubbling behind his blue eyes. His jaw twitched, and I readied myself for whatever he had to say, but he said nothing. He stayed stone quiet as he stormed away back to his car, just a few spots away, taking the dress with him.

"If you think this has anything to do with having sex with him, then you don't really know my brother," Elijah commented as he strolled away from the truck. "He owns you, but it has nothing to do with that."

I stood there watching them pull away, biting my lip and wondering what I had done.

"You and Adrian had sex?" Jamie asked.

14

October 13th

Dear Diary,

    Ugh, I shouldn't have ever let that cat out of the bag. Now that's all Jamie wants to talk about. I really should have kept my mouth shut, but let's be honest, when have I ever been good at that? If someone flips my switch, my thoughts come right out… and seriously… what the hell is up with Adrian? He seemed so mature… so different from the others, but in truth, he's just like every other guy. Once you let them between your legs, they think they own you.

    Adrian isn't the first to act this way, but he's the first one I haven't just walked away from. The others I could easily dismiss and walk away from while their tongue was still wagging, but not Adrian. With him, it's different. I wanted… scratch that… I needed him to understand. We had to find a way to coexist, but he also needs to grasp his place in this dynamic. And maybe, just maybe, I need to soften my edges a bit too.

    I think it's the years of constantly moving around and being told who I am and what I can or can't do that have made me so touchy on this subject. Adrian just stepped on that nerve, and before I knew it, I exploded.

    He did text me just before I went to bed. It came in among the flood from Jamie that was still going on and on about what I let slip. I ignored those and read his. It was a simple apology. Well, it was a little more than an apology. If he had left it as just an apology,

I might have replied. The added comment, "I still think you should wear the dress," kept me from replying.

On a lighter note, I did help Jamie pick out her dress today. She went for this bright pink number that I wouldn't be caught dead in. But hey, to each their own. Her choice between her two homecoming date options was entirely up to her.

In the world of vampires, which is what this diary is supposed to be about, anyway. 0 tracks, and 0 kills. That's my awesome stat line. I have no maps to draw or notes to make. My grandfather is keeping this chase all to himself. The next one, he will share, or so he said again tonight. I hated to tell him there won't be a next time.

There was a minor training session tonight. It was another academic only period, and it didn't last that long. I got the feeling this was an impromptu one he hadn't planned before. He wanted to address the question I had asked last night about why we do this, and I use the word "address" loosely here. There wasn't much of an answer. Well, that's not really fair. The why it is done made sense. Vampires are evil. Hello, everyone knows that. They are cursed creatures and kill ruthlessly to feed. That's a no brainer. Someone has to stop them. The why "us" answered was a little less clear. It was a simple, because someone has to. The police can't. They would be killed if they tried. They lacked our training. I got that, but why aren't they trained like we are? They would be the perfect people to handle this, instead of some dark secret random society that doesn't even have a name. This just all sounded sketchy.

Later

Walking into school, I felt like I was wearing a scarlet letter on my forehead. Jamie knew my little secret. The question I wondered about was whether it was still a secret. I hadn't screamed it to the world, but in the days of social media, a whisper can be louder than a shout. Under normal circumstances, I could tell if I was the topic of some hot gossip, but thanks to all the Adrian-related attention I had received lately, those stares and glances my way were a constant companion.

I got to my locker without incident. Jamie soon joined me, as she had every morning since we met. The stupid grin on her face made me worried, and I motioned for her to zip it ahead of any flood that might come from her mouth. A silly giggle escaped, but she nodded her understanding. Thank God. The only place worse to start a rumor than social media, a high school hallway. I turned back to my locker to finish exchanging my books with what I needed for the first few classes. The location of my classes didn't allow trips between my first three classes. A cool breath brushed the back of my neck. Now it was my turn to have a stupid grin on my face. I wasn't expecting Adrian to be here, but he has surprised me before. I put my books back in the locker and spun around, ready to throw my arms around him.

A hand grabbed my shoulder and turned me around and shoved me back into my locker with a bang. The sound cleared every student around us. I was face to face with Miranda Starling. She was mere inches from my face. I had never seen this woman smile, and this morning was no exception. Whether or not the muscles in her face could form a smile, I seriously doubted. If she attempted, her perfect porcelain skin might crack. While I basked in Adrian's steely blue eyes, hers looked at me with murderous intent.

"I told you to stay away from my brother."

"You did, but I think we can both make our own decisions," I said, following a hard swallow. She didn't appear to like my answer, and leaned in closer, leaving not much more than a hair's width between us. Her rose scented perfume combined with the mint of the toothpaste she used this morning produced an over-powering aroma that threatened to bring tears to my eyes. Her hand pressed my shoulder harder against the locker.

"Oww!"

The more I squirmed to get free, the harder she pressed, and the more she seemed to enjoy it.

"Let me go."

We were now attracting a crowd. They circled around us, but not a single person attempted to step in and help. Instead, they kept their distance, almost as if they were afraid of Miranda, which I could now understand.

"Not until you promise to stay away from my family." She straightened her arm, pushing me harder into my metal locker. The metal latch in the locker frame dug into my shoulder. I squirmed for relief, and she smiled.

"What, am I not good enough?" I groaned, moving enough for some temporary relief. I still wasn't sure what I had done to this girl. Adrian said she was protective, but this is way beyond that. This was prejudice. That was what it had to be. She didn't know me. She didn't know anything about me, except what I looked like, and that I didn't fit into her perfect world. "Am I from the wrong side of the tracks? I don't fit in your little perfect world?" I baited her. Why? It was stupid. She already wanted to hurt me, and I just gave her more of a reason to do it. Another quick shove made me pay for it.

She leaned in, her cool breath tickled my ear, and whispered, "You have no idea who we are. If you think this hurts, just wait until you get to know the real Adrian."

"Miranda! Let her go!" Elijah's hand thrust forward and grabbed his sister, yanking her back. She stumbled through the crowd and then slammed into the lockers on the other wall. "Stop it!"

She leered at her brother for the longest two seconds of my life, then turned and walked away, but not without slamming into his shoulder. "Be careful which side you pick, baby brother. You might not like the outcome." As she walked, the hallway cleared a path for her. Those that dared to even look at her did so with fear in their eyes. I completely understood. I watched and expected to see her, her blonde hair in a tight bun, and that black shirt and those black leather pants disappear into some door of fire leading right to the underworld where she belonged. She was a devil spawn.

"You all right?" Elijah asked while I rubbed my shoulder.

"Yea, I think so." I wasn't, but I wasn't about to admit that to anyone standing around me at the moment.

"It's a good thing I was here. If my brother had been here instead of me, he would have thrown Miranda through the wall."

"Bad blood in the family?" I asked and rushed to grab the last of my books. My shoulder barked at me with every move. The first bell rang in the hallway. We had exactly five minutes to get to class.

"Let's just say Adrian and Miranda rarely see eye to eye and have had a few big blow-ups before. Me, well, I'm the peacekeeper of the family."

"I can see that," I replied, slamming my locker door shut. "I just wish I knew what she has against me. Is she afraid that a commoner might invade her precious family?"

"Nah. Miranda may be petty, but she isn't that petty. Remember what we told you about her? She is very protective."

"What is she protecting?" Jamie asked, walking behind us. I was in my own little world processing what had just happened and had forgotten all about her. "It sure seems like she doesn't want Raven in Adrian's life. It comes off as if you guys are too good for the rest of us."

Elijah nodded, and I felt my heart sink as I realized I was in one of those old fairy tales about a prince and a common girl. I was that common girl here. Those had happy-ever-after endings. It was too bad that real life rarely had those. "It may come off as that, but nothing could be further from the truth. Let's just say she's worried about monsters." Elijah cracked an odd smile.

"Monster?" Jamie asked, rushing up to join us.

"I'm no monster." Of course, considering what I had been trained to do might make people think the opposite.

"Of course not. It's just a bad joke. Ignore my sister and let my brother and I handle it."

Gladly, I just hoped it was possible to ignore her. It seemed I was under her skin and she kept coming after me. It wasn't like I was looking for her. I guess every family has some kind of drama, and a few in-laws that don't get along. I could live with that. "Speaking of where is your brother?"

"Off buying homecoming tickets."

"Is that why you guys are here today?"

"That's one reason. It's also our scene reading day in drama." He leaned over and bumped my arm with his, sending a shot of pain through my shoulder. "Isn't it also your day too?"

If my arms weren't full of books, I would have slapped my forehead. I had completely forgotten, and it wasn't like I didn't have any reminders. I had a sticky on my mirror at home, and Jamie and I even ran through it twice last night, where I fumbled a few words and planned to review the scene again when I got home, but I never did. "Yep, it is."

"It's basically the final for this grading period, so it's not something we could skip. Adrian's been a little obsessive about it for the last two weeks, wanting to run our lines multiple times a day, but I don't guess I need to tell you about that side of him."

"No, you don't," I muttered.

"It's, okay. You can admit it. He is my brother. I think I know him better than most. I've known him longer, that's for sure. Just cut him some slack. Surprisingly, he isn't as smooth when it comes to others, but there is a great guy underneath." Elijah leaned over. "I can't say the same for my sister. She is nothing but prickly poison."

"The dress thing was a bit over the top."

"Eh, what can I say? If you're going to do something, don't do it halfway." He shrugged.

Elijah turned and grinned while we walked. I looked back at him, absent the grin. This may be a joke to him, but it still bothered me. He stopped walking, and I stopped next to him. We were a pebble in the roaring current of students rushing to their classes. They passed around us, brushing a little as they did. Jamie was our breakwater, but she didn't need to be. This was, I felt, about to be a private conversation.

"Jamie, why don't you go on? I'll catch up with you later," I directed, while looking at Elijah. He resembled his brother, but at the same time, he didn't. His features were softer. It would seem the same could be said about his personality. Jamie didn't move, and again I directed, but this time looking at her. "Go on." She took the more direct hint and joined the masses passing us.

When we were finally alone, with several hundred of our fellow students walking around us, Elijah said, "Look, my brother really cares for you. More than anyone else I have ever seen. He, I think, doesn't quite know how to handle it. He came off a bit intense last night. Just forget about it and move on."

"More than anyone?" I laughed. "What about all the starlets and princesses?"

Now it was Elijah's turn to laugh. "So, you've done a few searches and found all his eye candy. That's all it is. Eye candy. His and theirs. Beautiful people like to be seen with other beautiful people, but rarely do they care for them. He cares about you."

"I just…" I started and then stopped. Was I making a big deal out of something that really wasn't? Maybe I was. I didn't know. Come to think of it. I cared for him more than anyone else I can remember, too. Maybe we were both just being stupid and needed to figure this out together. "Ugh…," I continued, looking around, feeling sillier by the moment. "Maybe I am overreacting. The dress at the ball, demanding that I come with him, blowing up at me when I had other plans, and then demanding that I wear the dress he bought for homecoming. I don't like that. I am my own person. And can make my own decisions." I said, realizing the irony that just yesterday I was putting our names together as if we were one.

"He knows that. This is just all new to him. For as long as I have known him, he has kept himself locked away and not trusting himself to really become close to anyone. Now that he is out, maybe he needs a leash to help break him. This is his first time not just being arm candy." There was that grin again. "I hope you will use a light but firm touch on that leash."

Now, I even had to crack a bit of a smile at that. "I can't promise anything," I said with a quick shake to throw my hair over my shoulder, and to grab a quick look around to make sure no one was paying attention. This topic was embarrassing to me, but it could destroy his debonaire image. The rush of students still parted around us, but no one lingered long enough to take notice.

"He's going to screw up from time to time. Trust me on that. He is my brother, after all. I know him best. Hell, he probably already has."

We joined the rumbling horde and headed to English class. We were the last few to enter, and I mean the last few. Adrian was already in his new seat, next to the one I stole from him on my first day, with a stupid grin on his face.

That stupid grin stayed there throughout English, throughout lunch, and showed itself each time he glanced in my direction while running his lines with Elijah during drama. He and Elijah were outstanding in their scene from *Othello*. Adrian played Rodrigo and Elijah played Iago. They more than ran lines. They acted it out, walking around the classroom as if it were their stage, and none of us were there. I hated it when it ended, as did many.

Then it was our turn. I let Jamie pick the scene. I thought she would pick something more contemporary. Not! She went to the classics, and not even a popular classic: *Midsummer Night's Dream*.

She was Helena, and I was Hermia. It was bad enough it was a play I wasn't familiar with, but the awkward phrasing kept the lines from just rolling off the tongue. Having to go after Elijah and Adrian just highlighted that fact even more. They were an elegant ballet. We were a one-legged man in a three-legged race. Thanks to a last-minute cramming session at lunch, I didn't forget a single line. I didn't really perform them either, but we survived and got a B for our efforts.

The rest of the day settled into something that felt somewhat normal. I didn't have any classes with Adrian in the afternoon, but we passed each other in the hallway between each class. That wasn't a coincidence. His classes were in the other halls, so I knew he came out of his way just to say hello as he passed by.

When the last bell for the day rang, I went to my locker as normal and expected to find him there waiting for me. He wasn't. Jamie was, and her constant recap of the pros and cons about each of her two choices for homecoming dates didn't grate on my nerves as much as it had last night. Come to think of it, nothing did, not even the mountain of homework we had for next week on top of the English paper I already had to do. I felt, well, happy, and even felt a little bounce in my steps. Then I realized it. Good God, I was becoming Jamie.

We walked out and into the overcast afternoon, still going over her list. I contributed to it with a few pros of my own for both of her choices, even though I didn't know either of them that well. I just couldn't help myself. We were so involved in talking through her list I didn't notice the crowd we walked into around where I parked. Everyone parted as soon as I walked up. Gone was my beat-up Beetle. In its place, a brand-new white Mercedes, with a special hood ornament. Adrian, leaning against the front fender, holding out a set of keys.

"What… the…" I started to ask.

"I said we would have to fix it," he said, handing me the keys and leaning in to kiss me. I was so stunned I didn't kiss him back.

"Don't worry. Your Beetle is at our house for now, just in case you don't like this, but what's not to like?" Adrian extended his arm out toward the car and then proceeded to walk the full length of it.

"Why did you do this?" I asked. "I didn't ask for a car. I liked my car." There it was again, that something boiling inside. I tried to hold the lid on it, but anyone who put a lid on a boiling pot knew that was a mistake. The only way to head off the explosion was to remove the heat, so I turned away and looked right into everyone standing around us, taking in the scene. Out of the frying pan and into the fire, in a manner of speaking. I hated attention, and I turned back around. There was no stopping it. Here it came. "Stop trying to control me."

There was a murmur in the crowd behind us, but I had mostly blocked that out as I went from staring at the car to staring at Adrian. He had done it yet again. Over his shoulder, I saw Elijah stepping in. "Drive it for a day. See what you think. If you don't like it, we can bring your VW back."

"We can?" Adrian asked, spinning around and shooting a look at his brother.

"Yes, we can," Elijah said, putting his arm around his brother. Adrian shrugged it off and marched for me. This had a feeling of a repeat of yesterday, and I felt I was now in some kind of nightmare after-school special about toxic relationships.

Adrian grabbed my one hand that wasn't holding books. With his steel-blue eyes, he peered inside my soul, and spoke to me, not with words, but with shared emotions, that I felt. I felt every ouch of what he felt traversing through my eyes, and down my body, while a sense of comfort traveled through my hand and up my arm. "You have brought me such happiness. I wanted to do this for you, and maybe it is all screwed up. This is how our family shows… appreciation." He paused and gulped as he wrapped his arms around me. "That didn't sound stupid until I said it." He grinned sheepishly. "Drive it today, and we can swap it tomorrow after homecoming, okay? We'll have your old car washed." His fingers intertwined with mine and forced my hand open. Then he slid the key into my palm. "Just drive it for the day," he whispered.

That didn't make it any better, but I didn't see what other choice I had. "All right. Just for the day, and then tomorrow night after homecoming, you take me back to your place, and I can pick my car up."

"Deal." He pulled me in tightly against his chest, and then leaned down and kissed me. A wave of bliss overcame me, and for just a moment I had forgotten what we had just agreed to, why we had agreed to it, and the large crowd around us. As far as I was concerned, we were as alone as any two people could be. My hands roamed up and caressed his cheeks, then I brushed away the hood of the hoodie he wore, wanting to run my fingers through his hair. Adrian broke our embrace. A single hand bolted up, putting his hood back in place, and then he backed away. I wrapped my fingers around the keys as he backed away. His fingers hanging on to my arms, tracing down them and across my hand. I didn't want to let go and let the real-world in. "Want to go for a ride in my new car?" My hand grasping at his as it slipped from my grasp.

"I have something I need to do tonight, but I will text you later." Adrian stepped back away, and as I did my best to pout, he rushed back in and gave me another kiss. Again, I tried to hang on, but he slipped from my grasp. I watched, wanting, as he walked away, glancing back at me a few times. The clouds opened above us, bathing everything in a glorious light as warm as my heart felt. Adrian pulled the hood of his hoodie up over his head, and then ducked into the driver's side of his car and pulled off.

As he pulled off, the rest of the world returned, as did Jamie's squealing from the other side of the white Mercedes. Someone wanted to go for a ride, and how could I say no? With a click of the key fob, the driver's door opened, and that heavenly new car smell rushed out to greet me. I slid down on the ecstasy that was smooth, jet-black leather. I turned to open the passenger door but stopped when I saw a familiar white box in the seat, with a torn red ribbon. A half smile crept across my face as I picked it up and put it in the back seat.

15

October 14th

Dear Diary

It is now just after 4 in the morning, and I still haven't slept. Get this, I even went down to the basement after my grandfather went to sleep to do a little physical training with Henry and Bob all on my own, just to tire myself out. It didn't work. One might think it was the gift of a new car that was bothering me. Hell, I hadn't even given that a thought. There was something more pressing. My training or make that what I learned in my training last night. There was no physical training, nothing academic. We reviewed cases, including his current one. Page by page of his diary, and his process of acquiring all the information. My grandfather was thorough in every sense of the word. He knew everything, and as he told me this, he said he was done, and tomorrow was going to be "the" night. The night he made his move on the coven, which he felt was just a coven of two. If everything went well, we could be on our way in a week. If things went badly, we would be gone in hours. GONE!

I hadn't had time to figure out my plan. Now I wondered if I had time to figure anything out. Of course, I could be stupid for even writing this. What if he read it? Not that he had the chance. I kept it in my possession at all times. So, let's plan. Just like he plans in his diary.

1) When—whatever I did, I need to be gone by tomorrow night.

2) *Where—I could... I guess there were 2 ways to think about this. There was a short term where, the place I would go for a bit, and then the long term where, the place I would go forever. Well, that sucks. I hadn't considered that. I mean, I knew I needed to go somewhere, but if I do, I won't have Adrian in my life. That is... unless I take him with me. How in the H-E-L-L can I do that? It's not like I can just sometime tomorrow tell him the truth. "Hey, my real name is Maria, and me and my grandfather are part of a secret society of vampire hunters, and I want to escape. I have no money or anything. Do you want to run away with me and leave this awesome life you have behind?" Doing that might answer my where. I would be committed into a padded room.*

3) *How—well this was the simple one. Don't come home after the homecoming dance. That was the simplest way. Use that as my escape. Just drive off into the sunset in my nice new car, and that brings me right back to the where. There was one option. Disappear long enough for my grandfather to move on, and then come back.*

The question... was I forgettable enough for my grandfather to ever stop looking for me? I think I had finally found a way to make myself tired. My mind was exhausted from going in circles.

Later until the morning.

I woke up well after eleven in the morning. The gentle warm light of daybreak I saw on school mornings was long gone. The blinding light of the midday sun assaulted my room through the slats in the plantation shutters. One line of pain had moved with the progressing sun in the sky and lined up just perfectly with my eyes, and there was nothing I could do but wake up. When I noticed the time on my phone's display, I first panicked about missing school, but then I realized today was a planning day, and laid back down, listening to the silence of the house. That created another panic. My grandfather was usually up milling around early in the morning. I didn't hear any signs of him.

Then I remembered what today was, and I knew his routine on what he called "strike day". He would sleep in until early afternoon to prepare his body for a battle that could last all night long. That also reminded me of something else, and I rolled over to where my diary fell right after I passed out a few moments after I finished my entry. It was still open with my half-baked plan, full of holes, still showing.

A night of sleep, or make that half a night of sleep, didn't help clear things up. I still didn't have any answers, or even the start of any answers. There was one option I hadn't even considered when I was writing out my plan, but just driving off and disappearing and never coming back wasn't an option. The whole point was not to lose this life.

There was a momentary debate about going back to sleep myself, and I made a good argument for it, but my phone chimed a few times, and the pull of the awaiting messages settled it. I slung my legs out of the bed enough so I could sit up and reach for my phone. My heart raced, hoping for a sweet good morning, and there was one, just not from who I wanted to see it from.

"Good morning! I'm so excited about tonight."

"What about you?"

How to answer Jamie? I could lie and say I was excited, and that was what I did. *"Absolutely."*

It wasn't a complete lie. I was excited, but I was also full of dread and a host of other emotions that made my stomach queasy. This felt like this was one of those days where my life would change forever. Most people never felt those coming, but once they experienced it, they always recognized the feeling. I did. I had been through more of those moments than I could remember. It didn't hurt that my grandfather gave me a warning when he was about to complete his assignment, which meant we were about to leave and change our lives all over again. This was that feeling on steroids, because I was adding a twist to it.

Since I was already awake, there wasn't a second debate about going back to sleep and stood up face to face with another choice. Man, today was nothing but a day of choices. Both dresses hung on my closet door. The one I bought, and the one Adrian bought me. Which one to choose? The more I looked at them, the more the one he bought called me. I even reached out and rubbed the seams and fabric. It just felt different from the one I bought from the mall bridal store. What a moral dilemma. Showing up in the one he bought would give him the wrong message, but… what a dress.

After a quick good morning text to Adrian, I headed downstairs, trying not to make a sound as I passed my grandfather's room. My phone chimed just as I passed his door. In the silence that was our house, that chime sounded like the bells of Big Ben ringing in the hour. I froze and listened for a few moments for any rustling from the other side of his door. There was nothing. Either it didn't wake him, or he was just ignoring it. After a few tentative steps, not wanting to be done in by any old creaky boards, I continued moving and headed down to the kitchen to get something to eat. A bagel with more peanut butter than should be legally allowed, and a soda. Not exactly the breakfast of champions, but no one had objected before. My theory was it was heavy in protein and caffeine. I would have both strong muscles and be alert at the same time. While I was eating, I checked my phone, expecting a new flood from Jamie, but it wasn't there. It was Adrian.

"*Finally up?*"

"*It's a school holiday.*" I reminded him and put my phone down on the table next to my bagel drowning in the now very soft peanut butter. My own special touch, fifteen seconds in the microwave, made it almost taste like a desert.

Another chime, and while a finger on one hand collected the peanut goodness that didn't make it into my mouth with the last bite, the other picked up my phone, and I read the reply.

"*You missed a wonderful sunrise.*" Then a picture came through. It was a masterpiece of pinks and orange over rolling waves capped with white foam. It looked like a painting. He was at the beach house, and seeing it made me wish I was there too. "*I never miss a sunrise.*"

"*I never see a sunrise... I'm asleep lol. But it looks beautiful.*" I didn't put the phone down, and instead stared at the image, trying to put myself there while I took another bite of my bagel.

His reply came in with a chime, moving the picture up the screen. "*Its beauty doesn't compare to you.*"

Heat ran to my cheeks, and I had to put the bagel down to free a hand to cover my face. My other hand typed out, "*All right, Mr. Shakespeare.*" I wondered how many men have used some variation of that line from *Romeo and Juliet*. Knowing him, though, I would have expected the full line, recited word for word with the dramatic delivery of the best actors in the world.

"*Just telling you the truth. You are, by far, the most beautiful woman I have ever known.*"

A stupid smile crept across my face, and luckily, I was alone. Any attempt to hide one this big would be frivolous. "*You need to get out more.*" I deflected, letting more of my real personality show.

"*Send me a picture. I need something on my phone more beautiful than the sunrise.*"

"*No,*" my reply was quicker than any of my others had been. Then I crammed the last bite of bagel in my mouth, and I put the plate in the sink, leaving my phone on the table. It set off with a chirp and a quick vibration, calling me back to the table in a rush.

"*Please? I'm down on my knees begging.*"

The corners of my stupid smile curved up to meet the evil glint in my eye. "*That's a good position for you. You should get used to it.*" Shame, and shock, forced my hand to put the phone down, turned over face down as if that changed the fact that I actually sent that message.

Ding! *"Maybe I should. So, no picture?"*

He was persistent, and that was absolutely a no. I had just woken up. Hell, I hadn't even looked at myself in the mirror. I was probably nothing more than a rat's nest of hair on top of a face that made a zombie look alive. That didn't deter me from turning on the camera and looking at myself. My hair wasn't that bad. Nothing that a quick run through with my fingers would make gym class presentable. My face was a different story. Puffiness surrounded my eyes. Nothing was going to solve that, but I took a second look and almost hit the button, but I guess either my better judgement or willpower won out. *"It's a no to that request."*

The picture that arrived with the next ding melted away both. Adrian stood there, at his beach house, under the overcast sky with his shirt off. Beads of water dotted his skin as beads of sweat formed on mine. Every hair on my body stood on end. Before I knew it, my phone was at the end of my arm, and I heard the digital click of the shutter sound. It was sent before I saw it. The picture was me, at that moment. No makeup. No brushing out my hair first. Just me as I sat there, and I even thought I saw a spec or two of peanut butter in the corners of my mouth. Strangely, I didn't feel embarrassed. There was no desire to delete the picture from my phone. It was me. The me that slept in a bright green tank shirt and shorts. The me that didn't cake on dark makeup. He saw Maria.

"Now my day is complete, and I can die a happy man."

"Hey now, no dying yet. You still have to take me to homecoming tonight."

"I can't wait. Just 7 hours left. What are you doing with those 7 hours?"

Now that was a good question. A few of the hours had already been spoken for. Jamie was picking me up at three to go get our hair and makeup done. Her mom's treat. I tried to decline. There was too much on my mind. Too much I needed to figure out. Unfortunately, part of my ruse of who I was backfired on me and forced me to agree. She threatened to come drag me out of my house if I didn't say yes. Translation, she would march up the brick steps and on to the front porch of the two-story white colonial at the address two blocks away from my own that I have been picked up or dropped off at for the last ten days. That would have been a disaster. That left three hours, and I doubted my grandfather was going to be up soon for any training, but that wasn't a bad idea. I had homework, and lots of it, and since I was planning on being around here a while—"*Jamie's picking me up at 3 for a hair appointment, and before that, I am trying to make a dent in this weekend's homework.*"

I put the phone up and ran, silently, upstairs to grab my books. In the two hours I had, leaving one to get ready before Jamie picked me up, I could make a dent, a small dent, but still a dent in the pile. I had seen it before. Every school I was at was the same. If there was something big planned at that school or a big holiday coming up, they loaded on the homework.

When I returned to the table, there was a message and a picture waiting for me.

"*Have fun. I did mine last night.*" The picture was of his books on a desk positioned against a glass wall overlooking the dunes at his family's beach house. Neat stacks of paper sat on the desk next to each book. I could even see what looked like typed words. My god, he had already finished his English paper, and it looked like all of his other assignments too. How was that even possible?

"*You finished it all?*"

"*Yep, and you should get started. I'll pick you up at Jamie's at 7 ☐,*"

"*See you at 7.*"

I didn't want to admit to him that seven couldn't come soon enough. I put the phone down and spread out my books, debating which assignment to start first. The English paper would take a while, and there was no way I was going to finish it before I had to leave, but should I start it? I took another quick look at the picture in shock Adrian had already finished his. I found myself drawn to the scene through the glass wall. It was a sight I could get lost in. How he focused on his homework sitting there, I couldn't tell you. I know I wouldn't be able to. There was something peaceful about that view. There was something peaceful about the whole beach house. The location, the setting. It was so remote and out of the way.

"That's it," I whispered to the silence of the kitchen, and slammed my pencil down onto the table. The beach house. It's remote and out of the way. I got the feeling no one lived out there full time. It was almost like it was a party get away for his family. Could he stash me there, in hiding, for a while? At least until any attempts to find me blew over. I didn't see why not. My grandfather wouldn't think of looking there. Hell, he hasn't even asked who I was hanging around so much. Not exactly parent of the year material. He didn't know I was with Adrian, and to just cover the last bit of detail, my cell phone was a burner. He wouldn't have any access to it, or my call history.

So that was the where. At least that was the where in my mind. What I needed to figure out now was how to get Adrian to take me there. I couldn't tell him, or anyone, the truth. In this instance, the truth would not set me free. I believed in my diary I mentioned this truth would put me in a padded room. There had to be another way.

I pulled out a few sheets of paper and grabbed the pencil I had slammed down just moments ago, ready to draft out a few creative options. I sat for whoever knew how long. My phone even chimed the arrival of a few messages, and I let it sit right where it was, and focused on the task at hand. I had heard of writer's block. This was writer's cell block. I felt like any creativity I had was locked up for life, and it would never escape. Not that I didn't have any ideas. I had them, and a few of them even caused my hand to move to the top of the paper to write, but before lead hit paper, the idea had already fallen apart in my mind. Every idea still boiled down to what I couldn't do. I couldn't tell anyone the truth about what was going on. I couldn't tell anyone that my grandfather was harming me, and I needed to hide out for my protection. Both stories would make an awesome movie, but they wouldn't work in real life. Too many side effects that could blow up in my face. They were too… too… creative. I needed something more realistic.

Then it hit me. The most realistic idea of all. I all but leaped up out of my chair. It was too simple to even write it, and it was one I could float tonight to Adrian, and if he said no, there was no harm, no foul. It was perfect, and I looked down at my phone to check the time; it had only taken two hours to come up with. My homework would have to wait. With any luck, I would be sitting at that desk overlooking the dunes, working on it this weekend.

After a quick shower, I got dressed and packed up both dresses, still unsure which one I was wearing. I also packed up my books, a few spare changes of clothes and my essentials. I gave a quick look around the room. My insides turned, and a tear threatened to appear. This was the last time I would see this room. I had only been here ten days. I had said goodbye to other rooms I was in for months and never felt like this. This wasn't anything to do with the room. This was about saying goodbye to my life.

I turned and squeezed through the door and down the hall and stairs. The sounds of movement, and the television came from the kitchen. I had hoped to be gone before he woke, but then again, maybe this was for the best. He was the only family I had left; I needed to say my goodbye, even if he wouldn't understand. I dropped everything in the hallway and walked into the kitchen. He was sitting at the table drinking his coffee and reviewing his diary, just like he did every morning. The only difference was this was the middle of the afternoon.

"Jamie's coming to pick me up in about twenty minutes to get ready for homecoming," I said, fighting a quiver in my voice.

"Have fun tonight. Be a teenager."

I leaned down and hugged him around the neck. "You be careful tonight." Now a tear was more than threatening. It was rolling down my cheek.

"I will. I'm always careful," he said, unaware that I was crying behind him.

I let go and stood up, keeping my back to him as I walked out of the kitchen, pausing just outside the door to wipe my tears away. For just a moment, the question whether Adrian was worth all this slipped into my mind. The answer my brain gave was two parts. Yes, Adrian was, but even if he wasn't, someone someday would be, and I couldn't have that life living this life. With that, I picked up my bags, and headed out the door, and walked the two blocks to my pseudo address, where coincidentally I parked my new white Mercedes out on the street to sell the illusion. I put the bags I wouldn't need tonight in its trunk and stood there waiting for Jamie with both dresses thrown over my arm. Jamie was there right at three, and off we went for several hours of beauty treatment.

16

Two hours of hair shampoo, drying, curling, spraying and another hour of facial powder, blending, lipstick, and eyeliner later and I didn't even recognize myself in the mirror. Why had I let Jamie talk me into this? I didn't know. Oh yeah, I backed myself into a corner and didn't have a choice. I just hoped Adrian recognized me when he saw me in a few minutes. I stood in Jamie's bedroom, in just a towel, still undecided on which of the two dresses to pick. Jamie was still undecided about what we had talked about the entire time, which of her two dates to finally say yes to. That girl had strung those two boys along all week, and for some reason, they both agreed to wait by the phone tonight for a phone call. She wasn't making any progress on making a choice, and neither was I when it came to what dress to wear, when I decided to leave both to chance.

The suggestion was for Jamie, but I was tagging my decision along with hers. Let's flip a coin. Heads, she goes with Brandon. Tails, she goes with Scott. I did the honors, while Jamie covered her eyes. The quarter landed on her pink comforter, and I picked up her phone and selected Scott from the contacts and handed her the phone. While she informed him of her choice, I grabbed the dress Adrian had bought me and headed into the bathroom to get dressed.

When I came out, Jamie was dressed and still talking on the phone with Scott, which she promptly ended, and she dropped her phone on her comforter.

"Oh, my God. You're wearing his dress, and you look like a movie star."

I turned, having yet to look at myself in a mirror, and looked at my reflection in the full-length mirror in her closet door. My jaw dropped. Forget not recognizing myself after the makeover, but this wasn't me. It couldn't be me. "I just couldn't not wear it. It's…"

"A Jackie DeLane," Jamie completed for me. I still didn't know what that meant, but it was huge.

Jamie was still squealing about the dress when her mother knocked on the door, letting us know there were two gentlemen downstairs waiting for us. Butterflies danced around inside my stomach as I walked down the stairs. She was right. There were two gentlemen standing downstairs waiting for us, but I only looked at one. Adrian stumbled backwards when he caught sight of me. His hand grabbed the stair railing to steady himself. When we locked eyes, I knew he wasn't acting. His hand reached for mine, and I took it as I descended the last two steps.

"You wore it," he said, pulling me in for a quick kiss.

"How could I not? Someone special picked it out for me."

He let me back up and placed his hand over his heart and pounded it twice. "Your chariot awaits." He offered his arm, and we walked to the door as a series of flashes bathed the front room in a bright purple light. The time-honored tradition of parental pictures had trapped Jamie and Scott, and we weren't waiting.

I half expected the black car and driver, like for the ball, but not this time. Adrian had driven in his own car, and held the door open for me as I entered. Then we drove off just as Jamie and Scott escaped down the front steps.

"I'm so glad you wore that dress. It looks better than I even imagined it would," Adrian glanced over, and his eyes traced up and down me, and I felt my body flush, and squirmed. Not that I minded his attention. I rather liked it. "But, you know, you could have worn either dress and you would still have been the most beautiful woman in the world. I don't want you to think I am trying to control you or anything."

I looked out the window to keep Adrian from seeing the smile on my face, and I tried to hold it in for as long as I could, but there are limits to my willpower when I had a chance to nail someone on something, and I had the hammer, and he was the nail. I looked at him, my tongue buried in my cheek. "Elijah talked to you, didn't he?"

Now it was Adrian's turn to squirm and look away from me, the best he could while keeping his eyes on the road. There were a few dips and scratches of his head before he finally cracked and admitted, "Yep. He did."

I knew it, but I didn't care, as long as Adrian understood, and I was going to let it drop, but Adrian sat there, his mouth opening and closing. There was something else on his mind. We drove for two entire blocks that way until we stopped at a red light, and the dam broke.

"But Raven, it doesn't matter if he said anything to me or not. I was wrong about doing that. I don't know what came over me and why I acted that way. One of the reasons I like you is because you are you. You are your own person. You are real with me, not the person you think I want you to be to satisfy what I want. I am so tired of people that just do everything to satisfy and please me. I want a real person, and I am so sorry. If it ever happens again, slap me, please. I am begging you." His hand reached over and gripped mine. His cool touch was as comforting as always.

"Okay. I promise to slap you the next time you do it, but can you do me a favor?"

"Anything. Name it."

"Call me by my middle name, Maria. I can't stand the name Raven."

"All right, Maria. I like that name."

I did too, and since he wanted someone who was real, I decided it was time to be real with him. Or as much as I could get away with for the moment.

We pulled into the school parking lot and parked as close to the gym as we could. "Wait here," Adrian requested, as he stopped the car and got out. In just a flash, he was at my door, opening it and helping me out. Hand in hand, we walked down the sidewalk and into the gym amidst hundreds of gawking eyes. We walked in through the green and yellow balloon arch and into the packed gym, and again, eyes migrated toward us. We both stood there for a moment and took in the scene. This was a first for me, and it didn't disappoint. It looked exactly like every homecoming or prom scene on every television show or movie. I just hoped no one was up on the roof with a bucket of pig's blood. I was wearing a white dress. He led me further into the gym and around the edge of the dance floor to where there were tables for sitting. Elijah had already reserved one and was sitting there with his sister, who promptly evacuated the area as soon as she saw me.

Ever the gentleman, as it appeared the entire family was, Elijah stood up and pulled out the chair for me.

"No date?" I asked as I sat.

Elijah laughed it off. "Nah. Too many to choose from. Not worth my time. Plus, why choose one when I can dance with them all?" He leaned back in his chair, putting his arm around across the back of the chairs next to him as if he owned the world.

"My brother, the playboy," Adrian remarked. "Would you like something to drink or eat?" Adrian motioned toward the tables at the back of the gym with refreshments. Not the same spread that was at the ball.

"No, I'm fine."

"Would you like to dance?"

"Absolutely."

I was up and out of my chair before either of the two brothers could hold it for me. Hand in hand, we walked out to the dance floor. Adrian kept walking like he wanted to go to the center, but I stopped and pulled him back to the little spot I found right on the edge. It was cozy and didn't draw all the attention the two of us would get if we walked through everyone to the center, and that was just fine with me. Not to mention it appeared someone else had already claimed the center. Gracie and Scott were there under the disco ball that hung above the center of the dance floor.

Adrian locked his arms around me, and I leaned my head on his shoulder. This was no formal type of dance; this was just two people dancing to this soft and slow song. One of dozens of couples doing the same thing, but to us, no one else was there. It was just us until I felt a tap on the shoulder. I lifted my head from Adrian's shoulder and looked. Jamie stood there grinning wildly, like she did so often, waving a piece of paper in the air. She attempted to hand me the paper, but my hands were too busy wrapped around Adrian. She gave up and placed the paper on Adrian's shoulder so I could see it.

"Get out!" I yelled, and let go of Adrian, snatching the paper before it fell to the floor, and held it up in front of my face. Adrian moved behind me and read it. I heard him laugh while I was on the verge of a Jamie-esque squeal. "We're nominated for Homecoming King and Queen?"

"Yep" replied Jamie. Scott standing in the distance behind her.

"Wow," was all I could say as I turned and looked Adrian right in the eyes.

He shrugged, seemingly unimpressed.

"This is huge."

"We probably won't win," he said, pointing at the sheet of paper. "Look, there are five other couples nominated. What is it they say? It's an honor being nominated."

There were five other couples on the page, and possibly seeing Gace and Scott's name on the list just may have made me want to win. I playfully slapped him with the paper and then pointed at him. "Remember. You said I could do that if you ever speak for me or make a decision for me again."

"That I did." He grabbed the paper and handed it back to Jamie. In a single move, he spun me around and back into his arms. I wrapped mine around him, and put my head back on his shoulder, and once again everyone else disappeared, and it was just us and the song.

Once the song ended, we went back to the table for a bit and sat and talked. Well, we talked a little. Elijah and Adrian had a new game they played, which I found rather entertaining myself. It was "guess which guys had the guts to approach Miranda and ask her to dance." So far, Elijah was 3-of-4 in his picks. Adrian had only been right about one. Miranda shot down each poor sucker with the quickness of an assassin, just as I would have expected them to be. I don't believe there was a guy alive that could crack that ice queen.

Adrian and I danced twice more. Each song was a classic slow song from some era I was too young to remember; a teacher probably put together the play list. After the second song, there was a brief announcement from the DJ that voting for king and queen would end in thirty minutes. I felt a little jump inside, but I tamped that down. After another round of "who will be turned down by Miranda now," and "20 questions with the Starling brothers" around everything pop culture, which surprisingly they both seemed to be old souls opting for favorites from decades past, I saw Jamie pulling Scott to the dance floor and I felt inspired. I grabbed Adrian by his hand and yanked him out of the chair. He playfully resisted, but all it took was pouty lips and he was up, following me to the dance floor.

I was drifting off into paradise again when a force abruptly shoved Adrian and my bodies apart. It was Miranda, and I was about to explode on her right then and there. Then Elijah shoved a cell phone against Adrian's ear looking very grim.

"What's wrong?" I asked over the music.

Elijah just shook his head, eyes wide. Adrian said two words, and then stormed off the dance floor, dragging me by the hand. Elijah and Miranda followed. The ice queen cut a look at me and said, "This isn't for you. Can you get a ride home?"

"What is going on?" I again asked, as we ran through the arch of balloons and out the door.

"What?" Adrian yelled above the music as he exited the gym. He paced around and his free hand flailed the air with malice. Distress pulled at his face as he dropped the hand holding the phone down to his side. He was breathing heavily and tried to speak. The words were stuck behind something heavy. "Something's happened. We need to go. Now!"

Miranda and Elijah ran into the parking lot. Adrian looked up at me. Tears tore through his chiseled features, his rock-solid chin shook, while his eyes danced around the world, looking for relief. "My parents were attacked. My father's dead, and my mother is badly hurt. We need to go."

"Oh my God," my hand reached up to cover my mouth as I gasped. I couldn't believe my ears. "Absolutely," I said, rushing up to him and grabbing his hand and pulling him toward where we parked. His whole body shook.

He stopped, pulling me to a halt. "You can't come. I'm sorry."

"Why not? Let me drive you." I offered, hoped to help. I could see how shaken he was by all this. His eyes struggled to focus on anything, looking everywhere and nowhere all at once.

"I can take her home," Jamie suggested. I didn't realize she followed us out with Scott in tow. "Go be with your family. I'll get Raven home."

"Thank you," Adrian said, but it was more air than voice. His features were now gaunt and lifeless. I hugged him again, hoping to pull even a part of his grief away into my vessel, but it didn't work. He rushed off, broken, toward his car where Elijah waited, and I stood there watching as the brothers pulled off shortly before the two-seat black sports car driven by their sister. Both cars disappeared into the darkness, trailed by the roar of their engines just as my phone rang, and I pulled it free from my clutch, hoping to hear Adrian's voice.

"Maria," my grandfather's voice cried weakly. "I need you. I'm hurt bad."

17

"Raven, be careful." Jamie gripped the dashboard with one hand, while her other hand hid her eyes from the scene out of the windshield.

"Sorry," I exclaimed, after clipping yet another curb with Jamie's truck. I wouldn't have snatched the keys out of her hand if I hadn't already ridden with Jamie a few times. She was speed limit and rules of the road all the time. This wasn't the time for either. After my grandfather hung up, I called him back a dozen or more times, and he didn't answer. Our school was only twenty minutes from my house, and I made it in under twelve, slamming to a stop and clipping the curb in front of my faux house. I practically threw the keys at her while pulling them from the ignition in one move. "Go on. Things will be fine," I said as I bolted out the driver's side door.

"I'm coming with you." Jamie opened the passenger side door, but before the first creak of its hinge, I slammed it shut.

"No! I will handle this. You go on." I motioned for her to slide over to the driver's seat, and Jamie took the hint and slid over slowly. My foot tapped on the sidewalk with a woodpecker's pace, and I made mincemeat of the inside of my lip while I waited for her to crank it.

"You sure? I can help," Her truck roared to life.

"No. Go!" I leaned back away from the door, giving her room to pull away. She did, and I stepped back on the sidewalk, watching her pull down the road. Before she reached the corner, I took a few steps to the side, moving me closer and closer to my actual home.

"Come on. Come on," I begged under my breath until I saw the faded and patina blue paint job on the side of her truck disappeared around the corner and I sprinted off, letting my high heels fly off my feet wherever. Once they were off, I could truly run. The dress only inhibited me a bit when I reached the front steps and attempted to leap up them two at a time.

The door was closed and locked, and I plunged my hand into my clutch for my key. My cell phone was the only other thing in my clutch, but that didn't keep the search quick. The brass key on a simple metal ring kept slipping through my fingers' frantic search. I finally grasped it, ripping it out and shoving it into the lock, giving it a twist that threatened to break it in half. With a violent shove, the door flew open, crashing against the limits of his hinges. It slammed shut behind me.

"Grandfather!" I waited for a reply, but one never came. It was dead silent, almost too silent, and I flattened myself against the doorway leading into the hall and noted my surroundings. Nothing was out of place. Not that I expected anything to be. The shadows looked familiar, and if there was anything there, the hammering of my heart in my ears blocked their sound. So much for the training, I thought. With a quick slide of my feet, I rounded the corner and inched my way down the hall, looking up the stairs for any moving shadows. The moon of the night cast a perfect spotlight against the wall on the second floor. If anything, no matter how fast, made a move for the stairs, I would see it.

"Grandfather," I whispered up the stairs, not sure he could hear me, but at the moment I wasn't sure who else was up there too. There was still no response. Another slide step down the hall. My head jerking up to check the stairs, and then down again to check the kitchen door. Another couple silent slides of my feet, and I spun across the hall to the opposite wall, next to the kitchen door. I turned my head just enough so one eye could see through the door.

The sight I saw was all it took to forget all my training about being cautious. I ran into the room, collapsing to the floor next to my grandfather. Vampires could have lined the walls of the room; I wouldn't have taken notice. My entire world was lying on the floor. His hand wrapped around his throat, trying to stop the pulsating of blood, while more blood seeped from around one of my grandfather's own wooden stakes, now plunged deep into his stomach.

My hands fumbled for my clutch. "I'm calling for help."

His free hand reached up and grabbed one. "No, it's too late," he said. Every word gurgled.

"No!" I shook my head. "It's not. I'm calling!"

His hand gripped mine with an unnatural strength and pulled it down to his side. His other hand adjusted its grip on his throat, and he coughed. A spittle of blood dotted my dress. "Maria, it's my time. Nothing can be done," he wheezed, the gurgle returned for the last few words. "I won't survive. You have to finish this." His grip became weak, and the color vanished from his face. There was a little roll to his head as his neck went weak and it settled against the floor.

"No!" I screeched, grabbing his head and propping it up. "You can't leave me." Tears ran down my face. My heart was more than hammering in my ears now. Each beat a swing of a sledgehammer, shattering the fabric of my life. "You're my only family left!" Images of my father and mother flashed across my eyes.

His head turned and looked up. Two glassy marbles searched for me. Neither ever found me. "Those who die never really leave you. Whether or not they are really family."

Those were the last words my grandfather said. Those were the words that echoed in my head as I sat there and held him, hoping he would take another breath. He never did. His hand grew cold in mine. Not the cool comforting feel like Adrian's, but the cold and limp of death.

There was a protocol I was supposed to follow when this happened. We spoke of it often. In fact, we spoke of it every time the night before he made his move on the coven, every time except last night. It never came up this time, which was an odd omission. My grandfather was a creature of habit. Why had he forgotten part of his ritual? Maybe he was getting old and forgetful, and slow. That might explain what happened, but I didn't care about that now.

Fighting the desire to sit there and hold him, I laid his head down flat, and ran through the prescribed steps I was to follow if something happened. It was a three-step plan. First, grab his bag. Second, drive an hour away and find a hotel. Third, make the call to the number. I stood there looking at him for a few moments with tears rolling down my face, and my fist clinched, wanting to punch out at the world for taking everyone in my family. Forcing myself to do it for him, I searched the kitchen for his bag and found it by the back door. I grabbed it, locked the front door, and walked out the back. Using the backdoor was the required exit under any expedited exit. That meant crossing through the kitchen again. Seeing my grandfather laying there lifeless buckled my knees, and I caught myself against the table, and stumbled out the backdoor and down the steps. My legs wobbled for the first few steps away from the house, then I steadied myself and sped up, needing to make that call, knowing they would come tend to my grandfather. The longer I took, the longer he laid there. That drove me into a full-on sprint, up the same sidewalks I had run down just a few moments ago, past my high heels. I grabbed them. Why? I had no clue.

When I reached my car, I tossed them and my grandfather's bag in the backseat and started the ignition before I even had the door closed. I drove off with the plan to head north for no specific reason. I just needed to pick a direction and knew there was an interstate running through Savanah that went north and south. Now, I needed to find it. I pulled up the satellite navigation screen and scrolled around until I found the interstate and clicked on a ramp. A woman's voice began rattling off the directions, and at that moment my body collapsed back into the seat and a wave of grief came over me. The stream of tears increased to a flood, and I pounded my fist on the steering wheel. I knew tonight was going to end with me on a path to take me away from this life, but not like this. This was not what I wanted at all. The image of my grandfather laying on the floor flashed in front of my eye in between huge sobs. It was that image that pushed me to put the car in gear and pull off, following the pleasant-sounding voice.

I had driven for about half an hour when the tears stopped. I think I was out of them. The hurt and anger were still there. Well, let me correct that. The hurt was still there. Anger joined the party at just about South Carolina mile marker 23. I wanted to find who did this and put a stake through the cold black heart. That lasted until mile marker 37, and the tears returned. I think hearing my phone go off triggered it this time. Tonight was going to be emotionally charged, as it was. I was going to leave one life behind for another. Now I was driving north, leaving both behind.

I found our traditional no-tell-motel several miles off the interstate in Coosawatchie, South Carolina. Normally I would be full of jokes about a name like that, causing several odd looks from my grandfather, but I was empty on so many levels. I pulled in and requested our typical type of room. Outside facing. I handed over my ID, sweating bullets, but the tired and half-drunk clerk never did the math on my birthdate and handed me over the room key card. I walked in and went to our routine of cleansing the room. The cloves of garlic, which took me three strikes to attach to the door, the holy water, the crucifixes, and the salt. I finished my tasks and then put my grandfather's bag on one bed and sat on the other. I didn't really need a double room, but it was our typical setup. I had one last task, and it was the hardest of them all. It was the signal of the finality of my grandfather's existence. With the grief threatening to pull me to the floor, I leaned over and searched through his bag for his phone and the white card. After a deep breath, I slowly dialed the number, hesitating before I pressed send, but finally did as a lump gathered in my throat. Luckily, I wouldn't have to say anything. I let it ring twice, and the number answered. Then I counted to five, hung up, and collapsed back on the bed.

18

    The motel I chose was close enough to the interstate to hear the rhythmic droning of the traffic passing by. It was a lullaby that normally put me to sleep, but not tonight. I just laid there, on the bed in the dark room, staring up at what I guessed was the ceiling. I hadn't even turned the television on. Something we usually did as we slept. That was something I just couldn't do. I had already looked over at the bed half a dozen times expecting to see him lying there. He wasn't, and I knew where he was. That image was all I saw, and it tore at what little remained of me. I was just a shell there on top of the bedspread, waiting for the phone to ring.

    My grandfather had prepared me for this inevitability, but I never really considered it would happen. This moment was not one I had ever imagined how I would handle. Not for one minute, yet here I was, again, feeling like my six-year-old self in a dark room alone, having to deal with the realization that my family was dead and I was alone in the world. How similar this moment felt to that moment was startling. I wasn't still that six-year-old girl that sat there in a chair in an empty room at a hospital while both of my parents were being worked on in the next room. That child that heard everything the doctors said as they first called for the time of death for your father and then your mother just a few minutes later. A darkness settled in and I felt myself sinking down into it. That same darkness was now below me and threatened to pull me in. It was now official. I was alone again.

    My phone chimed next to me for the thirtieth time since I had checked in. I had resisted reaching for the phone. I just couldn't move to make it happen. This time, my hand reached for it and lifted it up. The screen was blinding in the darkness of my soul. It was Jamie.

How is he?

It was one of about thirty messages she had sent asking variations of the same question. I dropped the phone next to me without answering it as I realized I had broken one rule. I still had my phone with me. That was a major no-no for any quick escape. Even though under these circumstances, I doubted anyone was chasing us. They hadn't found us like all the times before. That didn't change the rules. My hand reached down and caressed my phone as I realized what I needed to do. I had to do it. I owed his memory enough to follow his rules.

There were plenty of opportunities on the drive up to chuck it out the window as I went over an overpass, if I had thought about it. Now, as I sat up, I considered my options, which were rather limited in the room. I could smash it. Make that I could try to smash it. Phones were tough these days, and my usual clumsiness had failed to break one yet. But I had broken a phone or two in my past, and how I had done that was available to me.

With the phone in my hand, I sat up and walked toward the bathroom, and turned on the faucet, filling the sink. I stood there, holding the phone, watching the sink fill, turning it off when the water line reached the edge of the sink. That should be enough, I thought, raising the phone up to drop it in. It chimed another five times while I waited. If this worked, those would be the last sounds it ever made.

My grip loosened, and it slipped in with a plop. I watched as it floated to the bottom, its screen still visible under the surface. If I remembered from the last time this happened, it wouldn't take more than a minute or two. It was at that minute I realized this was the end if what I had planned. There was no going back now, and I didn't know what the future held for me now.

The screen flickered and the surface of the water rippled. One last vibration before it died. One day Jamie would forget me.

They all did, or so I thought. Would Adrian? Even the possibility that he would forget me rattled what little bit of a soul I had left. I knew I wouldn't forget him, ever. He was everything I ever wanted. He was something I didn't think would be possible. He was messaging me on my phone. His name flashed on the screen, and my hand bolted into the water, pulling my phone out and reaching for the closest towel.

"Please don't die! Please don't die!" I begged while trying to dry my phone off with the cheap terrycloth towel, pushing the loops of fabric into every crevice. When I pulled it out of the towel, the screen was blank, and I screamed and tapped on it wildly. That was all it took. On the first tap, the display turned on, showing the same new message indicator from Adrian.

With a quick swipe, the message was up, along with the other, now totaling forty-seven messages from Jamie. I ignored those and went straight to the one from Adrian.

"Maria, are you still awake? I need to talk. My parents are dead."

My fingers betrayed my grandfather's rules and typed a reply.

"Adrian, I am so sorry. Are you okay?"

I sat down on the end of the bed, both hands holding my phone. Its screen shining straight up into my face, causing me to squint. The seconds it took him to respond felt like hours.

"Yes,"

"No.".

"Can you call me?"

I bounced the phone in my hand while I considered that. How much worse would calling be than texting? I had already broken that rule. I might as well pour gasoline on it and set it on fire.

"I need you."

That ended the debate. Maybe it was because someone other than my grandfather just told me they needed me. When my grandfather said it, he always said in the terms of needing me to be more responsible, needing me to pay more attention, or needing me to do something. This was a different need, and it touched me differently. My fingers roamed across the keypad and only paused at the send key for a second. It was the final decision to call that caused the hesitation. It was an opportunity to pull myself together.

"Raven.. I mean Maria. Can you come over?" He asked as soon as he answered.

"Are you okay? What happened?" I replied, ignoring his question on purpose. I couldn't come to him, and I didn't want to get into why.

"I'm fine. Wait," he paused, and I heard a loud sigh. "I must stop saying that. I'm not fine. I'm anything but. I'm not physically hurt, but…" a quiver developed in his voice. "Maria," he started. I could hear the telltale signs of a cry starting, and at the same time, I sniffed as a tear formed in the inside corner of my right eye. More were going to follow. I knew that. "My parents were murdered. Some asshole broke in to our house, and stabbed them." I heard sniffs and blubbering through every word.

"Oh Adrian. I am so sorry."

"Can you come over? I would feel better if you were here."

"Well…" I started.

"I mean Elijah and Miranda are here, but Elijah is just sitting in a dark room not talking to anyone and Miranda is pacing around screaming, but I need you."

"I can't."

"Why?" he cried. "I need you."

"I'm sitting at the hospital with my grandfather…."

"Whoa! What?" There wasn't even a sniff as he interrupted me. The shock of my announcement took care of that. It even surprised me. I hadn't really given it a thought before I said it, but it was a practical excuse. Jamie knew my grandfather was hurt, and called, so my alibi had coverage, and if I was here with him, I couldn't come see him. He wouldn't understand if I told him I couldn't come because I was sitting in a sleazy hotel an hour away.

"I'm at the hospital with my grandfather. He's been in an accident."

"Oh Maria, I'm so sorry. Was he in a traffic accident? Is he hurt bad?"

"It's bad," I said, lacking the strength Adrian had just found. My voice shook as my mind concocted my cover story. The story was more believable than the truth. It was my turn to sigh. "Someone mugged and stabbed him. He is in surgery now."

"I'm coming to you. I'm on my way."

"No! Don't!" I screamed, unintentionally.

"Maria, you don't have any other family here, and shouldn't have to sit up there alone. Let me come to you."

"No," I replied, a little less insistently this time. "Adrian, stay there. You have been through something far worse. I am so sorry to hear about your parents. Do you they know who did it?"

The quiver returned to his voice. "No," there was another sigh before rambling. "Whoever it was got pass our security system and cameras and everything. We don't even know how they got in the door. There's no sign of a break-in, and even stranger they didn't take anything. This place is loaded with pictures and vases and sculptures and all kinds of other shit worth a lot and they didn't take a single object. It doesn't even look like they touched them either."

"So, it wasn't a robbery?"

"I don't know!" he yelled through the phone, and then took a slow, deep breath. "Sorry. I don't know. It doesn't make any sense. The cops looked around, but they didn't find anything."

"Why would anyone want to hurt your family?"

"That I don't get," he bemoaned.

A knock on the door sent me falling back against the bed and my phone tumbling to the floor. Adrian's voice called from the phone just over the hammering of my heart in my ears. I looked toward the door and waited. There was a second knock, and I sat up, blindly reaching for the phone on the floor. I found it, and without paying too much attention to how close the phone was to my face, I said, "Adrian. I got to go. The doctors are coming." Then I hung up and dropped it on the bed before I stood up and walked over to the door.

With the world shrinking before my eyes, and my breath more of a wheeze, I looked out through the peephole. The image I saw caused my body to melt, and I opened the door, melting right into Uncle Mike's arms.

"Maria, I am so sorry this happened," he whispered, patting my back with his huge hand.

He held me against his hard, muscular chest for a long while. Almost wrapping me up in the trench coat he wore. There were a few beads of water on the collar. I guess it had rained outside. Eventually, he reached down, grabbing my hands and leading me over to the bed where I sat. He grabbed a chair and pulled it in front of me and sat down.

"I hate to ask this now, but I need to. Did he say if he completed his task?"

I shook my head.

"Is that a no he didn't complete it, or a no he didn't say?"

"He didn't say," I whispered, allowing my head to fall into my hands again.

"Did he say what happened?"

Again, I shook my head.

"All right." Mike reached up and rubbed the back of his neck, looking around the room. "Where is he?"

"In the kitchen, on the floor." The words barely escaped my mouth.

Mike pulled out his cell phone and typed for a moment before putting it back in his pocket.

"Uncle Mike, what is going to happen to my grandfather?" I asked through my hands.

"Don't worry about that."

"But I want to know." I pulled my head out of my hands and looked him in his brown eyes.

"He will be taken care of respectfully and given a proper burial befitting of someone of his standing in our world. We will let you know where his final resting place is so you can say your respects, and don't worry, he will be gone by the time you get back home."

"Get back home?" I asked curiously and shocked. "I'm not going back."

"You need to. Maria, I know it's hard…" Mike started, but I was already shaking my head no. There was no way in hell I was going back, especially tonight, and I knew good and well what that meant. That dream I had was gone, thanks to this nightmare. "Look, this is how this works. You need to go back home just like nothing happened. Go on about your life as if nothing happened." he paused and held up his hand to stop the fat-chance-in-hell reaction that I was about to give. "The best you can. That is all we ask. You have been trained and you need to confirm if his targets are dead, and if not, finish it."

I bolted up straight to my feet exclaimed, "That's a big hell no." My hand sliced across the air between us just to make sure he got the message. "You are going to send someone else, and you are going to get me out of here. And aren't we supposed to leave the minute we are found?"

"Maria," he said, dead calm. "In most cases yes. When you are found, you leave. But they didn't find him. He found them, and something went very wrong. You need to go back, confirm it's done, or complete the job, and then we will extricate you. You have been trained, and you're ready for this."

"No way. That's not going to happen." I turned and walked around the bed and stood in the center of the room, looking back at him defiantly. He didn't follow. Instead, he sat there as still and calmy as ever.

"This is how this works. Now what do you need?" He stood up and strolled over to my grandfather's bag on the other bed. "Do you have his notebook? I can help you find them."

"You can find them, but I'm not going back there."

Mike spun around. "Maria, we aren't going to do this circle all night. You are going back to finish things." He looked up at the ceiling, exacerbated, letting out a huff. "These creatures killed your grandfather. The only family you have left." he looked down at me and took a step forward. His size towered over me. Having a loose trench coat on that flowed behind him like a cape as he moved didn't help him seem any less imposing. "They took him from you. You have no one left. Your last member of your family is lying dead on the kitchen floor, and you just want to run." I guess I was wrong. I wasn't out of tears. Several formed in the corners of my eyes and then streamed in a race down my cheeks. "You could take revenge and keep them from doing this to anyone else ever again. You owe it to him to do that."

"I owe him?"

"Yes, you owe it to make his sacrifice, not a meaningless act. Think of what they took from you. Think of what you have lost. Feel that anger and use it. Take those that did this down and save hundreds of lives. These are not humans. These are not people. They are animals that will prey on people longer after your grandfather has turned to dust, causing family after family the hurt you are feeling. The hurt you are feeling for now the second time in your life."

"The second?"

"Your parents were the first. He never told you what killed them, did he?"

I shook my head, fearful of the answer.

"Vampires. They attacked and killed your parents." He took a step forward and grabbed me by the shoulders. "Maria, you are more than ready. Jonas knew that, but he was protecting you because of what you have already been through. That was his mistake. You need to do this. You need to end this coven's murderous behavior now. Save others from feeling this hurt you are feeling." He let me go and stepped back. "Then, once it is done, we will find you a new life. A life you want, and you can be done with us, if you want."

"What do I need to do?" I asked, not really realizing what that was. That carrot he just dangled in front of my face was a powerful motivator. It was a real smooth move by Uncle Mike. I had to give that to him, but that wasn't all. My anger had returned. Before, it was focused on me for not being able to help my grandfather, but now I had a new target. Something deep inside wanted to do this for him. Maybe to honor him. No, that wasn't it. That was too honorable for how this feeling grew. This was for me. My hurt grew inside as a hunger, and I needed to feed it.

"You know what to do. He's been training you."

"But I don't know where to start," I said. A slight shake had developed and radiated down my arms. "And how? My grandfather knew what he was doing, but they still killed him. I'll just be dessert for them." There was a bit of a whine to my voice and gave myself a quick pep talk to snap out of it. The next time it appeared, I might just slap my own face.

"Maria," Uncle Mike started, and then walked over to me, grabbing both shoulders in his big, strong hands. He was gentle as he held me there. "I love your grandfather like a brother. You know that, but we have to accept that he was getting old, and age slows you down. Maybe that step he had lost was just enough for them to get him. You won't have that problem," he said with a little shake of my shoulders. "And I will help you find where they are. Do you have his notebook?"

I pointed over at the bag, and Uncle Mike let go for me and reached in, retrieving my grandfather's journal. Then he motioned for me to follow him over to the table. He sat and opened the journal, flipping to the last couple of used pages. That was where his study began, turning and twisting the book to read the sideways and upside-down writing. To me, it looked like labels or instructions on a type of map.

"Do you still have your phone?"

I shook my head no, not knowing if I was being tested or not.

He reached into his pocket and pulled out his phone and slid it across the table to me. "Do you know where Forsyth Park is?"

"Yes."

"Open the map on my phone and find it."

I did as asked. It was an easy ask. All I had to do was view the map of Savannah and look for the largest park in downtown. "Okay."

"Got it?"

"Yes." I held the phone up to show him.

"Jonas used an old-world format, but I can understand it." Uncle Mike pushed the book into the middle of the table so we could both see it. He spun it around to face me. "Do you see that string of numbers?" How could I miss it? His big finger pointed it out for me. "That is what we call a directional set. If you know where you are starting from, you will know where to go. So…" he grabbed his phone from my grasp and put it down on the table. Then his eyes looked at the line of numbers once more. "Start here, and go what you think would be 120 paces, which should lead right to that corner there." Yep, his finger hovered over the corner of the park. "Now a three-step shuffle to turn, followed by another ten paces, then turn right, and you are right there." His finger traced each step as if he knew the exact distance of a stride. "That is where." His finger pointed to a big box on the map that denoted a large property. Which wasn't that odd. This was a very affluent section of town. The richest of the richest. I believe the Starlings lived in that area.

I looked up, my eyes meeting his brown eyes. "If I go do this tonight, you will help me settle into any life of my choice, correct?

"Yes, you have my word."

19

"Why am I doing this? Why am I doing this? Why am I doing this?"

The answer to that question was easy. I am stupid. It was now just after four in the morning. It was raining, and I was sitting in my white Mercedes parked on the street next to Forsyth Park, shaking. Each moment I sat here was a moment I hoped would help clear the images of my grandfather lying on the floor out of my mind. That never happened. If anything, it caused me to think of him more. I had questions I wanted to ask him. This was a moment his guidance would have been extremely helpful.

Why was I here? It was for him. My grandfather gave his life for this, and I had to finish it to honor his memory. Being motivated by some revenge didn't hurt. Uncle Mike pretty much had me with his speech about doing this for my grandfather, but when he threw in what really happened to my parents, that sealed the deal. The promise that I would be out of this, whatever it is, and be allowed to have the life I wanted was just the cherry on top.

I turned and looked at my grandfather's bag sitting in the passenger seat next to me. If I was going to do this, I would have only a few hours, else I would have to wait another day. Just the thought of that sent a shiver through me. I couldn't. I just couldn't. This had to end now. All of it. The creatures that took my grandfather had to die now, and while these weren't the exact vampires that killed my parents, that didn't much matter. This was for them, too.

One by one, I pulled objects out of the old brown leather bag and placed them on the seat. First was the vial of holy water, which Uncle Mike refilled for me. Next were the wooden stakes. His diary was next, but I didn't need that for this. It had already served its purpose. There were other objects I wouldn't need for this moment, but there was one I did, and my hand searched around in the darkness for it, cursing each time I felt something I didn't need. Eventually I found the small cloth bag, and pulled it out, debating whether to take the bag or just the crucifixes inside. I decided on just taking the small metal crosses by themselves, doubting I would have an opportunity in the heat of the moment to open the bag and pull them out. My lack of practical experience in all this was fueling a ton of doubts inside. I wish my grandfather was still around to help me.

I pulled the hood up over my head, and shoved the stakes, vial, and crosses into the center pocket of my hoodie and opened the door, heading for the expansive white mansion behind a black iron fence I had seen on the map. My focus was on the gate, which obviously wasn't open. Walking up and pressing the call button wasn't an option. Neither was climbing the actual gate. There was a camera on top of the fence pointed down right at the gate. I needed to avoid that, at all costs. So, like I was out on a walk, in the rain, in the middle of the night, just like any other sane person would be, I walked down the sidewalk right pass the gate and the camera.

I kept going until I left the cone of the next streetlight and then rushed to the fence at the corner of the property. With a single grab on a cross member, and a carefully placed foot, I was up on top of the fence, and over on the grass on the other side, in just a second. That was my average when my grandfather timed me going up and over a fence. I stayed low and crawled through the shadows to the side of the house. There were windows on the front, but few on this side. Not that there was much of a view. There was a vine covered brick fence separating this house from the one next door. The world was silent, minus the patter of raindrops on the ground. I reached the back corner, and peeked around, spying a large, enclosed patio space, with movement. My first sign, besides all the notes my grandfather made, was that a vampire lived here. Who would be up at this hour? Whoever it was, walked outside, into the rain and stood for a moment like nothing more than a shadow. I slipped back around the corner and pressed my body against the side of the house and listened. What I heard next was the creak of the hinges on the screen door that led inside. Did he go in, or did someone come out? There was no way to know for sure. Did I dare look? I dared and snuck a peek. He was gone, and the screen door was cracked open. This was my chance, and without thinking, I bolted for the door, keeping my steps light, slipping through the gap without touching it.

Now inside, I rolled to the side and ducked behind a huge planter of ferns. This gave me a great vantage point to check out the enclosed space. Something I probably should have done before I ran through the door blindly. As far as I knew, I had just run into a large gathering of vampires. My grandfather's notes said only one lived here, but as Uncle Mike and I were reviewing his notes, the thought occurred to me that maybe he ran into an ambush, and I had just repeated his mistake.

So far, so good. There was one else out here, and as I listened, I heard the faint sound of footsteps on tile coming from the door that led inside. Again, my heart pounded in my throat. Probably from the mere thought of what I needed to do. I needed to go inside and kill it.

It's an animal. It's a vicious, murderous animal. That was what I was telling myself as I took my first few steps toward the door, controlling the weight of each step to not make any noise, as I had practiced for over a decade. My hands reached into my pocket and pulled out both a crucifix and a stake. I crossed through the door, looking down the dark hallway. There was no one there, but the footsteps continued, lightly. I followed them down the hall, sticking close to the wall where the shadows were the darkest.

When I came to the first door, I paused and listened again. Let your ears be your eyes, is what my grandfather always told me. Even thinking about that saying drove a stake through my heart. I needed him, but he wasn't here. This was for him. It was inside this room. I knew it. The light steps on the hard tiles gave him away.

They sound more like a slide than a step. My best guess is he was somewhere in the middle of the room. I couldn't look first. If I looked first, it could see me, and then I would lose the element of surprise. All I could do was make my move and hope and remembering all the hours and days of training in dark and dank basements, I rounded the door and rushed into the room.

I hit it as he turned, and he tossed me off like I was nothing. My grandfather wasn't lying about their strength. Not giving it a chance to run, or attack on its own, the first movement my legs made when they hit the ground was to leap back in the direction I came from and I hit him again, knocking him to the ground. He was strong, his body firm as I landed on top of him. With a quick jerk of my hand, I pressed a crucifix against his forehead. There was a groan, and then he tossed me off again like a sack of air. I landed on my shoulder and slid across the room through a sliver of light coming in through a window, and then again into the shadow and up against the wall.

By the time I was back up on my feet, I had lost him, and this felt very familiar, and I crouched down, making myself as small as possible while listening and waiting. Where would he come from? He couldn't come from behind me. That was a wall. Every possibility was out in front of me, which made it so much easier than any of my training was. I heard him.

First, he was to my right, then to my left, then in front of me. Dang, he was fast. Another point my grandfather made but failed to properly explain just how fast. Even if I wanted to react to the sound, he would be gone before I ever got there. I had to wait, and let him make a move, maybe a mistake, and I had to be ready. Gripping the stake in my right hand. I was only going to get one shot, and I had to make it count.

He continued to move back and forth in front of me, faster each time, and never stepping into the sliver of light that separated us, but he made a critical mistake. He never mixed up what he was doing. It was back and forth, left, center, right, and back, and never stopped. I shifted my weight to my right leg, ready to pounce, and waited. As soon as I heard him right in front of me, I leaped to my right, swiping down hard with the stake.

His hand caught my wrist, stopping me from hitting my target. I tried to force it down, but his arm held me in place like a statue. We struggled in silence, and I reverted to one of my grandfather's tricks and let my left leg sweep into his knees, sending us both rolling to the ground with a thud, through the sliver of light.

"Brother!"

I heard the voice call from down the hall, but I couldn't believe my ears. My hand dropped the stake and shook. I looked down at the vampire holding my wrist. Elijah's frightened blue marbles stared back up at me.

"Brother, where are you?" Adrian's voice asked again from down the hall.

"Go," whispered Elijah as he released his grip. "I'll handle him. Just go." Elijah stood up and walked out, glancing back twice before walking out the door. I slipped back into the shadows once more.

"Are you all right?" Adrian asked. "I thought I heard something."

"You did. You heard me punching a wall. It's been a hell of a night."

"Be careful, you might break your hand."

"More likely I will hurt the wall." Then I heard someone being slapped on the back. "How are you holding up, brother?"

"I'm broken, like you. I've been texting Maria for the last hour and haven't heard back."

"Brother?" Elijah replied with a bit of a laugh. "It's the middle of the night. She's probably sleeping. She'll reply in the morning. Let's go find something to watch on TV. We both need to unwind."

I heard footsteps moving away from me. "Yea, you're probably right. She's at the hospital with her grandfather and probably fell asleep up there."

After the footsteps disappeared, I let a few seconds pass before I left, moving as fast as I could down the hall and out the back, just like I came in. Instead of going around the house and out the front, I hopped the fence behind them, and went two blocks over before backtracking to pick up my car, gasping for air the whole time after the world I knew had fallen away from my feet. I collapsed into the front seat, unable to make sense of anything. It felt as if someone had put my life in a blender and turned it on chop, followed by puree. It couldn't be, could it?

That was a question I didn't want to answer, and I started the car, and chirped the tires, pulling off, and again heading north, just like I had hours earlier. This time, it wasn't because of some protocol or anything. I needed to get away. I needed to get far away.

As I drove, thoughts bounced around my head, attempting to make sense of what I had realized. I tried to fight them, but they were too strong. Was this why Adrian hated sunny days? What about his taste? He liked old movies and music. They both did. I thought they just liked things that were vintage. Maybe those were songs and movies from their past. Holy crap. Was this why he, Elijah, and Miranda always wore hoodies during the day? I figured I couldn't make too much of this because I did too, but the difference was they wore the hoods and I didn't, unless I wanted to hide. Oh wait, crap... Miranda, she's one too. I had just lumped her in without even realizing what I had done. Her warnings echoed in my ears. This had nothing to do with who they were, socially. This had everything to do with what they were. "Holy Crap!"

I pulled back into the same hotel, not worrying about the strange reaction I might get when I check-in for the second time in under four hours. My body felt unable to move as moment after moment between Adrian and me flashed through my mind and bit by bit I realized all the signs I missed. Not that I was looking. Why would I have been? Vampires were never in fairy tales. My head collapsed against my hands as I held on to the steering wheel. This couldn't be happening. Losing everything in one night. I wept again, this time silently. I was too tired for anything else. My phone went off, and I reluctantly reached over, hoping it was uncle Mike. It was then I noticed another 23 missed messages from Jamie, and seven from Adrian. The last was just before four in the morning. There was a new message.

"It's Elijah. We need to talk! Just talk!"

I put the phone down and looked up. The first glint of sun of the new day sprayed in from the east under the clouds of the evening storm, casting everything in a red hue. This was not over, and I was now in hell.

Up Next - Book 2 – Blood Tide

DAVID CLARK

BLOOD TIDE

THE VAMPIRE HUNTER'S DIARIES
2

Available for Pre-Order at -
https://www.amazon.com/dp/B0D6M61RZP

Stay in Touch

Dear Reader,

Thank you for taking a chance on this book. I hope you enjoyed it. If you did, I'd be more than grateful if you could leave a review on Amazon (even if it is just a rating and a sentence or two). Every review makes a difference to an author and helps other readers discover the book.

To stay up to date on everything in the Blood Moon world, click here to join my mailing list.

As always, thank you for reading,

David

A big thank you to my beta reading team. Without all your feedback, books like this one would not be possible. Thank you for all your hard work.

Blood Moon © 2024 by David Clark. All Rights Reserved.
All rights reserved. No part of this book may be reproduced in any form or by any electronic or mechanical means including information storage and retrieval systems, without permission in writing from the author. The only exception is by a reviewer, who may quote short excerpts in a review.

This book is a work of fiction. Names, characters, places, and incidents either are products of the author's imagination or are used fictitiously. Any resemblance to actual persons, living or dead, events, or locales is entirely coincidental.

David Clark
Visit my website at www.authordavidclark.com

Printed in the United States of America

First Printing: June 2024
Frightening Future Publishing

Printed in Great Britain
by Amazon

52934345R10136